A RUGBY ROMANCE

HEIDI STARK

CONTENTS

To everyone who's ever thought:

Where is all the rugby romance featuring hot, muscular men tackling each other and landing in a sweaty heap. And where the FMC doesn't have to choose, because she's a hero both on and off the field.

And to everyone who's ever had a bad roommate situation. May the memories of the smut in this book replace the ones of them.

AUTHOR'S NOTE

Unlike some of my other books, this one doesn't include an encyclopedia full of trigger warnings.

The main thing to note is that it does include graphic sex with hot rugby players. Quite a bit of it, in fact. So hopefully that's your cup of tea, coffee, seltzer, or your other beverage of choice.

Interested in the latest updates regarding new releases, promotions and life updates from Heidi? Sign up for my newsletter here.

Join my Team! Interested in receiving advance copies

of my new releases? Apply to be part of my ARC team here.

RUGBY POSITIONS

1. Prop (Loosehead Prop and Tighthead Prop):

- Props are strong and powerful players who form the front row of the scrum. They provide stability and power during set pieces.

2. Hooker:

- The hooker plays a crucial role in the scrum, responsible for hooking the ball with their feet to their team during scrums, and accurate throwing in lineouts.

3. Lock (Second Row):

- Tall and strong players who provide power in scrums and are essential in lineouts for lifting teammates to catch the ball.

4. Flanker:

- Flankers are versatile players who excel in both attacking and defensive roles. They often secure possession at the breakdown and make tackles.

5. **Number 8**:

- Positioned at the back of the scrum, the number 8 is a strong runner and ball carrier. They secure possession from scrums and lineouts.

6. **Scrum-half**:

- The scrum-half distributes the ball from the breakdown to the backs and organizes the attack, similar to a quarterback in American football.

7. **First-Five Eighth (Fly Half):**

- The first-five eighth is a key playmaker responsible for decision-making, distributing the ball, and often kicking for territory or goal. Occasionally called a quarterback in the US.

8. **Second-Five Eighth (Inside Center/Inside Back):**

- Strong runner who supports the fly-half and helps break the defensive line.

9. **Outside Center**:

- Description: Fast and agile player attacking the defensive line and creating opportunities.
- NZ Term: Centre

  ○ US Term: Outside Center or Center

10. **Winger:**

  ○ Fast players positioned on the edges to finish attacking moves by scoring tries.

11. **Fullback:**

  ○ Positioned behind the main line of defense, responsible for catching high balls, covering kicks, and launching counter-attacks.

Key Rugby Terminology

If you already know about rugby, feel free to skip!

Ruck:

A ruck occurs when one or more players from each team, who are on their feet, are in physical contact, close around the ball on the ground. It typically happens after a tackle, when the ball carrier is brought to the ground. Players from both teams then attempt to secure possession of the ball by driving over it with their feet. The ruck is a crucial phase of play for maintaining possession and setting up attacking opportunities.

Maul:

A maul occurs when a player carrying the ball is held by one or more opponents, and one or more of the ball carrier's teammates bind onto the ball carrier. Additional players from both teams can join, creating a pushing contest. The maul can move forward with the ball still in possession of the ball carrier, allowing the attacking team to gain ground. The defending team aims to stop the maul's progress or disrupt possession.

Scrum:

A scrum is a set piece formed by the forwards of both teams, binding together and engaging with each other in a contest for possession of the ball. The scrum typically occurs after certain infractions, such as a knock-on or forward pass, and is used to restart play. The ball is fed into the scrum by the scrum-half of the team awarded possession, and both teams compete to win the ball using their strength and technique.

Lineout:

A lineout is a set piece restart that occurs when the ball goes out of play along the sidelines. Players from both teams form parallel lines perpendicular to the touchline. A designated player from the team awarded the throw-in (usually the hooker) throws the ball into play between the lines of players. Teammates lift jumpers to catch the ball, allowing their team to regain possession. Lineouts are strategic opportunities to launch attacking plays or secure possession of the ball.

Rugby Scoring System

Try: 5 points

Conversion: 2 points (ie a converted try is worth 7 points)

Field goal: 3 points

"We're not playing tiddlywinks here, mate. This is a contact sport."

— Tana Umaga, New Zealand rugby legend

CHAPTER 1

Dylan

"It's your last dayyyyy!"

I groan as a pillow lands on my arm. Opening one eye, I glance at the clock. It's two minutes before my alarm usually goes off. Those precious final two minutes of sleep have been callously ripped away from me. Somebody clearly has a death wish.

"Two more minutes! Why are you waking me up early?" I open the other eye to glare at Kat, my roommate, who has apparently dared to wake me. I'm not sure whether she's brave or stupid.

"Because I'm going to miss you, and two more minutes of your precious time seemed like a good idea!" She's practically bouncing off the walls, already fully dressed in her practice gear.

"Wow, Kat. What time did you wake up this morning? And how much caffeine have you had already?"

"I got up at 3 so I could finish my assignment," she shrugs, her words spilling out of her mouth a mile a minute. "And I had a couple of double espressos. Nothing out of the ordinary. Why? Am I acting weird?"

I shake my head and roll my eyes. "Not for you, I suppose. But if you were anyone else, I'd send you off somewhere to be evaluated."

Another pillow sails through the air and bops me on the head. Sighing, and resigned to my fate, I tug off my covers and push myself off the bed. "I'm not going to miss these spontaneous early wake-up calls, you know!" I jut out my lower lip and glance at her sideways. "But I sure as hell am going to miss you."

The sun's first rays break over the horizon as I finish lacing up my cleats. The chill of the morning air snaps at my cheeks like the sting of a rubber band, but I welcome it as part of my pre-practice ritual. Stepping onto the pitch, the grass crunches under my feet, still glazed with dew.

I take a deep breath, filling my lungs with the earthy scent of soil and new growth. It's my favorite part of the day. I'm an early bird by nature—provided my alarm gets to go off when it's scheduled to, and some sick demon doesn't rob me of my precious last few minutes. I'm drawn to the peace this time of day gives me, far before most of the world has even thought about waking up. Taking a sip from my thermos, I savor the taste of freshly brewed coffee. I may be an early bird, but I'm not a monster. I need caffeine like everyone else, just not as much as my roommate. Nobody needs that much, including her.

The stands sit empty around me, but I can hear the cheers and the chanting as if they were packed with fans eager to watch us get dirty. This field is my second home—the neatly lined white chalk, the precisely manicured grass. They're all as familiar to me as my own living room, and I'm a hell of a lot better at keeping things in order out here on the field.

As I start my warm-up drills, I reflect on the journey that brought me here. Rugby has always been my true north, guiding me through the twists and turns of young adulthood. While friends were out partying, I was training. While they were sleeping in, I was conditioning. The discipline required to excel at this sport has undoubtedly shaped me as a person. It's almost like a religion to me at this point. So, as much as I'm going to miss this place, when I got the once-in-a-lifetime opportunity to make a professional career out of rugby at club level, I jumped at the chance.

My teammates start to trickle onto the field, breaking my thoughts. We exchange eager grins and focused nods—no words are needed to convey the anticipation we all feel. We know why we're here and what we have to do.

Kat gives me a playful smack on the shoulder as she jogs past. "Let's do this, Cap." I didn't even see her get to the field, even though we had the same starting point. She must have flown here on a rocket ship powered by caffeine.

I clench my fists, my adrenaline starting to flow. No matter how many games I play, this feeling never gets old. This team is my family, and this field is my sanctuary. Still, most good things must come to an end.

I grin at Kat's enthusiasm. She's been my right-hand woman on this team for years, a fierce competitor who leaves everything on the pitch. Her hit last week was one for the highlight reels. I'm going to miss her don't-give-a-shit attitude, and her dedication to her team that leaves her willing to throw her body down for the sake of winning. She basically single-handedly keeps our team's physical therapists in business. As well as the entire coffee industry.

More teammates arrive, our pre-practice rituals blending into a symphony of preparation. Stretches, drills, focused breaths—we flow through our routines with easy familiarity.

I make eye contact with each player, reading their game faces. Johnson looks cool and collected, eager to put her speed to work. Ali has that intense gleam in her eyes that spells trouble for our opponents. Lopez ties her hair up, her jaw set with quiet determination. It might only be a practice, but it's our last session before one of our biggest games of the season. And I know in everyone's mind it's kind of my send-off, too. They want to do me proud before I go.

An unexpected surge of emotion passes through me. This mix of personalities, playing styles and strengths is what makes us unstoppable. We've put in the work to get our teamwork down to an art. Now it's almost time to reap the rewards, and it's bittersweet having to leave before seeing everything come to fruition. Still, professional club rugby is calling, and I need to answer.

Coach gathers us into a huddle, his gravelly voice rumbling through a familiar pep talk. I let his words wash over me, the sentiment imprinting itself on my psyche. We are impenetrable. We are unbreakable. We are one. And I can't believe this is our last time all together as a team. I can't believe I'm leaving them.

We break apart, hyped up and hungry for the practice game. I take my position on the pitch, my toes digging into the turf. The ref's whistle pierces the air and we explode into motion. Despite not many people, including my family, understanding it, this is what I live for.

CHAPTER 2

Dylan

The clatter of plates and chatter of teammates fills the Irish pub as I slide into the worn wooden booth. Elbows knock and feet tangle under the table, already laden with steaming mugs of tea, plates piled high with sausage and eggs, as laughter bubbles over like the froth on Lily's cappuccino.

"Dyl, pass the ketchup," Jess says, her grin as cheeky as ever. She nudges me under the table with a sneakered foot. "Or what do you kiwis call it, Liv? T sauce?"

I toss Jess the bottle with a wink, while Liv nods excitedly.

"Careful, Jess, or you'll get it on that brand new jersey of yours. How much did that cost you, anyway? Like two hundred bucks?" Official rugby jerseys can be a complete rip-off, but Jess knows we're all not-so-secretly envious of her extensive collection, so she's okay about us giving her a hard time.

She snorts. "Please, I could sauce up my entire uniform and still look better than you out on the field."

"In your dreams!" I fire back, laughing and shaking my head. The banter comes as easily as breathing with this team. My team. But not for much longer. In fact, technically, as of this morning, I guess I'm not part of the team anymore. Even though I knew it was coming, I think I need food before I can fully process this.

I spear a sausage and swirl it in ketchup, my eyes roving over the familiar faces—some still flushed from practice, hair escaping ponytails, exhaustion etched in the shadows under their eyes. But the smiles come quick, and laughter is never far behind. A warmth fills my chest, even as I feel the undercurrent of something more substantial beneath our easy chatter. There's a real camaraderie here, and an unspoken trust.

It feels like we've grown up together on this team, weathered injuries and victories, heartbreak and new beginnings. In many ways, they know me better than anyone. The thought is bittersweet. I take a bite of sausage to hide my sudden pensiveness. The explosion of familiar flavors of herbs and beef comforts me as I wonder whether I'll ever have a chance to find something anything like this again. Life decisions are hard. Adulting is hard.

But, no matter what comes next, I'll always have these memories—lazy breakfasts and bad jokes with the best women I know. My gaze catches on Liv across from me, and I grin through my full mouth. She scrunches her nose but smiles back, the moment stretching long and full between us. I can't help but think about everything she gave up to move here to pursue her own rugby career. Leaving the lush Hobbit-like wonderland of New Zealand to join us in the Pacific Northwest must have been a tough decision, but we're lucky to have her on the team.

Liv's expression shifts, a touch of sadness in her eyes even as her smile remains. "So Dyl, have you told your new team you're a total ball hog yet?" I know she's sad I'm leaving, and humor has always been her way of deflecting her emotions.

I toss a piece of toast at her across the table. "Hey now, don't go spreading rumors before I even get there! Or I'll hunt down your Vegemite stash and replace it all with Marmite!" It's a longstanding joke that Liv is a traitor to her country, preferring the brown, salty substance of Australian Vegemite over the equally salty yeast spread made in her home country. I don't get the appeal of either, but people from her homeland tend to get quite fired up on the topic.

The team erupts into giggles and exaggerated accusations, the mood lifting even as I feel the undercurrent of wistfulness return.

"She's right, though," Stella says, leaning forward with her chin in her hand. "What are we gonna do without our star hooker controlling the scrum? Our captain guiding us to achieve greatness?"

I shrug, touched by her praise. "You'll manage just fine, Stell. You're all awesome at what you do, both individually and as a team. Though I don't know who'll yell at you all to get your heads in the game when you're slacking off."

"No one can shriek like you, that's for sure," Liv snorts.

"It's not shrieking. It's called projecting from the diaphragm!" I respond. She's right, though. As much as I try to project a deep, authoritative tone when I'm yelling to the team, at some point I get a little nasally and... well, shrieky.

The conversation flows easily as we reminisce about games gone by, yet there's no denying the lingering sense of things coming to an end. I meet Liv's gaze again, seeing my own reluctance to leave mirrored there.

But change is coming, whether we're ready or not. All I can do is appreciate these last moments together, and trust that the bonds between us will endure, no matter the distance. Nothing is going to make me prouder than seeing the team go on to succeed without me, even though I'm going to have massive FOMO.

"Well, I'm sure you'll miss us terribly. Especially me. But at least you'll have plenty of smoking hot male rugby players to keep you company," Liv says, waggling her eyebrows suggestively.

I roll my eyes, knowing she's just trying to get a rise out of me. "Is that all you think I'll be doing over there? Ogling men?"

"I mean, a girl's gotta have some fun too, right?" she laughs.

"Look, I'll be way too focused on training to get distracted by any of that," I say dismissively. Though a part of me wonders if I'll feel differently once I'm actually there, surrounded by athletic, driven people like myself. It would be nice to find someone with the same qualities that have been so hard to find in this town. Still, while it's not why I'm going, it just might be a nice side effect of being there.

Liv scoffs. "Oh please, you're telling me if some hunky flanker starts chatting you up, you won't even be a little tempted?"

I toss a grape at her, which she catches deftly in her mouth. "Maybe I'll be doing the chatting up," I say with a wink. "Plus, my track record will show that I'm more of a fan of wingers."

The team whoops and whistles, Liv's eyes dancing mischievously. But underneath the joking, I know she's poking at something real—my tendency to prioritize my professional goals over personal relationships.

"In all seriousness, though," I say, "I just want to focus on becoming the best player I can be. The rest will fall into place... or it won't. But rugby has always come first for me."

Liv nods, a glimmer of pride in her eyes. She knows me well. And knows I've never been one to let a dick get in the way of my dreams.

CHAPTER 3

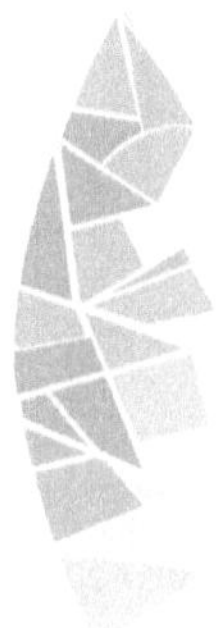

Dylan

The early morning sun streams through my apartment windows, lighting up the neat stacks of cardboard boxes that now contain my entire life. My tabby cat, Jonah, weaves between my legs as I finish packing the last few things—his favorite blanket and a stuffed mouse toy.

The gabapentin his veterinarian gave me to calm him on the plane has started to kick in, rendering his movements wobbly, as if he's just come back after a long night at the pub. I want to giggle, but my heart also clenches at his hopelessness, his complete dependence on me.

"Well, buddy, this is it," I say, picking him up and giving him a scratch behind the ears. "Just you and me starting over in a new city. But you know that no matter what happens, we'll always be together, little man."

Jonah purrs, nuzzling his face into my hand. I feel a pang in my chest as I take one final look around my now empty apartment. So many memories were made within these walls. Late nights laughing with friends over bottles of wine. Lazy Sundays curled up reading on the couch. A lot of time spent on the same couch recovering from various injuries and muscle pulls. In some ways, my first real adult home.

But it's time for a change. I can't stay in a dead-end office job and a stagnant life forever, always wondering 'what if?' This is my shot to follow my dream of playing pro rugby, even if it means leaving everything familiar behind.

I take a deep breath, gathering my courage. "Here we go," I whisper, more to myself than Jonah. I pick up his carrier and gently place him inside, tucking the blanket around him. He meows in protest but settles down quickly. I give him one last scratch behind the ears before zipping up his carrier. "Ready for an adventure, bud?" I ask. He meows back softly.

With a final glance back, I hoist my backpack over my shoulder, turn off the lights, and close the door behind me. My heart pounds with equal parts fear and excitement. I have no idea what lies ahead, but I'm ready to find out. This cat and I have some dreams to chase.

After an uneventful Uber ride, I pull my suitcase across the sidewalk and into the bustling airport departures terminal, weaving my way through crowds of travelers. The sheer size of the terminal is overwhelming, with endless check-in lines and blaring flight announcements. My nerves spike.

Is this crazy? Uprooting my whole life on the slim chance I might excel in this team and make my rugby dreams become reality?

I shake my head, trying to push the doubts away. No, you've made your choice, Dylan. This is your shot.

I check my watch anxiously, worried about missing my flight. The woman ahead of me at check-in is yelling loudly, causing a huge delay.

"This is unacceptable!" she shrieks at the attendant. "I demand to speak to your manager!"

I sigh, shifting my weight from foot to foot. Come on already. But the rude woman continues her tirade. With no other choice, I wait it out, finally getting through check-in and rushing to catch my flight.

Once onboard, I stash Jonah under the seat in front of me and try to relax as the other passengers shuffle down the aisle. My nerves are shot as I jam my foot between Jonah and the side of the seat to make sure passengers can't jostle him with their feet or luggage on the way past. For a moment, I wonder if I might have achieved the holy grail of an empty seat next to me, but that's short-lived. My seatmate ends up being none other than the rude woman from before, already jabbering loudly into her phone. Great. I settle in for a long few hours.

For a moment, I worry that this is a sign from the universe that I should grab Jonah and go running back off this plane into the more comfortable life I've built. But I hold myself back. This is just a blip. Stay focused on the future. My new team, new city, new life. In this case, it's about the destination and not the journey.

I'm jolted from my thoughts as the rude woman's shrill voice pierces the cabin.

"This is outrageous!" she exclaims. "They allow animals in here? I've heard about this foolishness! Emotional support peacocks and miniature horse service animals! This world is going soft, I tell you!"

I glance down to see Jonah fidgeting in his carrier. The woman glares at me before flagging down a passing flight attendant and explaining to her how outraged she is by my fuzzy little companion.

"Ma'am, I must insist you keep your voice down," the attendant says firmly. "The cat is allowed."

"Well I never!" the woman sputters. "It's completely unsanitary! What if I was allergic? I could... I could die!"

The attendant gives me an apologetic look. "I think she's right... it seems like it would be best for you and your cat to move...".

My mouth drops open. What's she going to do? Force Jonah and I to jump out the exit door?

She continues. "...up to first class, away from this woman."

I'm stunned. "Really? Oh, thank you!" My now-former seatmate fumes in shock and outrage as I grab Jonah and follow the attendant up front, settling into the spacious seat.

Jonah peeks out from his carrier, wide-eyed at the luxury surrounding us. I scratch behind his ears and sip champagne, feeling lighter than I have in ages.

This almost seems too good to be true. But maybe it's a sign that I'm on the right path after all. That taking risks can pay off.

As we climb higher, my doubts and worries fade away. A new city, a new team, a new life. I'm ready for this adventure.

As the plane levels off, I gaze out the window, watching the city shrink into a distant speck. A bittersweet feeling washes over me. This place represents so many memories—good and bad. But it's time to move on.

"Here we go, buddy," I whisper to Jonah, slightly unzipping the carrier so I can slip a few Greenies in and massage his neck. "No looking back now. Our new life awaits."

Jonah purrs softly, nuzzling against my hand. I take a deep breath, excitement and nervousness churning within me.

What will the new team be like? Will I finally get the chance I deserve, or will there be more politics and betrayal?

I shake my head. I can't go down that rabbit hole again. This time will be different. I just have to stay positive.

The flight attendant returns with a smile. "How's everything so far in first class?"

"Wonderful, thank you again," I say earnestly.

"Of course. We want you and Jonah to be comfortable." She hands me a cheese plate with crackers and grapes. "Here's a little something for the journey ahead."

I grin and give Jonah a little cube of cheese. Maybe this kindness is another sign of good things to come. I settle back in my seat, ready to see where this adventure takes us. The future is filled with possibility and hope.

CHAPTER 4

Dylan

The apartment building is sleek and modern, one of those cookie cutter types that developers have been putting up all around the city over the past few years. Stark white walls and dark roofs, row after row exactly like the other. Not my architectural preference, and a far cry from the ornate Victorian homes in my small hometown, but it's a roof over my head and that's all I need while I focus on my rugby career.

Plus, all the appliances should be fairly new. The website showed some nice amenities like a large pool and BBQ area, so that's something. Maybe I'll even make friends with some neighbors while I'm here.

I double-check the number on the door of the apartment in front of me. No need to embarrass myself first thing by trying to get into the wrong place. I knock, but nobody answers, and there's no sound of life from outside. Nice. I have the place to myself for a moment while I get my bearings.

Maybe I can be a bit nosy and try to suss out my mysterious roommates before we finally meet. I tried to find out who they were going to be before I got here, but the housing department said it was against policy. I know they'll be rugby players too, from one of the women's teams, but that's all.

Grabbing the hastily scrawled note from my purse containing the apartment's keycode, I carefully press each number and it beeps, opening on the first try. Nervously, I step inside.

The first thing I notice is the way the apartment smells. Not necessarily a bad scent. But just not what I expected for a place full of girls. There's no perfume here... instead, there's a masculine vibe to it. Like body spray and medium rare steak.

My gaze sweeps the living room and I wince. Mismatched furniture is buried under piles of wrinkled clothes. A few takeout containers and beer cans litter the coffee table. The carpet looks like it hasn't been vacuumed in a while. Not exactly what I pictured for my new home with the women's rugby team. I sigh, remembering the meticulously decorated apartment photos the housing office had sent over. Is this some kind of hazing prank? Maybe I should just turn around and crash at a hotel tonight.

But no—I'm here to prove I can handle anything they throw at me, on and off the field. I'm just being picky. So what? They're not a house full of Martha Stewarts, but the same could be said about me.

I straighten my shoulders, inhaling the stale air. I've got this. Time to show my new team I don't flinch in the face of mess.

Stepping further inside, I push aside the apprehension swirling in my gut. This isn't the fresh start I envisioned, but it's not a big deal. Nothing a quick tidy-up can't fix. I'll make it work. I'm ready for a new chapter, whatever form it takes.

I let Jonah out of his carrier and he eagerly jumps out and runs off to explore his new home. He's not one of those cats who cowers and hides away until they're comfortable. He's the curious one, the brave adventurer. I never thought a cat could inspire a human, but I admire his unabashed courage on an almost daily basis.

The kitchen is clean, but in a haphazard way, as if the counter was wiped down in a rush or an afterthought. A few stray dishes are piled in the sink, but they at least look like they've been rinsed.

I peer inside the fridge. Stacks of steaks and pork chops. And a ton of chicken breast. A humongous block of cheese. Barely a vegetable in sight. I cautiously open the vegetable crisper, and inside I find a combination of beer and electrolyte drinks. Maybe everyone here is on a keto diet or something? But it's definitely not what I expected. That said, rugby girls have a reputation for being a bit quirky–and god knows I am–so who am I to talk? At least I won't be short on protein.

I head to the bathroom, bracing myself for what I might find. The entire room has a light coating of something dark and... oh my god! I flinch away as I realize the substance appears to be body hair. Short, curly, dark. Now, I'm not afraid of body hair in principle, but everyone has their limits. It looks like someone bushwhacked a mountain of pubes and then blew it all over the room like dandelion spurs.

"What in the world?" I mutter. The sink is covered in globs of toothpaste and stubble trimmings. The mirror is so spotted and smeared I can barely see my reflection. I look down at the bathmat and recoil in horror—it's like a fur rug, totally coated in even more coarse, dark hair.

I was excited to meet my roommates, but now I'm a little terrified. Who exactly am I going to be sharing this space with?

I take a deep breath, steadying myself. I've got this. I'll keep an open mind and figure this out. Maybe it'll even be good for me, pushing me outside my comfort zone... I'm not sure how, but I need to believe in something positive.

The only good thing I can see right now in this room is the bathtub. It's fucking huge, and I get the feeling it hasn't been used in a while. It's one of the cleanest surfaces I've seen in the entire apartment.

Whatever's going on, though, I'm fairly certain that my roommates aren't who I thought they'd be. I pictured chatting over face masks with my female rugby teammates, not...this. If I'm honest, I feel totally blindsided.

I lean against the wall, trying to wrap my mind around the situation. Maybe this is all just a misunderstanding. But as I look around again, taking in the hair-clogged shower drain and hairy soap bars, I begin to realize there's no mistaking it.

My theory is confirmed as Jonah strides back into the room, proudly dragging what are unmistakably a pair of men's boxer briefs.

I'm living with men. Messy ones, at that.

My heart pounds as the reality sinks in. I've gone from expecting to room with my fellow rugby girls to apparently moving in with a bunch of total strangers—male strangers. This is so far outside my comfort zone, I can barely process it. There must have been some kind of mix-up with the housing department.

I shake my head in disbelief. How could this have happened? I thought I was finally going to find my place here. Instead, it seems like I've been dropped into the ultimate fish-out-of-water situation.

But, there are worse things I suppose. I can get this all ironed out. This is just another challenge to overcome on my way to proving my worth.

As I turn to leave the disaster of a bathroom, I lift my chin up. I didn't come this far to back down now.

I head back out into the apartment, determined to investigate further. There have got to be more clues here to explain this bizarre situation.

Jonah discards the newly discovered boxer briefs in the middle of the floor and accompanies me on the rest of my investigation.

I wander into the first bedroom. The decor is minimal, just a twin bed and a dresser. But the pile of dirty clothes spilling out of the hamper and the gym bag tossed haphazardly in the corner speak volumes.

Making my way to the kitchen again, I notice details that escaped me before. The protein powder jars lined up along the counter. The collection of bottle openers almost overflowing from the silverware drawer. The sophisticated gaming console that takes up most of the room around the TV.

My mind races, trying to make sense of it all. This has to be a mistake...right? I was so focused on making the women's rugby team, I guess I didn't pay close enough attention to the housing details. Some major miscommunication clearly went down.

I shake my head, laughing in disbelief. Of all the crazy situations I thought I'd encounter as a professional athlete in an elite club training program, suddenly living with a bunch of guys definitely wasn't one.

I guess there's only one way to find out for sure—meet the roommates face-to-face. My palms sweat at the thought, but my curiosity wins out. I've never backed down from a challenge yet. So I square my shoulders and get ready to face whatever comes next head on. This year is definitely not going to be boring.

I hear deep voices and heavy footsteps approaching. I freeze in place as the door's keypad beeps and then it opens.

Two men enter. What the hell? They both freeze as they notice me standing there watching them.

But... wait a second. These are no ordinary men. They are *massive*, each one well over six foot. When I say these men are titans, I mean it. Their arms bulge from their sleeves, tattoos proudly on display. Their rugby shorts cling to their quads like thick Christmas hams. And both of them have gorgeous faces to match their exquisite bodies—chiseled jaws, sparkling eyes.

When the universe was giving out attractiveness points, I swear it handed a few extra to each man who plays rugby.

The first has short dark brown hair, closely cropped. His eyes are a piercing green color. His shoulder and arm muscles bulge from his shirt, threatening to tear the fabric. And his huge arms are covered in tattoos. His mouth twists in a smirk as he glances at me, his gaze trailing over my body, leaving me blushing.

The other guy is about the same height and just as breathtaking. His hair is a slightly lighter, more sandy color, and he wears a neatly trimmed beard that highlights his angular jaw and high cheekbones. He also sports tattoos over his muscular arms and legs.

I don't know who these men are, but they are magnificent.

"What do we have here?" One of them asks.

"Yeah, haha. Did someone order a stripper?" The bearded one asks, his eyes roaming over my body.

I look down self-consciously, my crop top and shorts suddenly leaving me painfully bare rather than cute and put together like I'd felt when I dressed this morning.

"No, I'm not a stripper! I'm a hooker!" The audacity!

The men's eyes grow wide and I blush as I realize the alternate meaning of my words.

"Jeez, Coach wasn't lying when he said he had some weird shit planned for us this season." The cute one... well, they're both cute. The cute one without the beard speaks up. "And I thought you lot were meant to be referred to as sex workers these days?"

"A rugby hooker! I play the position of hooker in rugby!" I exclaim, exasperated, still blushing, but now starting to get slightly annoyed at the implication.

"Well, that's great to hear. We play rugby too. No offense, but... who are you and what are you doing in our apartment?"

"Um, I'm just as confused as you are. I'm supposed to live here now, but there seems to have been some type of mix-up. I'm... Dylan."

"*You're* Dylan?" The one with the beard quirks a brow and the two guys look at each other.

"Yeah, my mother was big on unisex names. I guess she read some study where they made women more likely to succeed in life than something more girly—" I realize I'm rambling and let my words trail off.

No-Beard snorts. "Well, it looks like she fucked up because you're the latest addition to apartment 403. Making us your new room-mates."

I glance at them and then back around the room. Suddenly the apartment makes a lot more sense. "That would explain the mess and the copious amounts of body hair everywhere."

"Yeah, this is a guys' apartment..." His voice trails off. "At least it was. Couldn't you tell?" He gestures around, and I smirk at the crunched-up beer cans and other trash. "And don't be so sexist. Girls can be messy, too. We have a few friends on the women's team, and you can bet their apartments are just like ours. Maybe worse."

I quirk a brow, but he's right.

"Let me give the housing office a call and try to get this figured out." I gesture at the suitcases I hauled in. "Luckily, I didn't bring much. My other stuff isn't arriving for a couple of weeks. And my cat doesn't take up much room."

"Excuse me, did you say *cat*?" asks Bearded Guy.

"Yes, I have a cat. It was on my application form."

As if on queue, Jonah strides past once again, the boxer briefs in his mouth and proudly trailing behind him.

"Well, clearly whoever processed your application didn't read it properly. Killian's deathly allergic to cats. Or maybe he just hates them. One or the other. I forget."

"Who's Killian?"

"Our other roommate," Bearded Guy shrugs. "You'd better get things sorted out. And what the hell? Are those my undies?" He snatches them from Jonah, who narrows his eyes and puts a paw out in a lazy attempt to take them back.

No Beard speaks up. "I guess we should introduce ourselves. You don't know our names either. I'm Noah," he says, and then gestures at Bearded Guy, "and this here is Jayden. And I suppose it doesn't really matter for you, but Killian is out of town right now, and it sounds like he'll be back in the next few days."

Bearded Guy nods. Neither makes a move to shake my hand or anything. They just stand there awkwardly.

"Nice to meet you, I guess?" My voice squeaks like two balloons rubbing together.

I can't believe it. Of all the apartments in this entire city, I land myself in a place with two more rugby jocks. Great, just great. My perfect living situation has been ruined before I even unpacked my bags.

"Listen," says Noah, glancing at his watch. "The housing office has closed for the day, so you're not going to be able to change anything until at least the morning. There's obviously a room available, so you can stay here the night so you don't have to worry about getting a hotel or anything. And then the housing office is just down the road, so you can go there first thing when they open."

Still feeling overwhelmed by the situation, I sigh and nod. While it wasn't the night I had planned, and I'd really hoped to be able to start making myself at home in my new room, he's right. The thought of searching around for a hotel with vacancies—one that's pet-friendly at that—seems like a step too far right now. And a room's a room.

"Thank you," I say. "And don't worry, Jonah and I will be out of your hair in no time." I blush. "And I'm so sorry about... that." I gesture at the boxer briefs. "He's got a thing for underwear. You should see what he does with my bras."

At the mention of bras, Jayden and Noah's eyes flick toward my chest as if on autopilot, and I find myself blushing yet again. I cross my arms protectively over myself.

They give me a spontaneous tour of the apartment which, while slightly awkward, thankfully goes off without a hitch. It's a little more leisurely than my earlier snooping, so this time I have an opportunity to take it all in. Aside from the mess, the space is exactly as I remembered from the photos—spacious and well-lit. Noah and Jayden are surprisingly considerate, albeit a bit flustered, as they show me around, making sure to point out the finer details of their bachelor pad that might've eluded my notice.

"This here's the gym," Noah gestures, in what I assume was once a garage. "Got everything you might need for a good workout, including a pull-up bar and some handy dumbbells. And over there," he continues, leading us back upstairs, "is the man cave, uh, I mean, uh, common room."

We return to the living room. "Okay, well, that's it!" Noah exclaims, visibly relieved that the tour is over. "If you need anything, don't hesitate to ask, alright?"

"Yeah, we're here to help, man—er, I mean, you know," Jayden stutters, elbowing Noah in the ribs.

"Thanks, guys, I appreciate it." I give them a genuine smile. "I'm sure we're all adults here, and we can make this work for one night."

"Absolutely," Noah nods. "Alright, well, we'll leave you to get settled in. We've got some errands to run, so take your time." He gives me another once over and I find myself blushing again under his intense gaze. "You know, if it weren't for the cat, we might get you to stay."

CHAPTER 5

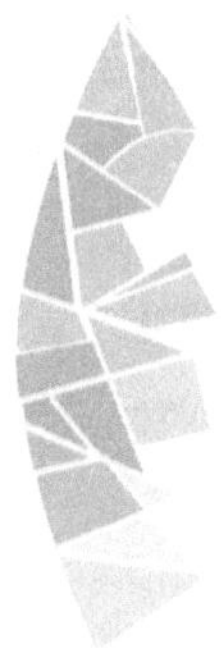

Dylan

I head to the empty room we saw on the tour—the same one I thought was going to be mine—and set down my suitcase and Jonah's carrier. I glance around, a wave of confusion and what feels like sadness washing over me.

The room itself is clean and spacious, as if someone put effort into making it nice for whoever claimed it next.

I walk to the window and glance out. It's dark out now, but it looks like this room will get a ton of natural light.

A little ensuite bathroom sits off to the side. Unlike the main shared bathroom, this one is immaculate, with gleaming surfaces and a nice shower.

It's a pity I can't take this entire setup with me wherever I go next.

Sitting down on the bed, which is made up with some generic sheets and a couple of pillows, I sigh. This isn't meant to be how this new chapter started. But as exhaustion hits me, I realize a good night's sleep will help to make things feel better.

As if reading my mind, Jonah jumps up onto the bed and curls into a ball beside me. I need to be more like this furry creature, unphased by uprooting his entire little life.

I lie back on the bed and find myself drifting away into the comforting arms of slumber...

The bedroom door creaks open and a shadowy figure slips inside. Even in the dim light, I can see the outline of broad shoulders and muscular arms. I immediately notice the figure is wearing a scrum cap, the rugby headgear that protects forward players in a scrum. It obscures his face, contouring around his head with a protective chin strap wrapping around his chiseled jaw. It's the rugby equivalent of wearing a mask, especially in the dark.

My heart pounds. Who is it?

As he steps closer, the moonlight illuminates a familiar smirk. "Miss me, Dylan?"

Jayden. Of course it's him. That cocky bastard. That cocky, hot as hell bastard.

Before I can respond, another figure fills the doorway. Taller and very muscular, also decorated in gorgeous tattoos. Noah.

"Sorry we're late," he growls, sliding onto the bed beside me. "Traffic was murder."

"Sounds like an excuse to me," I scoff, even as heat pools in my belly. Having them both here, now—it's too much. "What do you want?"

"What do you think?" Jayden's voice drops an octave, rough with need. He crawls onto the bed, bracketing me between their hard bodies. I'm in a rugby player sandwich and I have never been more excited to be squeezed between two other people.

Noah nuzzles my neck, his breath hot against my skin. "We're here to give you what you've always wanted, kitten."

I try to squirm away, but there's no escaping them. Not that I really want to. "I don't know what you're talking about," I whisper, staring up at him through my long eyelashes.

"Liar." Jayden captures my mouth in a searing kiss, thrusting his tongue between my lips. At the same time, Noah reaches down and strokes between my thighs, parting my pussy lips to find the slick evidence of my arousal.

They've got me, and we all know it. My traitorous body betrays the hunger I've tried so hard to deny. Hunger for them.

"Just relax," Noah murmurs, sliding a finger deep inside me. "We're going to take such good care of you."

A moan escapes my lips as Jayden swallows it with another kiss. My resistance crumbles, washed away under a flood of desire. Who needs to prove anything, anyway? I have everything I want right here.

I surrender to their touch, my body boneless between them.

Jayden breaks the kiss, trailing his lips along my jaw. "That's our good girl." He captures one of my wrists and secures it to the headboard with a silk tie.

Noah repeats the action on the other side, binding me in place. Helpless. Vulnerable. My arousal spikes, hot and needy.

With my limbs immobilized, they turn their attention to the rest of me.

Jayden pulls the front of my tank top down, baring my breasts. He sucks one nipple into his mouth, teasing it with his teeth until I whimper.

Noah settles between my splayed thighs, nudging them wider apart. His breath ghosts over my exposed pussy as he presses soft kisses along my inner thighs. Each brush of his lips edges closer to where I need him most.

I strain against my bindings, torn between arching into Jayden's mouth and using my hips to push Noah's face lower.

They're in no hurry, content to take me apart piece by piece.

"Please," I gasp out. Jayden's eyes gleam in the dim light, predatory.

"Please what?" Noah prompts, his voice a low rumble. "Tell us what you want, Dylan."

Heat floods my cheeks even as slick heat pools at my core. But I can't deny them. Or myself. Not anymore.

"Touch me," I whisper.

Noah obliges, dragging his tongue through my lips.

I cry out, my back arching off the bed as much as my restraints allow.

He finds my clit, circling it slowly before sucking the sensitive bundle of nerves into his mouth.

Sparks dance across my skin, and my thighs tremble.

Jayden abandons my breasts to capture my mouth in a searing kiss, muffling my moans.

Noah slips two fingers inside me, crooking them to stroke my G-spot on every thrust.

The dual sensations overwhelm me, pressure building at the base of my spine.

I'm so close, teetering on the edge of oblivion.

Jayden breaks the kiss, trailing his lips along my jaw to nip at my earlobe. "Come for us, Dylan."

The quiet command undoes me. My orgasm crashes over me in waves, pulsing around Noah's fingers as I clench helplessly around them.

They work me through the aftershocks, not relenting until I go limp against the mattress.

Jayden brushes my hair back from my face, pressing a soft kiss to my forehead. A sweet contrast to their earlier roughness.

Noah eases his fingers from my body, and I whimper at the loss. But I have no time to mourn before he's sliding up my body to take Jayden's place, claiming my mouth in a deep, hungry kiss.

I can taste myself on his lips, and the realization makes me squirm against my bonds. They're nowhere near done with me yet.

This is going to be a long night.

I break the kiss with Noah, panting for breath. My lips feel swollen and sensitive, my body buzzing with arousal.

Jayden moves up to the head of the bed and kneels in front of me. He strokes his cock, swollen and flushed, and nudges the head against my lips. "Open up, sweetheart. Time for your reward."

I obey without thinking, parting my lips. He slides his gorgeous, swollen cock into my mouth in one smooth thrust, hitting the back of my throat.

I gag around him, but he just groans in pleasure, tangling his fingers in my hair. "That's it," he murmurs. "Just like that."

He sets a brutal pace, fucking my mouth with abandon as I struggle to keep up.

Drool leaks from the corners of my lips, tears pricking at the corners of my eyes. But I revel in his loss of control, in the way I can reduce him to base instincts.

It's intoxicating.

Noah, having moved down the bed, chooses that moment to thrust into me with his impressive girth, filling me in one hard stroke.

I cry out around Jayden's cock, my back arching off the bed as they both fill me with their hardness. They find a rhythm, Jayden's hips snapping forward every time Noah bottoms out inside me.

The dual assault on my senses is almost too much to bear. I feel deliciously used, nothing more than a vessel for their pleasure. Heat coils in my belly, tension building with every thrust, and I know I'm going to come again.

Noah bites down on my shoulder, his pace faltering for a moment. "Fuck, you feel so good. I'm gonna come deep inside you, Dylan."

Jayden pulls out of my mouth just as I tumble over the edge again. Thick, hot spurts of his cum coat my face and chest.

The filthy display sends Noah chasing after me as warmth floods my core.

They collapse on either side of me, chests heaving.

I'm still trembling through the aftershocks, wrists sore from tugging at my restraints.

Jayden disappears for a moment, while Noah unties my bindings, and quickly returns with something in his hand. He wipes my face and chest clean with a warm washcloth, his fingers lingering over my sensitized skin.

I hum in contentment, my limbs liquid and heavy in the aftermath of passion.

"You did so well, baby," Jayden murmurs, pressing a soft kiss to my temple. He hands the washcloth to Noah, who uses it to wipe my pussy and my thighs as his cum still drips from me.

Once he's done taking care of me, Noah moves up the bed until he's nuzzled against my neck, his arm draping over my waist. "That was perfect. You're perfect." His stubble grazes against the crook of my neck, sending little shockwaves throughout my already sensitized body.

Their praise, and their taking care of me, makes me flush, a warmth that has nothing to do with the activities we just engaged in.

I turn to press a kiss to Jayden's jaw, and then Noah's forehead.

"Maybe this whole living together thing won't be so bad after all." I yawn, my eyes drooping shut in satisfaction and relief.

Noah chuckles, the sound rumbling through his chest. "Just think, kitten. We've only just begun."

A delicious shiver runs down my spine at the promise in his tone. Living with two hot as hell rugby players certainly won't be without its challenges. But if this is any indication of what's to come, I think I'll manage just fine.

My lips curve into a satisfied smile as I drift off to sleep, cocooned between their warmth.

My eyes flash open as I wake with a start, prepared to see a burly rugby player on either side of me.

Shit! Don't screw the crew, Dylan! Everyone knows that. And they're not even meant to be my crew!

I look down at the warm figure pressing against me. I feel a surge of immense relief but also disappointment as I realize I'm the only human in my bed, and the warmth is being provided by my sweet cat, Jonah, who enjoys being the little spoon but will occasionally spoon me from behind while we sleep.

Jesus, I'm only one night in, and I'm already fantasizing about my very fuckable new roommates.

This might only be a temporary arrangement, but that dream was *hot* and I'm more than wet.

Luckily, I'm going to fix everything very soon and I can reset this whole situation. Because I moved here to get away from politics and other complications, and this whole situation has complicated written all over it.

Sighing, I gently move Jonah to the side. He lets out a soft meow in his sleep as I groggily push myself out of bed.

Yep, I'm going to fix this before I soak my mattress completely with dreams of what these men could do to my body.

CHAPTER 6

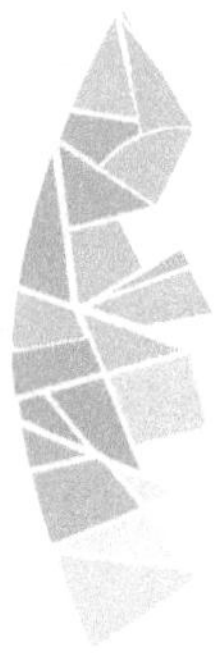

Dylan

The housing office is utter chaos—a den of harried students and overwhelmed staff. Numbers glow red on the ticketing machine as it spits out slips by the dozen. Forms shuffle across the front desk in unorganized stacks. Conversations meld into a steady murmur that bounces off the walls.

For whatever reason, places like this never seem to keep up with advances in modern technology. Everywhere else, you can make appointments and speak to people on your phone, but the places that have your life in their hands? Long lines, in-person visits, and questionable wait times.

I slip through a gap in the impatient crowd and step up to the counter. Time to tackle this housing mix-up head-on.

"Excuse me," I say, planting my elbows on the desk. The administrator peers at me over her cat-eye glasses, unimpressed. "I'm Dylan. I just got here yesterday and, well, you put me in an apartment with a bunch of guys from the men's team?"

She blinks. "Right. You're the girl named Dylan."

"Yes, that's me. The *girl*." I try to keep my tone light. Patience, Dylan. "Not sure how I ended up assigned to the men's apartment?"

"Housing is full this year. You're just going to have to wait for an opening." She grabs a form and shoves it toward me. "Here's the waiting list application."

Seriously? I picture myself stuck in an apartment with guys for four months rather than building rapport with my own teammates. No thanks.

"I really can't stay in a guys' apartment," I insist. "Isn't there any other option?"

The administrator gives a bureaucratic shrug. "You'll just have to be patient."

"There must be other places I can rent in this city. But I realize accommodation is part of my club contract. Can't we adjust it so I just pay my own way somewhere else?"

She shakes her head without a pause. "I'm afraid not, Ms. Morgan. It's a requirement of your contract that you stay inside the compound in one of our club-owned apartments. Staying anywhere else isn't financially viable for the club, and there's concern that being too far away will only lead players to... distractions."

As if living under the same roof as the two smoking hot rugby players I've already had a steamy sex dream about isn't enough of a distraction. Thanks, lady.

"There are no exceptions, I take it?"

"Absolutely not." The woman shakes her head again, a move I have a feeling she practices often.

Patience isn't really my strong suit. But getting riled up won't help. I take a breath and nod, taking the form. "Got it. I'll fill this out."

As I step outside the bustling office, I weigh my options. I could march right back in there and cause a scene—demanding to speak to the housing office's manager—but that isn't really my style. Or I can accept the temporary solution for now. As an athlete, I know all too well that sometimes you have to accept what you're handed and make the best of it.

I pull out my phone to call Liv. "Well, it looks like I'm rooming with players from the men's team for a bit," I say.

Liv gasps. "Seriously? That's insane. I know I was teasing you about meeting hot rugby players, but I never thought it would be because you're all trapped under the same roof together. Rooming with a bunch of messy men sounds absolutely vile. Are they hot at least?"

"I know, but no use fighting bureaucracy. I'll make it work." I pause. "And yes, they are two of the finest specimens I've ever seen. Apparently there's a third guy, but he's out of town, so I haven't seen him yet."

"If you say so," Liv laughs. "Look, at least it'll be entertaining, and you'll have some stories to share by the end of the season."

"Here's hoping." I take a deep breath as I push through the housing office doors again. It's time to embrace this new, unexpected chapter. I can do this. After all, I've endured much worse on the rugby pitch.

I march back up to the front desk, resignation settling in my gut. But I keep my chin up. No point in letting them see me sweat.

"Okay, I see I don't really have any options other than to accept the temporary housing arrangement," I tell the administrator as I hand them the form. I'm in a different line from last time, and now I'm talking to a bespectacled, slightly balding man who looks like he'd rather be anywhere than here. Me too, buddy, me too.

He nods, shuffling through a stack of papers. "Alright, this form acknowledges that you understand the placement is only temporary until we can find you alternate accommodations. You forgot to sign here," he says, pointing at the bottom of the form.

As I scribble my signature, I ask, "Any idea when that might be?"

"Could be a few weeks until something opens up, maybe longer." He gives an apologetic shrug. "Beginning of the season is our busiest time. Not many people move mid-season, but we do have some overseas players occasionally transitioning in and out at unusual times."

A few weeks or longer? I stifle a sigh. "Got it, thanks."

I step outside into the bright afternoon sunlight, watching other incoming players lugging boxes and suitcases around the compound. The first day of a new chapter. Usually, I love the rush of a fresh start. But knowing I have to bunk with the boys dampens my enthusiasm.

Still, there's no point dwelling on what I can't change.

I hitch my duffel bag higher on my shoulder and stride towards the apartment. Game on. It's not ideal, sharing with the guys. But I'll make the best of it.

Maybe we'll all get a good laugh out of this ridiculous mix-up.

CHAPTER 7

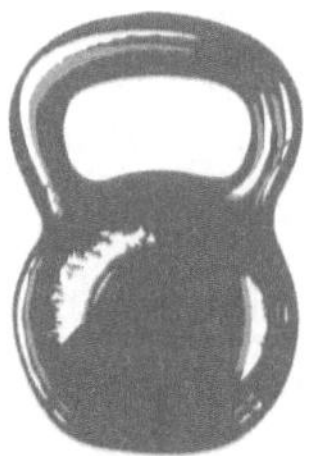

Noah

I can't freaking believe this. Here I am, Noah Spencer, international rugby sensation—or, at least, that's what the tabloids say—and I'm about to open my door to let in a complete stranger who's been shoved into my life due to some sort of twisted cosmic prank.

A part of me is amused, because this is straight out of a spicy rom-com—you know, the kind where two people who can't stand each other are forced to live together and end up tearing each other's clothes off by the end of the movie? Yeah, right. That's not happening with this chick.

To distract myself, I start preparing a protein shake. I lug a massive tub of whey protein from the pantry and thump it down on the counter, the silverware rattling from the impact.

"Careful," snorts Jayden as he strolls into the room, wearing only a towel slung low over his hips. "You need to start being more gentle now that we have a... female roommate."

I snort. We're going to get a lot of mileage out of this one, presuming she has to stay with us for a while. "You should probably keep your dick in your pants seeing we have a female roommate," I gesture at his loosely slung towel. "Wouldn't want to poke anyone's eye out."

Sensing my amusement, Jayden quirks a brow. "How do you think she's getting along at the housing office?"

"Well, she's been out for a while, so I figure nothing has changed," I shrug. "I don't know if you've checked the message boards lately, but the housing inventory seems to be extra lean at the moment. So, my guess is she isn't having much luck, and she's going to be stuck with us for a while at least."

Jayden shrugs and grins. "I mean, we'd have to up our game, wouldn't we?" he teases, nudging me with his elbow.

"Oh, no doubt about it," I agree. "We'd need a whole new routine, mate. Early morning workouts, less takeout, and maybe even remembering to do the dishes more than once in a blue moon." I gesture at Jayden's skimpy towel outfit. "Wearing more clothes around the apartment..."

We share a laugh, continuing to speculate about the return of our new surprise housemate. The doorbell rings, interrupting our conversation.

"Maybe that's her... this could be the moment of truth, Jayd."

Jayden feigns a shudder. "As long as she doesn't steal all the hot water, we'll be fine."

I open the door, and my jaw nearly hits the floor.

Standing in the doorway is a vision in spandex and a sports bra, drenched in sweat and more gorgeous than I could've ever imagined.

It's Dylan, but she looks different from yesterday. She's refreshed, wearing a light slick of makeup, her hair framing her face in a way that accentuates her delicate features. I thought she was pretty even when she was exhausted, but damn, this woman is smoking.

"Uh, hi," I manage to croak out, my brain scrambled by the sight before me. "I'm sorry you had to use the doorbell. Here," I say, turning to head in the direction of our catch-all basket in the hallway. "Let me get you the spare key, at least for now. Usually you just need the code but sometimes we forget and lock the other latch…"

Dylan's cheeks turn a light shade of pink as she dabs at her forehead with the back of her hand. "Oh yeah, thanks… I might be needing that for a little longer than any of us hoped."

Jayden appears at my side, and his jaw drops slightly at the sight of her. He's thunderstruck by this beauty, too. Normally not at a loss for words, Jayden is speechless as his eyes roam Dylan's body. She's curves and strength, and I can't blame him.

Dylan's eyes fly to Jayden and I swear her cheeks grow slightly pink as she surveys him in nothing but a towel, his tattooed, hard body on display. I can't blame her. He's a decent-looking guy.

I elbow him in the ribs, and his face flushes as he tries to regain his composure. "Right, well, come in, come in," he stutters, ushering her inside. "We were just… uh, discussing… er, the… the situation."

Dylan's lips twitch into a half-smile, as if she can read our minds. "Look, I know this is awkward, but I don't have anywhere else to go. The housing office has said it might take a while until I can move, and that it's probably only going to happen based on some international player transitioning out partway through the season."

Jayden and I exchange glances. "Well, okay then. It sounds like there's not much we can do except try to make this work," I say.

"So, this is going to be... interesting," she says, her eyes dancing with amusement as she glances between us before scooting her way through and heading to the room that appears to officially be hers now, at least for a while.

"Can you believe this?" I ask, shaking my head in disbelief as I type out a message to our other roommate, Killian.

Noah:

> *Bet you're sad to miss the drama here, Killian. Dylan's mix-up has turned her into our newest roommate, at least for now. Oh, and she has a cat. Sorry, bud.*

I send the text, a smirk playing on my lips.

Jayden types out his own response.

Jayden:

> *Yeah, imagine that. House meetings will never be the same again. The cat is cute, but the girl is hottttttt*

Jayden:

> *PS You're not really deathly allergic, are you?*

We both laugh as we wait for Killian's response, which comes through moments later.

Killian:

> *Ha. I never thought this would be an apartment full of pussy. But yeah, I'm not actually allergic. I just said that to put off my psycho ex girlfriend from getting one. She was using the cat as a way to tie me down in some kind of a serious relationship. The gateway to a proposal or something.*

I grin and shake my head. Killian's taste in women has gotten him into a fair bit of trouble over the past couple of years.

I laugh and head to my room, the conversation with Dylan and the group chat still fresh in my mind as I wonder how this whole situation will pan out.

The thought of living with her, even for a short while, sends a thrill through me. It's been a long time since I've been this intrigued by a woman, let alone one as talented as Dylan.

Since she showed up, I've spent a fair amount of time perusing her stats online and she's a solid player, an impressive hooker with a talent for developing new players.

I shake my head, trying to clear my thoughts. I'm here to focus on rugby, after all. We all are.

Still, I can't help but wonder how things will play out with the new addition to the team... and the house.

After a post-practice nap, I wake to the smell of coffee brewing.

I peek one eye open, blinking blearily. My memories of the previous night and this morning come flooding back, and I can't help but smile as I remember the text exchange with Killian.

I swing my legs out of bed, yawning and stretching as I pad downstairs in search of the caffeine that calls to me like a siren's song.

I'm not at all prepared for the sight that greets me in the kitchen.

Dylan, clad in nothing but a baggy T-shirt and short shorts, is bent over the counter, her heart-stoppingly toned ass on display as she searches the cupboards.

The longing that pools in my stomach takes me by surprise, and for a moment, all I can do is stare.

"Hi again, Noah," she says, not turning around. "I was just about to make myself some toast. Want any?"

My brain short-circuits. Her voice is like honey, dripping over me like a drug I can't get enough of. "Uh, yeah... thanks... I mean, yes, please," I stutter, cursing my own ineloquence.

She straightens up as she turns, her cheeks flushing a charming shade of pink, and I realize I've been caught ogling. "Sorry, I didn't... I mean, I thought you were... nevermind."

Dylan laughs and hands me a mug of steaming coffee, which I gratefully accept. "You're fine. I should probably put some pants on, huh?" she says, her eyes twinkling with mischief.

I choke on my coffee, barely managing to splutter a response. "Ah, no rush... I mean, you're... you look... I mean, toast sounds great."

Dylan laughs even louder, the surprisingly resonant sound like music to my ears. "I'll be back in a second. Don't spill the beans... or the coffee," she adds over her shoulder as she saunters away.

As I wait for her return, I take a deep breath, mentally preparing myself for the day ahead.

With Dylan in the picture, this season is going to be anything but boring.

CHAPTER 8

Dylan

"So yeah, guys," I say, glancing between Noah, and Jayden who is sprawled on the couch. "The housing office wasn't really much help at all. Couldn't give me an estimate of when I'd be able to move out. So it looks like I'm your new roommate for the foreseeable future. Surprise?"

Jayden grins, eyes glinting with mischief. "Did we just win the lottery, or is this the universe playing a cruel joke?"

Noah stretches, his muscles rippling beneath his t-shirt. "Guess we'll find out soon enough."

I fight back a shiver, forcing nonchalance. I'm used to commanding a field, but this is new territory. Still, I won't let them see me sweat.

"Well, go easy on me at first. I promise not to leave my dirty socks everywhere...yet."

Jayden chuckles. "No promises. We might just have to haze you a little, newbie."

I cock an eyebrow. "Careful. I don't haze easily."

The banter comes naturally, like a scrimmage warming up for the real game. There's an undercurrent here, a subtle push and pull.

I don't know the rules yet, but I'm no stranger to strategy. And I don't give up at the first sign of trouble.

Game on, boys.

The playful back-and-forth is interrupted by the sound of the balcony door sliding open. I turn, a quip on my lips, but the words die unspoken.

The door opens with a slight squeak, and I'm face-to-face with a mountain of a man. His muscular frame fills the doorway, wild dark hair with blonde highlights falling to his shoulders. He looks like he just stepped off the cover of a steamy romance novel.

My breath catches in my chest as my heart begins to race. God, one look at this man and he's got me feeling woozy.

"Dylan, meet our other roommate, Killian," Noah says. "Killian, this is our new roommate, Dylan."

Killian's piercing blue eyes rake over me. "Wow, this is the smoking hot roommate you were talking about?"

I almost faint as I notice his Irish accent.

Jayden grins. "She's pretty fucking cute."

I cross my arms. "I'm standing right here. And I'm not just some piece of groupie meat."

Killian smirks. "We've heard. You're a hooker."

My jaw drops. What an asshole. I narrow my eyes, heat rising to my cheeks. He might be gorgeous, but he's already getting on my last nerve. "Excuse me? No one would ever talk that way to a male athlete."

"Relax, newbie. I'm just messing with you," he says with a chuckle.

I'm fuming. I know I should be used to this crap, but it still grinds my gears. Of course a man who looks like a Greek god would have a glaring flaw—misogynistic tendencies.

But I'm not going to let some cocky jerk rattle me. I came here to prove myself on the field, not take shit from arrogant men.

I lift my chin and stare him down. "Don't underestimate me. I might surprise you."

"Well, that's fine with me. I love surprises." He winks, and the teasing sparkle in his eye only serves to infuriate me.

The way he tilts his head causes the overhead light to glint off his chiseled jaw, leaving him looking more than perfect. I bet he practices his angles in the mirror, the handsome son of a bitch.

My mouth goes dry. Come on, get it together! I force a relaxed smile, hoping he doesn't notice the hitch in my breath.

"So you really are the famous new roommate?" His gaze sweeps over me, and damn if that smirk doesn't make my knees weak. "I didn't know whether to believe the boys when they said a hot chick was moving in. I was thinking they were pulling a prank on me, and you were going to be some dude with a broken nose and half his teeth missing."

I lift my chin, my cheeks flushing at the way the other guys have clearly described me to this god. "Well, here I am, in the flesh." I gesture down at myself breezily, like I'm not hyperaware of his eyes tracing my body. "Not a myth, just a girl standing in front of her roommates..." I bite my lip, holding back a grin. "Asking them not to make it weird."

Killian laughs, a rich sound that does nothing to calm my racing pulse. "No promises there." He leans against the doorframe, all casual grace and barely leashed power. "But we'll try to behave."

His smile promises the opposite. I don't know if I'm ready for whatever game he wants to play.

I take a deep breath to steady myself as Killian saunters into the kitchen. Noah trails behind, and Jayden pushes himself up off the couch to join us. It's our first time all together in one room. I'm not sure what I expected, but the undercurrent of electricity sparking between us takes me by surprise.

Noah catches my eye, offering an easy grin. "Welcome to the madhouse, Dylan. Make yourself at home."

I smile back gratefully. At least someone is trying to be somewhat normal here.

Jayden rummages through the fridge, emerging with a diet soda. He pops the tab, his eyes glinting mischievously. "Yeah, mi casa es su casa. Within reason." He waggles his eyebrows. "Clothes mandatory in shared spaces."

I laugh, hoping it sounds more nonchalant than I feel. "Duly noted. I'll keep the streaking to a minimum."

From the corner of my eye, I see Killian's gaze drop appreciatively down my body. "That's a shame," he says, his voice like velvet. "I was looking forward to the free show."

Heat floods my cheeks. I resist the urge to fan myself. Get it together, Dylan.

I straighten and meet his eyes, arching an eyebrow. "Careful what you wish for."

His lips curve. "I can handle anything you want to show me, sweetheart."

Oh boy. These three are going to be trouble, I can tell. I clear my throat, trying desperately to steer this runaway train back to solid ground.

"So!" My voice comes out too loud. I wince. "What's the plan for dinner? How do meals work around here? I was picturing lots of salads and brown rice, but based on the contents of the fridge and the coffee table," I point at the mess in the living room, "it looks like you've expanded your culinary horizons more than the typical professional athlete."

Noah claps his hands together. "I'm thinking takeout. Burgers sound good?"

There's a general murmur of assent.

In less than thirty minutes, we're gathered around the dining room table with a spread of greasy fast food bags between us. I snag a fry, savoring the comfort of carbs.

"To new roommates." I lift my soda in a toast. "May we not kill each other."

"I'll drink to that," Noah chuckles.

We clink our cans together. As we settle in to eat, things feel almost normal. But there's an undercurrent I can't ignore, especially when I catch Killian watching me, heat in his eyes.

This could get complicated. I just hope I'm ready for the ride.

I try to focus on my burger, but my eyes keep darting to Killian. He's unfairly attractive, all sharp angles and hard muscle. It doesn't help that his t-shirt clings to his sculpted chest.

I force myself to stare at my food.

"So, Dylan," Jayden says after swallowing a bite of his burger. "How are you feeling about moving in with a bunch of dudes you barely know?"

I toy with a fry, considering how to answer. "It's fine. I needed a change of scenery. And you guys had a room." I shrug. "Seems like fate."

"We're happy to have you." Noah smiles warmly. "Even if the circumstances are a bit unconventional."

"To say the least." I huff a laugh.

"Nothing wrong with unconventional." Killian's gaze bores into me. "Makes life more interesting."

I shiver, his intensity hitting me like a shockwave. Get a grip, Dylan.

I shovel more food in my mouth so I don't have to respond.

"You'll have to let us know if we start getting on your nerves." Jayden bumps my shoulder playfully. "We can be a lot to handle."

"I think I can take whatever you guys dish out." I toss my hair back.

Killian's eyes darken. "Careful, or I might take that as a challenge."

The way he looks at me...like he wants to devour me...it makes my pulse skitter.

I drain my soda, needing a distraction.

This attraction is dangerous. I know where it could lead. But maybe a little danger is exactly what I need.

"I'm sure you have a ton of stuff to organize, and your cat misses you," says Noah. He gestures at the plates on the table. "Let us take care of this. Consider it a welcome present."

I smile and nod, grateful for the opportunity to exit and start sorting out my stuff. And he's right. Poor little Jonah has been in our room all day and I'm sure he's itching for company and the opportunity to explore.

I close the door to my new bedroom, leaning against it as I let out a breath. What a day. Moving in with three hot guys I barely know. Not at all how I saw this going.

I fan myself, still feeling a bit flushed from dinner. Especially with Killian eyeing me like I was a juicy steak.

Get it together, Dylan. Ogling the roommate is asking for trouble.

The truth is, the mere sight of Killian is making me wet. And that's being fueled by his banter... as much as his words irk me, I'm eating up the tension they're creating between my thighs.

With a groan, I peel off my clothes and change into shorts and a tank top. The cool air feels good on my overheated skin.

I reach out and scratch Jonah's head and he nuzzles his ear into my hand, right where he most likes to be scratched.

I pull out my phone and text Kat.

Dylan:

So I just met the hot third roommate.

Jonah hops up on the bed next to me and snuggles into my side while I wait for their reply.

Kat:

Spill! Is he as gorgeous up close as you imagined? Of course I've been stalking his social media ever since you mentioned him, but I don't think he keeps things up to date.

Kat:

I need all the details!

Dylan:

Well, he's certainly nice to look at. But his personality could use some work.

Kat:

Uh oh. What happened?

Dylan:

He called me a hooker within the first two minutes of meeting me. It's like the running joke of the apartment and I'm so over it.

Kat:

Yikes. What a jackass. But, to be fair, it is your rugby position.

Dylan:

I know, right? He's got that cocky jock vibe in the worst way. And I know it's my position, but that's not what he meant.

Kat:

So much for my fantasies of a dreamy sports romance.

Dylan:

Yeah, he's no Prince Charming, that's for sure. More like the villain who tries to sabotage the heroine.

Kat:

Or the misunderstood bad boy who needs the love of a good woman to redeem him.

Dylan:

Wow, we clearly read too many books. But this is real life. Let's not get ahead of ourselves here. As of now, he's just an obnoxious god. Emphasis on the obnoxious.

Kat:

Dylan:

Kat:

I sigh as I put my phone away. Something tells me living with Killian is going to be an adventure, whether I like it or not. But I refuse to let some egotistical jock intimidate me. Next time he tries to get close, I'll be ready and waiting.

Flopping onto the bed, I stare at the ceiling. Killian is temptation incarnate with those piercing eyes and muscular frame. And that ac cent...swoon.

Focus! I give myself a little shake.

But Jayden's boyish charm is adorable. And Noah seems so genuine and kind. Plus, have you seen those arms? All of them have arms that could pick me up and do deliciously wicked things...

"Get your head in the game, Dylan," I mutter. "You're here to play rugby. Not drool over your roommates."

Even if said roommates are crazy hot. And living one or two thin walls away.

I groan again, rolling over and smooshing my face into the pillow. This arrangement is going to test my willpower big time. But I'm not about to jeopardize my spot on the team over some eye candy.

No matter how sweet the view is.

CHAPTER 9

Dylan

I'm out on the practice field, but it looks different. A thick mist swirls over the immaculately trimmed pitch, making it hard to see more than a couple of feet in front of me. The cold air wraps around me in a cloak, leaving me covered in goosebumps as the damp layers caress my bare skin.

Wait... bare skin?

I look down. Oh my fucking god. I'm naked on the practice field.

I glance around, my cheeks on fire, desperately searching for something to cover myself with, but of course, there's nothing in sight. I contemplate running back inside, but my body feels strange, as if I can't move more than a step in either direction. I feel exposed, but there's an eerie calm. Through the darkness, I strain my eyes but don't seem to see anyone else nearby.

"Well, well, if it isn't our resident rugby goddess, Dylan," a sultry voice drawls from behind me in an Irish lilt. Killian. Figures. Of course, it would be him.

He's one of the only guys who can make me feel like a shy little kitten one moment and completely on fire the next. The other two being my other hot new roommates.

"Cover me!" I hiss, trying and failing to sound composed.

"With pleasure, love," he purrs, wiggling his eyebrows. "And I'm pretty sure I have the proper equipment to do the job."

Ugh, Killian Baxter, why do you have to be so damn hot?

I stomp my foot, which isn't as intimidating as I'd hoped with no shoes on. "I meant with something to... you know!" I gesture at my nakedness, wishing the earth would swallow me whole.

He grins, slow and wicked, taking his sweet time before handing me a spare jersey. "I know what you meant, Dylan, but where's the fun in that?" he says, his eyes roaming over my body like a predator stalking its prey.

I snatch the jersey and yank it over my head, tugging it down as far as it'll go. "You're a pig, you know that?" I sputter, unable to meet his eyes.

"Yeah, but you like it," he teases, winking. Before I can form a witty retort, he adds, "But seriously, are you okay, Dyl? You've been distracted all practice."

Dang it, he noticed. "I'm fine, just...thinking about... stuff," I mumble, tying my laces in triple knots.

"Care to share with the team, princess?" he asks, using the pet name he knows I hate...love.

"None of your business, Baxter," I huff, but I can't help the small smile tugging at my lips.

"All right, all right," he says, holding his palms up in surrender. "But you know if you ever need a... hand... with anything," he trails off suggestively, "my locker room's always open. In fact," his gaze roves over my body, "I don't think I can wait that long..."

"Killian," I moan as he approaches me, this unstoppable wall of pure hotness coming toward me. "We shouldn't..."

"Shh..." he whispers, capturing my lips in a searing kiss that would melt my panties if I were wearing any. His hands roam my body, and I moan as his fingertips graze my bare skin. He growls, "So fucking sexy, kitten."

Killian's eyes darken, and he grips my hips, lifting me up against the cold metal fence that lines the field. "I've always wanted you like this," he grunts.

This is where he'd probably tear my panties off, but I'm not wearing any.

"Me too," I confess, my voice husky with desire.

He hoists me up further, and I wrap my legs around his waist as he slams me against the fence.

He enters me roughly with his massive cock, his tongue finding mine as our bodies move in sync.

The metal bites into my back, but I don't care because being in his arms feels like home.

"Damn, kitten," he growls, his hips grinding into mine with a ferocity I didn't know he had in him. "You feel... so... fucking... good. And the sight of you in my jersey... it makes me want to fuck you until your legs are like jello."

"Killian, oh god, don't stop," I moan, my nails digging into his broad shoulders.

His pace intensifies, and I know I'm teetering on the edge.

"I. Can't. Hold. Off. Any. Longer," I pant in between moans.

"Neither... can... I," he grunts, and together, we shatter, our cries of ecstasy echoing through the empty field.

Breathless, we cling to each other, our breaths coming out in ragged pants. "Well, that was," I start, laughing breathlessly, "unexpected."

Killian chuckles, setting me down gently. "A kitten's got claws." He smirks, rubbing at his back where my fingernails made their presence known.

"Oh, you haven't seen anything yet, Killian," I wink, deciding I quite like this bold, confident version of myself.

I swing my leg over his waist, straddling him as he lays back on the cold, damp grass, and take him in my hands, admiring his hardness. "Ready for round two, big guy?" I say, winking at him, trying to hide the vulnerability I feel.

"Oh, kitten," Killian grunts, his eyes smoldering with desire, "I've been ready since you first walked onto this field. Ride me."

With a coy smile, I lower myself onto him, his cock filling me perfectly, like a key in a lock.

I moan, savoring the feeling of him inside me. It's been too long since I've felt this alive.

We move together, our bodies slapping against each other, our moans echoing across the empty stadium.

I bend forward, my breasts bouncing enticingly, and grind my hips into his, eliciting a groan from Killian.

He wraps his hands around my waist, guiding my motions, thrusting up into me as if his life depends on it.

"God, Dylan," he pants, "You feel so... so..."

"Tight? Wet?" I finish for him, gasping as he hits just the right spot within me.

"Both," he grunts, his fingers digging into the turf, his abs tensing beneath me.

The stadium lights flicker on, bathing us in their harsh glare, but we don't stop.

We're lost in each other, caught up in the moment, in the intensity of our union.

Neither of us care about the potential audience, or the consequences.

All that matters is this... this connection, this passionate, all-consuming need to be one with the other.

I throw my head back, my hair cascading down my naked back as I moan loudly, my climax building, coiling deep within my core.

Killian buries his face in my neck, his teeth nipping at my sensitive skin as he spurs me on. "That's it, baby, come for me. Let go."

With a scream that would put any good rugby cheerleader to shame, I shatter around him, my inner walls clenching against him as I orgasm harder than I ever have before.

Killian follows suit, his body rigid beneath mine.

"You're mine, Dylan," he growls out, his voice guttural and animalistic as he pulls out, his hot seed spraying across my chest, and the scoreboard lights up to reveal the final score.

"It's a draw," I whisper.

I stir awake, my heart pounding and my body on fire, the damp sheets tangled around my legs.

Blinking in the dimly lit room, I take a moment to orient myself.

It was just a dream. A vivid, hot as hell dream. And not the first one I've had about my new roommates.

I run my hand over my slick thighs, still tingling with the residual phantom sensation of Killian's touch.

"Shit," I mutter beneath my breath, burying my flushed face into my pillow. Of all the times for my subconscious to be distracted like this. I should be visualizing my moves on the field, not straddling my roommate's giant dream cock.

Giving Jonah a quick snuggle, I roll out of bed, grab my duffel bag, and head for the shower in an attempt to wash away the memory of the scorching hot dream.

As I stand under the cool spray, however, I can't help but replay the scene in my mind. Killian's eyes dark with desire, his hands on my hips, guiding me.

"Focus, Dylan," I scold myself, lathering up with body wash. "I'm here for rugby, nothing else." But even as I say it, I can't help but wonder what it would be like if it had been real, if Killian and I...

Forcing the thought away, I step out of the shower, dress, and head toward the kitchen.

I need a strong cup of coffee, some banter with my new teammates at practice, and to stop thinking about my very off-limits, very gorgeous roommates.

CHAPTER 10

Dylan

The crisp morning air invigorates me as I hit the streets, adrenaline pumping through my veins as I push myself to outrun my lust-addled mind.

If my old team's administration could see me now, they'd be eating their own shorts. "Oh, she's too distracted, short, tall, fat, thin, smart, stupid to be any good," they used to sneer. Always some reason why I wasn't good enough. And after I stood up for one of my teammates who was being harassed by a member of the management team? I basically kissed any chance of being in the starting lineup goodbye.

Well, I'll show them. The call from this club couldn't have come at a better time. I'll work my ass off here and earn that starting position, respect, and maybe even help the team to earn a Victory Cup title.

As I round the corner, I nearly collide with a naked muscular god, who's out for a run as well. I take in his rippling, tanned body and his tattoos, and gradually I realize they look familiar.

Fuck, it's Noah, looking hotter than ever, clad only in a pair of gray shorts and running shoes.

"Sorry!" we both exclaim, my cheeks flaring redder than the rising sun that gleams off his glistening skin.

"No worries, Dylan," he smiles, his abs rippling in the morning light as if they're taunting me. "Fancy a run together?"

I hesitate, but he's my roommate, and he's asking me for a run, not a one-night stand. "Sure, why not?"

As we jog side by side, our breaths synced, I silently curse my stupid hormones for making me notice how his biceps flex with every stride.

I clear my throat, channeling my inner coach for some much-needed seriousness. "So, Noah, any tips for fitting in with the team or the club in general?"

He smirks, "Well, Dylan," he drawls, "if you want to fit in, you gotta loosen up." I nearly trip over my own two feet. "I meant on defense," he clarifies, saving me from further mortification.

"You—you've seen me play?"

"Yeah," he shrugs. "I got curious and checked some of your games out on YouTube when I was having trouble sleeping. You're good, and I can see why you're on the team. But you're too rigid. You need to be more fluid."

I choke on a mouthful of air. "Fluid?"

Noah laughs, "Relax, Dylan. It just means to go with the flow."

We share a laugh, and for a moment, we're just two players bonding over a shared love of the game. The sun's rays warm my skin as we run, and I can't help but think that maybe this won't be so bad after all.

As we approach the apartment and part ways, I shoot one last glance at Noah's toned back and his tight butt. Not to mention his massive thighs that could probably crush me to death without him even trying.

No harm in looking, right?

But when I turn around, Jayden and Killian are both there, suppressing grins as wide as the front door.

Damn. Already off to a great start, Dylan.

Killian's eyes spark with amusement. "Enjoying the view, Dylan? Did we totally just catch you perving out on Noah?"

"Er, no, I just—" I stammer, my cheeks on fire.

Noah comes to my rescue, his amusement obvious by the giant smirk on his face that I'd love to smack right off. "Sure, she was. I can't blame her, though. This ass looks good from every angle." He pats his own behind and winks, diffusing the tension.

"Mate, why don't you and your over-inflated ego get a bloody room," Killian retorts, shoving Noah playfully.

It's like they make fun of whoever is the easiest target, and I experience a sense of relief as their focus turns to Noah.

Laughter erupts and, as I head to my room, I can't help but feel a little lighter.

Maybe this living situation isn't so bad after all.

I mean, with roommates like these, I have all the entertainment I could possibly need right here.

CHAPTER 11

Dylan

The grocery store is a buzzing hive of activity, shoppers weaving in and out of the aisles like bees.

I breathe in the scent of fresh produce and baked goods, grateful for the normalcy after the tension-filled morning at the apartment. I grab a cart and set off to gather some things, my mind swirling with anticipation of my first practice with the new team.

As I toss items into the cart—spinach, eggs, almond milk, and a few healthyish treats—I can't help but feel the stares of other shoppers. I know they're probably just curious about the new girl on the championship rugby team, but it still makes me self-conscious. I'd hoped to blend in here, not be under a microscope.

Lost in thought, I pick up a bottle of cold-pressed olive oil, and my fingers brush against someone else's. Squeaking, I look up into the deepest blue eyes I've ever seen, curiously familiar in their intensity.

"Sorry, I—" I start, before recognizing the owner of the handsomeness in front of me. "Jayden?" I stammer, my cheeks flushing. Great, just what I need—to run into one of my roommates while looking like a tomato.

Jayden smirks, a glint of amusement in his eyes. "Fancy meeting you here, Queen of the Roommate Mix-Ups."

I roll my eyes. "Harsh, but fair," I retort, feeling my cheeks burn even hotter. I'm sure that having a female roommate isn't their dream either. It probably cramps their style for all the girls they no doubt usually bring around.

"Seriously, I'm sorry you haven't had the easiest start here," he says, his smile softening. "And I'm sorry I haven't made you feel more welcome. It was as much of a surprise for us as it was for you, but we've had the benefit of being settled in for a while."

"It's fine," I say, waving it off, even though it isn't. But I don't want to make things more awkward than they already are.

The tension between us crackles like lightning. I swallow, desperately trying not to stare at his lips or the way his biceps flex as he places a bag of protein powder in his cart.

Focus, Dylan, I scold myself.

"So, what's on the menu for you this week?" Jayden asks, changing the subject. "You gonna make us suffer through overly healthy girly crap, or can we live a little?"

I huff. "My cooking is not that bad," I reply, poking him in the abs playfully.

"Ouch, hot stuff," he jokes, feigning a wound. "Don't hit a guy where it hurts."

I feel my cheeks ignite as we both become painfully aware of our proximity in the aisle.

"Well, I should probably go... grocery shop," I mumble, gesturing vaguely towards the rest of the store.

"Wait, Dylan," Jayden calls out, his voice tinged with something I can't quite place. "Want some company? I could help you carry the groceries, since, you know, you... forgot your key." He smirks, holding up the spare key I apparently left on the counter. "Noah keeps forgetting and double-locking it, remember?"

My jaw drops. "How did you—"

"I've got my ways," he winks, an impish glint in his eye. "Besides, I could use some more tips on how not to suck on and off the field."

My face catches fire. "You're insufferable, you know that?" I groan, but my lips twitch into a reluctant smile.

"I know," he grins, tossing the keyring back to me. "But you love it." And with that, he winks and saunters off, leaving me flustered and giggling at his audacity.

As I watch him go, a warmth blooms in my chest. Maybe having Jayden around wouldn't be so bad after all.

The rest of the shopping trip goes by in a blur, and I can't get Jayden's smirk or his innuendos out of my head.

After a while, we almost literally bang into each other again. We banter our way through the aisles, surprisingly in sync as we throw items into each other's carts. It's actually fun, I realize with a pang of disbelief.

When we finally make our way to the checkout lines, I can't help but feel a twinge of sadness that this unexpected moment of levity has almost come to an end. "Well, this has been... unexpectedly bearable," I admit, swiping my card to pay for my groceries.

Jayden flashes me a dimpled grin. "Told you. I can be charming when I want to be. And you're not so bad yourself."

"Yeah, well, don't get used to it," I huff, but my smile gives me away.

With our groceries in tow, we head back to the apartment, the tension between us having shifted from slightly antagonistic to something else, something that makes my stomach flip-flop. As we reach the door, we exchange a brief moment of understanding before Jayden keys in a new security code, replacing the one I'd memorized just hours ago.

I shot him a pointed look. "Really?"

"What? Can't have just anyone barging in on us now, can we?" he winks, ushering me inside. As I pass him, he leans in close, and whispers in my ear, "But I'll be sure to barge in when you least expect it, love."

He straightens and his voice returns to normal. "Here's the new code," he says, handing it to me on a piece of paper. "And stop losing your keys."

I feel my cheeks catch fire as I scurry off to my bedroom, flustered and aroused in equal measure.

Later, in the middle of the night, I find myself craving a snack.

Creeping downstairs in my pajamas, I tiptoe to the fridge, careful not to wake my sleeping housemates. I rummage around, grabbing a tub of ice cream and some chocolate chip cookies, before realizing I left my water bottle upstairs.

"Bugger," I mutter, using a word I learned from my friend Liv, debating whether it's worth going back to get it.

Before I can make up my mind, heavy footsteps thud down the staircase, and the landing light flicks on. I freeze, cursing my luck as Jayden descends the stairs, wearing only a plush gray towel slung low over his hips, water droplets glistening on his bare chest.

Rivulets of water leave slick lines down the V-shaped contour leading from his obliques to his groin... a V-line or Adonis belt I guess are the technical terms, but Kat always preferred the term 'cum gutters' and right now I can't get that out of my head.

"Sleepless too, sunshine?" he drawls, a smirk playing on his lips.

My cheeks flame as I clutch my midnight snack, trying to think of a witty comeback but failing miserably. His low-slung towel has rendered me speechless once again.

"Oh, come on, Dylan, I thought we were past the awkward stage," he teases, sauntering over to the fridge, his toned abs rippling with each step.

"What do you want, Jayden?" I huff, craning my neck to avoid his gorgeous, near-naked body.

"A drink, and a spoon," he smirks, nodding at my ice cream. "And maybe some company, if you're offering."

I roll my eyes, but my heart hammers in my chest. "Fine, take one," I mutter, tossing him a spoon.

As we sit in the darkened kitchen, devouring the ice cream, the tension between us is thicker than the creamy treat.

Jayden shifts closer, dabbing at my lips with a paper towel. "You've got some...," he trails off, his warm breath grazing softly against my skin.

I hold my breath, my gaze locked on his.

Slowly, he leans in, his lips brushing mine, gentle and achingly soft, his stubble tickling my skin.

I melt into him, the ice cream forgotten, as we succumb to the simmering chemistry that's been building between us ever since we first laid eyes on each other.

Breaking apart, both panting, I gaze into his eyes.

"I've been wanting to do that since we met," he says, his voice husky.

I feel a flush creep up my neck.

"So, tell me about Jayden Bishop," I say, feigning nonchalance and eager for a distraction. My brain is still processing the kiss.

He smirks, leaning back against the counter. "What do you want to know, Dylan?"

"Tell me something I don't know about you..."

"Let's just say I'm more than a pretty face and a mean tackle."

Our eyes lock once more, and my heart skips a beat. "Oh yeah? What does that mean?"

"You'll see, in good time. Good things shouldn't be rushed," he smirks again.

"I'd be a fool not to believe you," I say, my voice husky with desire. "But I still think you need to prove it."

"I'm glad you said that," he growls, swooping in for another searing kiss. "Wouldn't want to disappoint the new assistant captain of the women's team," he murmurs against my neck, sending shivers down my spine.

"We'll see about that."

Just as quickly as everything started, Jayden pulls away. "I—I should go," he says, his hardness evident underneath his towel as he makes his way out of the kitchen. "That was a mistake. I'm sorry," he says, walking away.

"Wait, what just happened?" I arch a brow at his retreating back. A muscular back covered in tattoos. Ugh. My weakness. "Did I do something wrong?"

But he doesn't reply, just continues to walk away, leaving me alone with a rapidly melting pint in my hand.

I look down at my ice cream and sigh. This is going to be harder than I expected. Strange and hard. Usually a fun combination.

But in this setting, I'm suddenly not so sure.

CHAPTER 12

Dylan

I'm carrying the heavy box of training equipment down the hall, my arms burning from the weight.

As I pass the living room, the guys call out.

"Hey Dylan, you need a hand with that?" asks Jayden.

I stop, glaring at them. "No, I've got it," I snap.

"You sure?" says Noah. "That looks pretty heavy."

My grip tightens on the box. They're only offering because I'm a woman. I don't need their help.

I always feel so conflicted about this.

There's something we're taught as girls where a guy holding a door open for us is meant to be polite... and I don't mind it from time to time.

But expecting a guy to carry every heavy fucking thing heavier than a purse? I work out hard, I'm strong. I don't need a man for that.

For other things, perhaps. But not for this.

"I'm fine," I say sharply. "I can carry a stupid box by myself."

The moment the words leave my mouth, I realize I'm being a bit of a bitch.

"Whoa, calm down," Jayden holds up his hands. "We were just trying to help."

His words make me feel worse, because he's right. They are just trying to help. It's just the implied assumption that I can't do it for myself that irks me.

"Yeah, don't get your sports bra in a twist," Noah jokes.

I scowl, stomping towards the kitchen.

Jerks.

I'll show them I'm just as strong as they are.

My stubborn Taurus nature is coming out. The box digs into my arms, but I keep going, ignoring the pain.

I don't need their help, even though they would probably have made this whole ordeal much easier.

I stomp into the kitchen, dropping the heavy box on the counter with a thud. As I straighten, rubbing my sore arms, laughter erupts from the living room.

What the hell? Are they laughing at me?

Fuming, I march back down the hall to confront them. Noah and Jayden are cracking up on the couch.

"What's so funny?" I demand, crossing my arms.

"Um, Dylan..." Jayden grins, averting his eyes. "Your shirt."

I glance down. To my horror, one of my nipples has slipped free of my tank top.

No wonder they were offering to help—the weight of the box must have tugged my shirt down.

My face burns crimson. How long has my nipple been exposed?

"Oh my god!" I gasp, quickly tucking my boob back into my tank top.

The guys erupt into laughter again.

Mortified, I whirl around, fleeing back to my room. I'll never live this down. Stupid top.

I hear Noah call after me, "Hey, don't be embarrassed! It's nothing we haven't seen before!"

I slam my door, throwing myself onto the bed. I can't believe I flashed them. This is so humiliating. But at least now I know they were just trying to help, not patronize me. Still, I'm never leaving my room again.

I bury my face in my pillow, willing the mattress to swallow me whole. How can I ever look Noah and Jayden in the eye again after this nip slip fiasco?

Jonah saunters up to me and plops down by my armpit, purring loudly, as if he's getting huge amusement from the situation as well.

A knock sounds at my door. "Dylan? Can I come in?" Noah calls out gently.

"No! Go away!" I yell, my voice muffled by the pillow.

The door creaks open anyway and I sense Noah standing over me.

"Hey, don't beat yourself up over this," he says. "It was an accident. Even the best of us have a nip slip from time to time."

I narrow my eyes. "Like you've ever had a nip slip."

"Dude," he laughs. "One of my balls straight up slipped out of my pants in a scrum drill once."

I can't help but snort, and lift my head to glare at him. "That did not happen to you! And as for my 'accident', as you put it, you and Jayden both seemed to find it hilarious."

Noah grins. "What can I say? You have nice nipples."

I smack his arm, but can't help cracking a smile. His teasing makes me feel a little better.

"There's that pretty smile," Noah says, brushing a strand of hair from my face. "It's just us here, Dylan. No need to be embarrassed."

I sigh, sitting up. "I know. I just hate feeling like the butt of some joke. And it really felt like you guys just didn't think I could carry the equipment by myself, even though I've done it a million times before."

Noah tilts my chin up to meet his gaze. "You're not a joke to me. Never could see you like that, especially after watching you in those game recordings." His voice is earnest now. "Nipple aside, we likely would have asked you if we could help anyway. Just like we would have asked any of the other guys, too!"

My heart flutters as his face inches closer to mine. When his lips meet mine, the lingering awkwardness melts away. Before I can think too much about it, I'm kissing him back.

Kissing roommates wasn't on my agenda, but it sure as hell is fun, especially when they look like this.

Maybe this nip slip wasn't such a disaster after all.

CHAPTER 13

Dylan

I slide into the passenger seat of Noah's car, my gym bag at my feet. The equipment box is safely ensconced in the back seat, and I eventually let Noah help me carry it there without freaking out again. My stomach is a bundle of nerves, but I try to play it cool.

After kissing me, he'd simply left the room, and neither of us have brought it up again. It's almost as if I imagined it. And now, here we are, a new day. It's clear he doesn't intend to bring it up, and there's no way I can let my focus be derailed by one—okay, two—roommate kisses.

"Ready for day one, captain?" Noah asks, flashing me a grin as he pulls out of the parking lot.

"Assistant captain. And as ready as I'll ever be," I say, letting out a shaky laugh. Get it together, Dylan. I'm still blown away that the club has taken a chance on me, let alone in a leadership role like this. It feels like everything I've ever dreamed of is all finally starting to happen.

Noah goes on about how stoked he is for the leadership program, even if some of the exercises sound a bit fluffy.

My thoughts drift as I stare out the window, psyching myself up. It's cute that he's excited, but I need to get my head in the game. This is my chance to prove I've got what it takes. No more bench warming or politics blocking my path.

"Earth to Dylan?" Noah's voice breaks through my inner pep talk.

"Huh? Oh yeah, sorry," I say, feeling my cheeks flush. "Just getting in the zone. I heard there's some woo-woo stuff too, but I'm into that."

Noah chuckles. "Let me guess—crystals, vision boards, sage smudging?"

"You know it," I say with a dramatic sigh. "I'm a total woo girl."

The other rugby girls used to make fun of me for it, but they shut up a little after I bought them each a custom crystal and they started seeing the results a tiny bit of what manifestation can do if you put your mind to it.

Noah shakes his head, amused. As he pulls into the parking lot, I feel a nervous thrill run through me. This is my time to shine.

"So what's the deal with Jayden?" I can't help but ask, trying to sound casual as we walk into the training center. Clearly, I'm not very good at compartmentalizing, but I just can't let this go. "Does he always blow hot and cold like this, or is it just me?"

Noah holds the door open for me. "Nah, don't take it personally. Jayden's just kind of territorial in general. He likes his space."

"Yeah, I got that vibe when he practically bit my head off for touching his precious kitchen tools this morning," I say, rolling my eyes. "Not like the kitchen was spotless to begin with. Which made it worse. It's not like you can mess up a mess. He complained because I put the spatula face down."

Noah laughs. "See what I mean? Total diva when it comes to his cooking domain. But he'll warm up to you, eventually."

I nod, reassured. Maybe I'm being overly sensitive—this is a fresh start, and I can't let past drama cloud things.

Noah gives me an encouraging pat on the back. "You've got this, Dylan. Forget about Jayden and his nitpicking. Remember why you're here. Go show them what you've got."

With renewed confidence, I head into the training room, ready to prove my worth. Noah's right —I can't let Jayden or anyone else shake me. It's time I take my destiny into my own hands.

I take a seat on the floor next to some of my new teammates, feeling their curious eyes on me. I know I'm the new girl, the unknown entity, but I'm determined to show them I belong here.

As the instructor starts leading us through a series of yoga poses and breathing exercises, I feel myself relaxing into the movements, the stress of the past few weeks melting away. This may look like woo-woo nonsense to some of the guys, but I can already feel it centering me, getting me in the zone.

It's hard to lead a group when you're flustered and all over the place in your own mind. Putting your own emergency mask on before helping others, and all that.

Out of the corner of my eye, I notice Noah across the room, contorting his tall frame into awkward yoga positions. He looks utterly ridiculous and I have to stifle a laugh.

He catches me watching him and winks dramatically, nearly toppling over in the process.

I shake my head and turn my focus back to my own breathing, but I can't help the smile tugging at my lips. For a rugby player, especially one of his size, he's actually quite bendy.

It's when he contorts his body into happy baby pose that I finally lose my shit, earning a stern look from the instructor when I laugh so hard I snort and end up doubled over on the floor.

This huge man, his bulging, muscular thighs squeezed against his chest, desperately trying to wrap his fingers around his pinky toes but not quite making it. He's flailing around like an ant that's fallen on its back and can't get up.

Unable to help myself, I discreetly whip out my phone and take a brief video to share with the other guys later. All's fair in love and roommate war.

Maybe this captain training program won't be so bad after all. With classmates like Noah lightening the mood, I might even enjoy myself.

CHAPTER 14

Dylan

After our mindfulness session, it's time for lunch.

I can't get the first taste of mac and cheese out of my head as I follow Noah across the lawn. The warm, gooey cheese still coats my tongue, a delicious distraction from the butterflies in my stomach. For a sports program, they certainly put on an impressive display of food.

I really like how the nutritionists here focus on a balanced approach, taking overall macros and calories into account rather than banning 'bad' foods. It's a far cry from the more restrictive food regimes I've heard other clubs subscribe to, and, as a foodie, I'm so grateful this was the club that picked me.

Noah waves over three hulking guys who are tossing a rugby ball back and forth. "Mike, Sione, Hone, come meet Dylan!"

My palms sweat. Will Noah's teammates like me? I know how cliquey teams can be. But Mike's smile is as warm as the mac and cheese. "Welcome to the madhouse! How are you liking it so far?"

Sione claps my shoulder. "We heard you're a hell of a hooker. Can't wait to see your skills on the pitch."

"I bet she can drink us all under the table too," Hone says with a wink. His easy banter sets me at ease, almost as if he's treating me like one of the guys. Maybe I've found my people.

We chat about our favorite teams and playlists until we're called back to the session.

As we walk, Noah murmurs, "Told you this would change our lives."

With his team already feeling like family, I'm starting to believe him.

I slide into a seat next to Noah in the auditorium as the day's guest speaker, Nigel Nesbitt, takes the stage with Cynthia, a handsome, angular woman who manages the club's leadership program. Her no-nonsense ponytail and sharp blazer contrast with Nigel's surfer dude vibe.

"Leadership," Nigel begins. "It's a word that gets thrown around a lot in sports. But what does it really mean?"

Cynthia clicks to the next slide. "Leadership is influence," she says crisply. "It's about inspiring others towards a common goal."

As they discuss pivoting strategies and overcoming resistance to change, Noah and I exchange glances. It's like they're describing our own situation—and maybe, just maybe, this course will teach us how to pivot the way we both so desperately need.

CHAPTER 15

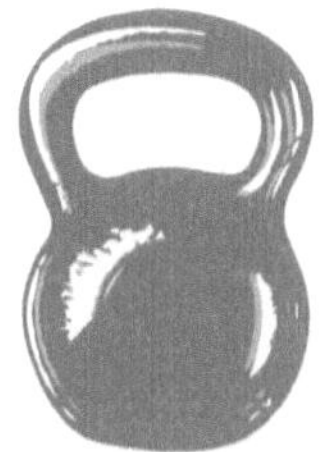

Noah

The sun beats down on my neck as I stare across the empty rugby pitch, my mind full of leadership terminology after the day's classes. Heat radiates off the grass in shimmery waves, reminding me of my childhood summers with Jayden. We'd play one-on-one rugby for hours, collapsing in exhaustion as the day faded to dusk.

Jayden's always been wary of strangers. I know why. His stepdad Walt waltzed into Jayden's life when he was ten, all charismatic smiles and big talk. But behind closed doors, Walt was a mean drunk. I saw the bruises he tried to hide.

So when someone new comes along, Jayden blows hot and cold and occasionally bares his teeth. Like with Dylan. I get that he's protective of our team, but she seems harmless. Eager to prove herself, yeah, but she's got no agenda other than playing her best.

So why's Jayden giving her such a hard time? She's not like Walt. I mean, have you seen her smile? It lights up her whole face. And she's got a wicked sense of humor too. Just the other day, I heard her sassing our other teammate, Luke, about his terrible finesse on the pitch. She's kinda perfect, actually...

Wait, do I have a thing for Dylan? Is that why I jumped to defend her against Jayden?

No way. I barely know her. But I do feel this urge to shield her. To make her feel at home here.

And the kiss we had came out of the blue, but that was just spontaneous. A way to dispel the tension. That's all there was to it.

At least Jayden's not trying to treat Dylan like he tends to treat his fangirls, though. Using them and discarding them without a thought before rapidly moving onto the next one. I've seen him in action, and it's both alarming and impressive, the simplicity with which he's able to pull hot chicks and then treat them like utter shit. No consequences to make him stop, I guess.

My phone buzzes, jolting me from my thoughts.

Jayden:

Why do you have such a boner for Dylan?

I laugh out loud. He can be a real mind reader sometimes. Maybe I do have a little thing for her. But it's more than that. She deserves a real chance here. And I'm gonna make sure she gets it.

I shake my head and start typing a reply:

Noah:

Dude, I don't have a 'boner' for her. I just think she deserves a fair shot on the team. Put yourself in her tiny ass shoes. She just moved here and is trying to fit in. Cut her some slack.

A few moments later, my phone buzzes again.

Jayden:

> *Whatever, man, she's cute and all, and maybe I just haven't gotten to know her as well as you. I want to like her, but I don't know if I can trust her. Something about her seems off.*

I frown and start typing furiously.

Noah:

> *You've got to give her more of a chance. Help her feel welcome here. It must be lonely and overwhelming being surrounded by a new team of guys. She's new to the city, too. Just give her a chance. And of course something seems off… anyone would be acting off with a giant man-child like you breathing down her neck and being nice one moment and mean the next. Stop being so moody and get yourself together.*

I hit send and wait, wondering how he'll respond. I get why he's being prickly, but it's misplaced, and I just want to help her feel at home here.

My phone buzzes one more time.

Jayden:

> *Fine, I'll try to be nicer or whatever. But I've got my eye on her.*

Noah:

> *I knew you'd come around. She's gonna be great for the club and the women's team. Just watch.*

I set my phone down, hoping I've made some progress with Jayden. Dylan deserves to feel accepted. And I aim to make that happen, no matter what it takes. Even if it means standing up to my stubborn friend.

I usually don't get involved in team politics or take sides. But for some reason, I feel drawn to Dylan.

Maybe it's because her situation reminds me a bit of my own past. When I first joined the rugby team, I was an outsider too. The hazing and teasing was relentless until I proved my worth on the field. It was a lonely, isolating time.

I see that same look in Dylan's eyes—that deep hunger to belong. She's trying so hard to fit into the team, taking any insult or joke with forced laughter.

I know that feeling of never quite measuring up. Of having to work twice as hard just to be seen as an equal.

And I'm a giant man, the stereotypical image of a professional rugby guy. I can't even imagine what it would be like to add on being a woman. I can only imagine a huge deal of frustration and, at some point, a certain resignation that we're all stuck within an entrenched, misogynistic framework that will take years or decades to shift. Not that I'd ever say any of this out loud.

Or maybe it's more than that.

There's an intensity about Dylan that intrigues me. She seems to wear a tough exterior, but I sense a vulnerability underneath.

When we talk, her emerald eyes bore into mine with startling focus. Her quick wit and sarcastic humor make me want to banter with her for hours.

She makes me feel energized, alive, as if I have to be on high alert to keep up with her witty sneak attacks.

She knows how to pester and prod, but in an intellectual way that's hard to poke holes in. And, as I think about it, I realize that I love every second of it.

I shake my head, confused by my own tangled emotions. I barely know this girl. Yet I feel oddly drawn to her in a way I can't fully explain.

All I know for sure is that I want to protect Dylan from harm. I want to see her thrive and succeed here.

And I'll do whatever it takes to make that happen.

CHAPTER 16

Dylan

I walk into the training room and stop short when I see her. A petite blonde whirlwind in hot pink yoga pants and a "Girls Run the World" tank top practically bounces up to me, her ponytail swinging halfway down her back.

"You must be Dylan! I'm Loretta, the team physical therapist. So great to finally meet you!" She pumps my hand enthusiastically. I'm actually shocked by her grip, given her size. Any firmer, and I might need physical therapy.

Before I can respond, a tall brunette in a crisp pantsuit strides over. "And I'm Keeley, the PR manager." Her handshake is brisk, but her smile is warm. "We are so thrilled you've joined us this season!"

"Thanks, me too," I say, still a bit stunned by their exuberance.

Loretta claps her hands. "Aren't you just going to take this team by storm? I can feel it!"

"We need someone with your talent and experience," Keeley agrees. "I can already envision all the great coverage we'll get with you leading the forward pack."

Their confidence buoys me. No veiled agendas or political mind games—just genuine excitement at my arrival.

I can't help but grin back. It's the first time I've been in an all-female leadership team, and I don't even know how to explain how the energy just feels different. Not that I mind being around a group of testosterone-charged men, of course. It's just nice to have this experience.

Based on what I've seen so far, I have a feeling that maybe this time will genuinely be different. A fresh start, and my chance to finally prove myself on a team that truly wants me.

Loretta's enthusiasm is infectious as she chatters on about her passion for bringing women's rugby into the spotlight. "The women's game has come so far, but it still doesn't get the respect or attention it deserves compared to the men," she says, her green eyes flashing with conviction. "That's why I love working with this team—helping pave the way for the future!"

I nod, impressed by her dedication. "So you sought out working with a women's rugby squad?"

"Absolutely!" Loretta laughs. "When I first moved to the city, I figured I'd be working with big, burly dudes. But then I discovered this team and never looked back. The sisterhood and spirit here are like nothing I've ever experienced. In fact, the club is so passionate about progressing the women's team—I'm sure that's part of why you took your position here...". She pauses, and I nod. "We actually get to try out some of the most progressive rehabilitation techniques in the world before the men's team."

I quirk a brow, not wanting to dampen her enthusiasm by pointing out it sounds like the women's team may be being used as guinea pigs for trial treatments.

She squeezes my bicep playfully. "And don't worry, I'll have those muscles of yours in tip-top shape in no time!"

I chuckle at her boldness.

Keeley smiles knowingly.

"Loretta's right about the special bond here," she says. "As the PR manager, I want to showcase that to the world. Women supporting women—that's what it's all about. Lifting each other up and putting all types of professional athletes in the spotlight where they belong. I can't wait until Shay, the captain, arrives... her club wouldn't let her out of her contract in time for the first game, which isn't ideal, but you and she are going to get along like a house on fire."

I nod along as Keeley speaks, her enthusiasm lighting a fire in me.

Their passion is contagious. For the first time in ages, I feel that spark—the thrill of being part of something bigger than myself. Something groundbreaking.

"The women's game has come so far, but you're right—we still have a long way to go to get the same respect and visibility as the men's leagues," I say.

Keeley's eyes shine. "Exactly! That's been my mission since joining the team. Giving women's rugby the coverage and hype it deserves. And now, with you leading the squad, I just know we're going to take things to the next level."

She gives me an appraising look. "You're the perfect poster girl to spotlight what we can achieve. Talented, driven, not to mention gorgeous." She winks.

I blush, not used to such direct praise. But her belief in me and in the future of the women's game is empowering.

"Well, I'm honored to help carry that torch," I say sincerely. "This team, this sisterhood—it already means the world to me. I'll do whatever I can to help you shine a light on what we're building here."

Keeley grins and pulls me into an enthusiastic hug. "Just you wait, we're going to take this league by storm!"

As we chat and laugh together, I feel lighter than I have in years.

Like I've finally found my people.

With these women by my side, I know I can soar.

The future for women's rugby has never looked brighter.

CHAPTER 17

Dylan

The whistle blows and my feet pound against the grass, adrenaline pumping through my veins. I dart left and right, dodging defenders as I make a break for the try line. The ball feels like an extension of my hand, the perfect oval shape gliding between my fingers.

I spot an opening and push forward, my legs burning as I sprint the last few meters.

With a final burst of speed, I smash through the tackle and slam the ball down across the line.

The ref's hand shoots into the air—try!

My new teammates let out a roar and rush over, surrounding me in a mass of grinning faces and high-fives.

I'm shocked. Hookers don't usually score tries. But here I am, at my first practice, and I can't even be accused of being a ball hog because it literally landed in my hands, and I saw a clear path so I took it.

"That was insane!" A girl with spiky black hair claps me on the back. "Dylan, right? I'm Sarah."

Another teammate squeezes my shoulder. "Seriously impressive footwork there. I'm Beck."

I can't stop smiling, their praise warming me from the inside out. After feeling overlooked for so long, it's incredible to finally be seen for my athleticism.

"Thanks, you two played great as well," I say. We fall into easy conversation as we walk towards the locker room, the three of us laughing and joking like old friends. They seem just like the type of teammates I was hoping for. No interest in politics or drama—just the sport we love and the chance to prove our worth.

"So get this," I say as we reach the locker room. "As you know, I just moved here, and there's been a total mix-up with my housing."

Sarah's eyes go wide. "What? Girl, spill!"

"Well," I sigh, "I was supposed to stay with some of the other new recruits, but when I got to the house, it was already full. So the housing office stuck me with..."

"Don't tell me," Beck says. "Killian Baxter?"

I nod, and they both gasp dramatically.

"No way!" Sarah whispers. "Living with the poster boy of the men's team himself?"

"I know, it's crazy," I say, shaking my head. "I don't even know him..."

Beck leans in, voice low. "Honestly, no one does. He's friendly enough, but keeps to himself."

"Total mystery man," Sarah agrees. "But so talented and focused. You should see him on the pitch—poetry in motion. He's also quite focused... at the bars and clubs, if you know what I mean. Has a reputation for having a different girl on his arm every day of the week."

"Not that you can blame him," says Beck. "The way he looks, he could get any girl he wanted. Even some of the lesbians on the team, myself included, don't mind staring at his bum."

I laugh. "Well, I'm sure he's great and all, and I have seen him in his undies and can confirm he's... well-shaped in that department. But I'm here for one reason—rugby. I'll leave the swooning over Killian's dreamy eyes or chiseled abs... or exquisite tattoos... to you guys." I quirk a brow. "Wait, how did you guess I was living with him? There must be a ton of team apartments here."

"Oh, he and the other guys have been going around telling everyone how they have this hot new female roommate. Which is obviously you. You're the talk of the men's team, that's for sure."

I roll my eyes and shake my head. "Great, just what I always wanted. Burly neanderthals group texting about my tits. It doesn't help that I had a nip slip in front of two of them the other day."

We grin, camaraderie warm between us as I tell them the story of Nipplegate. They empathize and share a laugh with me and it helps me to realize it's really not a big deal, just a good story. With teammates like these, I feel like I could thrive here, on the field and off.

I smile and give them a nod. "Thanks for the heads up about Killian, though. I'll try not to drool too obviously over the mysterious dreamboat."

We all laugh again as we head out of the locker room.

"In all seriousness, though," Sarah says, "living with Killian and the other guys could be good for you. They're all leaders on their team. Get some extra pitch time, inside tips, maybe even a management role for the men's team one day if you play your cards right, and if that's something you want to do."

She waggles her eyebrows suggestively and I roll my eyes.

"Doubtful. I don't even know if he likes me yet. I'm not here to cozy up to anyone, remember?"

"Yeah, yeah," Beck waves her hand. "All business, we know. We can tell that about you already. But never say never!"

I just shake my head with a grin. "You two are incorrigible. Now come on, I'm starving!"

We chat and joke all the way to the dining hall, their infectious enthusiasm making me feel like I'm already part of the team.

With drive, skill and friends like these, even my unruly roommates stand a chance against me for long.

CHAPTER 18

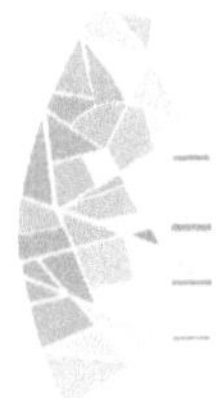

Dylan

I t's later in the evening, and things have progressed to the local bar, a popular post-dining hall watering hole known for live music and cheap drinks.

That's when I notice a man standing at the bar.

Fuck. It's him.

I hadn't thought about him in ages, but I'd recognize those tattoos anywhere.

I'd shoved him out of my mind, because I'm not a one-night stand type of girl. Whatever that means. No shame in anyone who enjoys the thrill of finding a cute guy at the club, taking him home and fucking his brains out, and then sending them on their merry way. It's just not my usual style.

But there was something about the night we met. The intoxicating beat of the bass in the club, and the way the drinks went down easily, leaving me in a state of comfort and lowered inhibitions. I felt sexy and free, extra empowered by it being my visit to check out whether the rugby program was right for me. And, given the city's population, I thought there'd be no way I'd ever see him again.

Yet, here he is in all his muscly glory. And he's wearing tight shorts and a shirt that leave his muscles bulging in all the right places. Good god, he's looking even better than the first time I met him. His thighs are enormous, bulging so firmly they threaten to tear his shorts. And I know from experience his thighs aren't the only thing bulging in his pants.

I freeze in place, my heart pounding. Do I say something? Act like I don't recognize him?

Before I can decide, his gaze slides over me. And there's not even a flicker of recognition in his eyes. Like I'm just another stranger in the crowd.

Anger and embarrassment flare in my chest. How dare he not remember me? I may not make a habit of one-off encounters, but I'm memorable, damn it.

He sure seemed to be having a good time when he was plowing me in every sex position we could think of, and some that I think we just made up on the spot.

I lift my chin and stride forward, determined to make my presence known. "Kai, isn't it?" My tone is deceptively light and casual.

A frown creases his forehead. "Sorry, do I know you?"

The words are a slap in the face. I plaster on a smile, all teeth. "Don't worry about it. My mistake."

Without another word, I turn on my heel and stalk away, my fists clenched at my sides. So much for proving my worth. I'm just another faceless woman to add to his list of conquests. How humiliating.

"Dylan, wait up!"

Noah jogs up beside me, brow furrowed with concern. "What was that all about? I saw you talking to our teammate Kai and then you just took off. Did he say something to upset you?"

I give a jerky shrug. "Nothing. It's fine."

"It didn't look fine." Noah folds his arms, leveling me with a piercing look. "If I didn't know better, I'd say this wasn't the first time you two had met." He pauses, and recognition dawns in his eyes. "Did you hook up with him or something?"

My face flames. Am I that obvious? Trust Noah to cut right to the heart of things.

I can't bring myself to admit the truth, so I stare down at my shoes and mumble, "It was just a one-night stand. A while ago. No big deal."

Noah's eyes widen. "Seriously? With Kai?" He gives a low whistle. "No wonder you're acting so weird around him."

I glare and punch his arm. "Shut up! It's embarrassing enough as it is."

"Sorry, sorry." He rubs his arm, though my punch couldn't have hurt. The jerk is just trying to get a rise out of me. "So he didn't recognize you then?" His gaze trails over me and he shakes his head. "What an idiot."

The anger and hurt rise up again, and I have to fight to keep my voice steady. "Nope. Just another notch on his bedpost, I imagine."

Noah's expression softens with sympathy. "His loss. You deserve better than that, Dylan."

I give him a weak smile. "Thanks, Noah. I know it's stupid, getting worked up over a guy like him. He's not worth it."

Noah slings an arm around my shoulders. "Exactly. Now come on, let's go get a drink. Forget all about him."

I nod, straightening my spine. Noah's right. Kai isn't worth another second of my time. I'm going to walk away from this with my head held high—and find someone who will actually remember my name.

After about half an hour, and emboldened by another drink, I decide to give it one more try. I plaster on a smile and walk over to where Kai stands with a few of his teammates. "Hey guys, just wanted to say congratulations on the win the other day."

Kai turns, and for a moment his gaze brightens in what appears to be recognition. My stupid heart leaps in response.

But then his eyes shutter, and the easy grin he offers feels impersonal. Polite. "Thanks. We appreciate the support."

His teammates chime in with similar platitudes, but I keep my focus on Kai, searching for any flicker of our connection.

There's nothing.

I was a fool to think a single night together meant anything to him.

Anger and hurt curdle in my gut, and I have to fight to keep my tone light. "Well, I should get going. Early practice tomorrow." I nod to the group. "I'm Dylan by the way, from the women's team. Have a good night, all."

Kai lifts a hand in farewell. "You too. Thanks for coming out, Daria."

"Dylan. My name is Dylan," I say, my mouth involuntarily contorting itself as if I just chugged a gallon of sour grapes.

I turn on my heel and stalk away before I do something I'll regret, like throw my drink in his stupid, forgetful face. How dare he act like I'm just another ditzy fan!

Like I didn't rock his world that night, and he didn't promise we'd do it again. Promises, promises. What a joke.

Based on what I've seen so far, I reckon the club would do better if it just threw the whole men's team away.

Noah is waiting by the exit, his expression grim. "That bad, huh?" God, how embarrassing. He must have seen the entire awkward thing. And how desperate must I look, going back over to him only to be unrecognized a second time. My cheeks flame at the thought.

"I don't want to talk about it." I march past him toward the door. "Let's just go."

Noah falls into step beside me. "Should I kick his ass for you?"

I huff out a bitter laugh. "I'm not worth the trouble, remember?" Although, his offer makes me think about what it would look like, the two giant men with their enormous muscles bulging and rippling as they fought over me.

Despite my humiliation at Kai's dismissal of me, my pussy still clenches as the fantasy plays out in my mind.

"Hey." Noah grabs my arm, forcing me to stop and face him. "Don't you dare let that arrogant jerk make you feel worthless. You're amazing, Dylan, and any guy would be lucky to have you. If Kai is too stupid to see that, it's most definitely his loss and not yours. You really do deserve way better."

His fierce loyalty makes my throat tighten.

I pull him into a hug. "Thanks, Noah. I know we haven't known each other for long, but at the moment, I really don't know what I'd do without you."

He hugs me back, hard. I stifle a moan as his hard chest presses into my neck. "Now come on, let's go drown your sorrows in ice cream."

I smile against his shoulder. "You always know just what to say."

Noah presses a kiss to the top of my head, a friendly gesture that leaves my head spinning slightly all the same. "That's what I'm here for."

Maybe Kai turning out to be a waste of time is a blessing in disguise.

Because maybe I have everything I need right here.

CHAPTER 19

Dylan

The grocery store aisle tilts sideways as my feet leave the floor. For a split second, I'm weightless, suspended mid-air. Fear spikes through me and I flail, grasping for something stable to grip onto, knocking boxes of cereal to the floor.

"Hey!" a familiar voice laughs behind me. "Chill out, it's just me."

I crane my neck around to see Killian grinning up at me, his muscly arm wrapped around my waist, holding me aloft like I weigh nothing.

"Killian!" I gasp, swatting his shoulder. "Put me down, you oaf."

He chuckles but complies, setting me gently on my feet.

I straighten my shirt and turn to face him, hands on my hips, trying to ignore the humming sensation everywhere he just touched me.

"What's the big idea, grabbing me like that? You scared the crap out of me."

Killian rubs the back of his neck, looking sheepish. "Sorry, I was just messing around. Wanted to see if I could lift you. What do you run, like 170 or so?"

I roll my eyes, but can't help the little thrill that courses through me. His casual display of strength makes my pulse quicken. I bite my lip, imagining what those powerful arms could do...

Shaking the thought away, I punch his shoulder again, lightly. "That's a rude question to ask a girl. But 180, for your information. And next time, give a girl some warning, yeah?"

He grins. "Duly noted."

I bend to gather the fallen boxes, hyper aware of his eyes on me. As annoying as that was, I can't deny it—I like knowing I have Killian's attention.

I stack the cereal boxes back on the shelf, trying to ignore the fluttering in my stomach as Killian watches me intently.

"So..." he says, leaning against the shelves casually. "You've been avoiding me since we became roommates."

I stiffen, keeping my gaze fixed on restocking. "No, I haven't."

"Yes, you have." He steps closer. "Every time I enter a room, you leave. You never sit near me at dinner. And just now you tensed up when I touched you."

I turn to face him, indignant. "That's because you grabbed me without warning and lifted me into the air!"

"Maybe," he concedes. "But I think it's more than that." His eyes burn into mine. "I make you nervous, don't I?"

My breath catches at his proximity, his musky scent enveloping me. I force nonchalance. "You don't make me nervous." I'm such a liar. My heart is racing, my knees are weak and my palms are sweating profusely, just from being in his presence.

He smiles slowly. "Yes, I do. And you know it."

Suddenly, he presses me back against the shelves, caging me in with his arms. My heart pounds wildly as he leans in close, our faces inches apart.

"But that's okay," he murmurs. "Because I'm going to spend every day breaking down those walls of yours, Dylan." His fingers trail down my arm and I shiver. "Before long, you'll be like putty in my hands."

My lips part, shock and desire warring within me.

Just as quickly, he smirks and pulls back, sauntering away.

"See you at home, roomie," he calls over his shoulder.

I slump back against the shelves, my pulse racing.

Oh boy. I'm in trouble.

I take a deep breath to steady myself as I watch him walk away, his taut ass bouncing pleasantly in time with his long strides. My skin still tingles where he touched me.

I can't deny there's an intense magnetic attraction between us. And, living together, it seems impossible to resist. That close proximity, and the intimacy of sharing a space even though we sleep in separate rooms. So many chances for accidental nudity.. we've already had a nip slip incident, for goodness' sake. The situation just seems ripe with opportunity and risk.

As I continue my shopping, I can't stop picturing Killian shirtless after a workout, his muscles rippling. Or emerging from the shower with just a towel wrapped around his waist. If only I could make that towel fall down. If only I could be that towel.

A flush creeps up my neck at the thought. Get it together, Dylan.

But my mind keeps wandering to all the tantalizing possibilities of having a roommate who looks like Killian. Lazy weekend mornings lounging in bed together. Steamy showers where we "conserve water." Curling up on the couch, his strong arms wrapped around me.

I bite my lip, desire simmering within me. Maybe this arrangement is just what I need.

As I head to the checkout, I make a decision. No more running away from Killian. It's time to stop fighting this magnetic pull between us.

I'm going to embrace every moment of having this gorgeous man as a roommate. And let him break through these walls I've built.

One searing kiss at a time.

CHAPTER 20

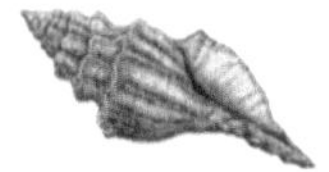

Killian

The hum of my engine is the only sound cutting through the silence as I cruise down the empty back roads. My hands grip the steering wheel, my knuckles turning white as a riot of thoughts storm through my head.

Despite her obvious strength, she was all curves and softness when I picked her up at the grocery store, a jolt of desire shooting through me at the contact. And that brief, accidental touch of her butt cheek... God, what's happening to me?

I shake my head and sigh, shifting in my seat. The memory of Dylan's body pressed against mine floods my senses, my body's instant reaction proof that the chemistry between us is undeniable. But is it worth the risk?

"No screwing the crew. That's the rule," I mutter under my breath.

I've always followed it to avoid complications, but Dylan is different. There's an energy about her, magnetic and intoxicating, that threatens to override my better judgment. Plus, I've never had this temptation of a woman like her living under the same roof.

Not that I've ever met anyone close to a woman like her.

The late afternoon sun dips lower in the sky, shadows lengthening across the road. I know I should resist this temptation and maintain professional boundaries, but I can't stop replaying that fleeting moment in the store. Her startled gasp as our bodies collided, the softness of her curves molding against me, the apple scent of her shampoo—every detail is seared into my memory.

By the time I pull into the driveway, the sun has nearly set, but its golden glow still filters through the windows. I sit in the car watching shadows dance across the interior, buying time before I have to face the source of my distraction.

With a sigh, I turn off the engine and step outside. The apartment is dark and silent, but I know she's in there. Waiting. And despite my best intentions, I can feel my resolve crumbling with each step towards the door. This is going to be complicated.

I pause outside the apartment door, steeling myself. When I finally turn the key in the lock, the hinges creak ominously.

Dylan glances up from the sofa, a flicker of surprise crossing her face before it smooths into a smile. "Hey, you're back."

My heartbeat kicks up a notch at the sight of her. She's wearing a tank top and sweatpants, her hair piled haphazardly on top of her head, but she still manages to look casually gorgeous.

I swallow hard, torn between bolting for the safety of my room and crossing the space between us to see if she tastes as sweet as she smells.

"I, uh..." Words fail me as I struggle for composure. She arches a brow, and I clear my throat. "How was the rest of your day?"

"Uneventful." Dylan shrugs, a wry twist to her mouth. "Yours?"

"Same." I shrug, too aware of her gaze tracking my every movement. The weight of her attention is a physical thing, and I shift restlessly.

Silence falls as we study each other, both aware of the current of attraction flowing between us.

I know I should say something, do something to dispel the tension, but I'm paralyzed.

"So, about what happened at the store..." Dylan finally says.

My heart leaps, and I brace myself for the rejection I'm sure is coming. She's going to tell me it was a mistake, that we should forget it ever happened.

I open my mouth, unsure of how I'll respond, when she continues.

"Do you want to maybe pick up where we left off?"

I stare at her, stunned into silence. Did she really just...?

Dylan laughs, a throaty sound that sends heat flooding through my veins. She unfolds from the sofa and prowls across the room, stopping just inside my personal space.

"Well?" She tips her head back to meet my gaze, eyes glinting with challenge and something more intimate. "Are you going to kiss me or not?"

I swallow hard, my mouth suddenly dry. "Dylan, I..."

What am I going to say? That I want her, more than I've ever wanted anyone, but I have rules against this sort of thing? That she's already disrupting my carefully ordered world, and if we start something, there'll be no going back?

One look at her face, open and vulnerable in a way I've never seen, and all my reservations crumble into dust.

Who am I kidding? There's no resisting this woman. She's gotten under my skin, awakened something primal I can't ignore. Not anymore.

"Oh, to hell with it," I mutter, grabbing her by the hips and pulling her flush against me.

Dylan's answering grin is triumphant. "That's more like it."

And then her mouth is on mine, and I'm lost.

The kiss is hungry and deep, weeks of pent-up desire unleashed in the slick slide of lips and tongues. Dylan kisses like she does everything else: with single-minded intensity and razor-sharp focus.

I groan into her mouth, my hands roaming over the sweet curve of her ass and the strong planes of her back.

She arches into my touch, rocking her hips in a way that makes my vision go hazy with lust.

This is insanity. I'm kissing my roommate, breaking every rule I've ever set for myself, and I don't care.

All that matters is Dylan, here in my arms at last.

When we break apart, panting for breath, Dylan grins. "I knew you'd come around."

I shake my head, still dazed. "What have you done to me?"

"Improved your quality of life exponentially, I'd say." Dylan laughs and kisses the corner of my mouth. "You can thank me later."

CHAPTER 21

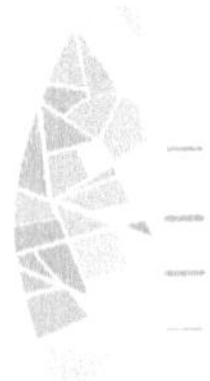

Dylan

I step into the brightly lit conference room, a blend of excitement and nerves swirling in my stomach. The large open space is abuzz with energy, packed with rugby players from both the men's and women's teams.

There's a vibrant and eclectic mix of us, some having traveled from far away to be part of the club and its progressive program, but despite our differing journeys to get here, we're united by the same fiery passion for rugby.

My gaze drifts across the room and lands on Jayden. He exudes an easy confidence, those sculpted muscles flexing with even the slightest movement. His neatly trimmed beard gives him a type of rugged sophistication. Like he would be just as comfortable chopping wood—maybe even chasing me through the woods—as he is out on the rugby pitch.

I have to admit, he's ruggedly attractive in that glossy magazine kind of way… a pinup rugby player of sorts. But that smug look on his face makes me want to watch the opposing team wipe the floor with him on the field.

Sure, he could probably bench press a truck, but I bet his ego weighs even more.

This room is designed for collaboration—round tables with just enough space to encourage interaction, with rugby posters and memorabilia covering the walls. Normally, some of the punny quotes on the posters would make me laugh.

But all I can focus on right now is Jayden.

Our inexplicable rivalry bubbles just beneath the surface, an intoxicating blend of competitiveness and undeniable chemistry. I have a feeling this seminar will only stoke the flames, but that's fine with me. I'm more than ready to put this pretty boy in his place.

Jayden's hand shoots up during the Q&A. "I mean, it's great we're all here," he says with an arrogant smirk, "But let's not pretend the women's game is as tough as the men's. It's just biology, right?"

There are some chuckles from a few men, and eye rolls from nearly every woman around the room. I see my opportunity to knock him down a peg.

"Interesting point, Jayden," I say, matching his smirk with one of my own. "But tell me, does having all that muscle make up for your lack of speed, or is it just to compensate for something else?"

The room erupts in laughter and applause as Jayden's face reddens. He clearly wasn't expecting me to hit back so hard. I feel a rush of satisfaction at wounding his pride.

On a break during the seminar, he approaches me, irritation lingering in his eyes. "Nice jabs back there. You have a sharp tongue. Do you always fight with your words?"

"Only when the opponent is worth the effort," I retort. "You planning on taking cheap shots at women's rugby all season, or was today just a special occasion?"

As much as I enjoy putting Jayden in his place, I can't deny the exhilaration of our verbal sparring.

This rivalry is just getting started.

The seminar progresses, and to my surprise and frustration, Jayden and I are paired up to demonstrate a tackling drill for the group.

I inwardly groan, dreading the forced proximity. It's not enough that I have to endure living under the same roof with this guy, or attend this seminar in his presence. But now we have to physically touch each other, intentionally, in front of a room full of people.

Sure, we kissed one time, but I was delirious in a late night ice cream haze so it doesn't count.

As we take our positions on the mat, Jayden leans in close. "Don't worry, I'll go easy on you," he murmurs.

I scoff, shoving him away. "Oh, I have plenty of surprises up my sleeve," I whisper back. "You might learn a thing or two if you paid attention to the game instead of just running your mouth."

We lock eyes in challenge.

When the instructor blows the whistle, Jayden comes at me hard.

I stand my ground, using his momentum against him to execute a perfect form tackle that takes him down swiftly.

A couple of people in the room gasp at seeing my much smaller frame take down this big brute. But it's all physics, using the force of Jayden's own momentum and manipulating his energy and gravity like putty in my hands.

I smirk down at Jayden as he lies stunned on the mat. "How's that for biology?"

Around us, the room buzzes with impressed murmurs. Despite our rivalry, Jayden and I move in seamless synchronicity. As we help each other up, a spark of electricity passes between us. There's no denying the chemistry brewing beneath our antagonism.

Later, I replay the moment in my mind. As frustrating as Jayden is, there's something about the way he challenges me that's unique.

As the seminar ends, Jayden approaches me with a grudging look of respect. "Not bad today, Dylan," he says. "I still can't believe you took me down like that. I was mad at first but, if I'm honest, I'm mainly just very impressed. It's clear why you were selected to be part of the program."

I nod briskly, trying not to let my surprise show. Was that actual sincerity from the insufferable Jayden? "Yeah, thanks," I reply, before turning to leave.

"See you at home, princess," he calls out after me, and I roll my eyes.

I mull over the day's events as I walk to my car. Jayden is infuriating, no doubt about it. But working together in close quarters has only magnified the intense connection between us. As much as I hate to admit it, I felt alive in a way I haven't in ages when I was sparring with him.

There's something about Jayden that challenges me, that forces me to bring my A-game in a way I take for granted with most people. I have a feeling this season will be anything but boring with him around.

As frustrating as it is, I can't deny the attraction simmering under our rivalry. Jayden is cocky and competitive, but he also makes me feel seen—really seen—in a way few people ever have. In some ways, despite a rocky start, I have a feeling this is just the beginning for us. What that means exactly, I have no idea.

"Damn him," I mutter under my breath, smiling despite myself as I exit the training building.

No matter how much we clash, Jayden has lit a fire in me. This is going to be one hell of a season.

By the time I reach the apartment, I'm still replaying the day's events in my mind. As much as I want to write Jayden off as an arrogant jerk, there's something about him that lingers in my thoughts.

The whisper of his voice saying, "See you at home, princess," sends an involuntary shiver down my spine. I hate the pet name, but can't deny the way it made my pulse quicken when he said it.

I shake my head, as if the physical motion could dislodge Jayden from my mind. This is ridiculous. I've just met the guy, and here I am obsessing over every interaction we've had like a teenager with a crush.

No, this isn't a crush. This is a rivalry, plain and simple. I refuse to let Jayden think he can get under my skin that easily.

I'm here to play rugby, not get distracted by arrogant pretty boys who are all talk, and who seem to think they're entitled to what amounts to royalty status just because they were born with a dick.

As I go inside and begin preparing dinner, I make a promise to myself: I won't let Jayden or any other man distract me from my goals, no matter how hot they are. No matter how worked up they may make me. Every barbed word between us will only make me more determined to put him in his place however I can.

This season is mine, no matter how much Jayden wants to get in my head. I've fought way too hard for far too long to let anyone take this from me, least of all him.

Let him whisper all the pet names and veiled challenges he wants, I will answer only with the scoreboard.

This princess is out for the crown.

Game on, Jayden.

CHAPTER 22

Dylan

The sun beats down on my shoulders as I sip my iced coffee.

Beck nudges my arm from across our patio table. "So, come on, spill! What's going on with you and the hotties since we last spoke?"

My cheeks grow red, and it's not from the sun. "Nothing! I told you, I can't go there."

"I think you ought to go for it!" Sarah pipes in. "You only live once, right?"

"But I'm here to play rugby, not date half of the men's team."

Beck leans forward, her eyes glinting. "Why can't you have both?"

"Yeah!" Sarah chimes. "Don't turn down an opportunity that could be life-changing for you, especially in the bedroom." She wiggles her eyebrows suggestively.

I roll my eyes, but can't help laughing. "You make it sound like a plot from a porno or something."

"Well, you're the one acting like it's an after-school special," Beck teases.

"Come on, Dyl!" Sarah grabs my hand excitedly. "You're living the dream! Three smoking hot roommates ready to cater to your every need?"

I know they mean well, but I came here to prove myself as an athlete after everything that happened on my old team. I can't afford any distractions, no matter how tempting.

But maybe I am taking myself too seriously... after all, they're right. My situation is pretty unique, and one that many women would just about kill for.

"Alright, alright!" I raise my hands in surrender, unable to hide my smile. "I'll think about it, okay? Now can we talk about something other than my non-existent love life?"

Beck and Sarah exchange a knowing look, but they let me off the hook. For now, at least.

I sip my coffee, already dreading their interrogation at our next girls' night...

I take a long sip of my coffee, savoring the rich aroma before setting it down with a sigh. "It's not just about my love life, though," I say, tracing my finger along the rim of the cup. "Or lack thereof."

Beck tilts her head, studying me intently. "What do you mean?"

"It's just..." I pause, trying to find the right words. "I want to be taken seriously here, you know? As an athlete. I feel like I'm finally getting a real shot to prove myself."

Sarah nods in understanding. "After everything that happened on your old team."

"Exactly." I absently shred a napkin on the table. "I got screwed over because of politics and drama. All that behind-the-scenes BS. Nothing to do with my actual ability to play rugby. And I'm scared the same thing could happen again if I get distracted."

"By three hot roommates," Beck adds with a smirk.

I roll my eyes again but can't help laughing. "Yeah, yeah. But truly—I just want to focus on rugby right now. I need to keep my eye on the ball, literally and figuratively."

"We get it," Sarah says gently. "We're going through our own versions of the same challenges. Balancing everything is tough. But Dyl, you do also deserve to have a life outside of rugby, too."

"I know, I know..." I trail off, staring into my coffee.

"And there are other balls that clearly wouldn't mind having your eyes on them."

Her words almost make me spit out my coffee, and for a moment I begin to choke.

Beck reaches over and squeezes my hand and passes me a glass of water. "Hey. Don't be so hard on yourself. You're allowed to have fun too. And sorry. I wasn't trying to cut off oxygen to your brain."

I greedily take a sip of water and my breathing returns to normal.

Sarah nods emphatically. "Absolutely! Listen, we know it's a very real fight to be taken seriously as female athletes. Trust us, we've been there."

"But that doesn't mean you can't also enjoy yourself along the way," Beck adds with a wink.

I chew my lip thoughtfully as their words sink in. Maybe they're right. I have been taking myself too seriously lately. I'm so focused on proving my worth that I've forgotten to come up for air.

"Alright," I say finally. "You've convinced me. I'll try to loosen up a bit."

Beck and Sarah exchange a triumphant high-five.

"Atta girl!" Sarah grins. "You gotta get a little wet and wild in the process, too."

I burst out laughing, shaking my head. "You two are incorrigible."

"But you love us," Beck sings.

"Yeah, yeah." I can't fight the smile tugging at my lips. "I really do."

I chuckle as I take another sip of coffee, feeling lighter than I have in weeks.

Beck and Sarah are right—the situation with my roommates really is absurd when I think about it objectively.

Here I am, living with three extremely attractive professional rugby players who I have undeniable chemistry with. It's like something straight out of a romance novel.

Aside from a couple of stray kisses here and there, I've been so focused on proving myself as an athlete that I haven't stopped to enjoy the delicious possibilities.

Maybe it's time I loosen the reins a little and have some fun.

I'm young, unattached, and living with three hunky men. I'd be a fool not to explore that tantalizing dynamic.

A delicious shiver runs through me as I think about all the flirty banter, the charged looks, the 'accidental' and not so accidental touches.

My roommates seem more than willing to play. And I have to admit, the idea of being the center of their attention is incredibly appealing.

I meet Beck's eyes, my own sparkling with newfound mischief.

"You know what? You're absolutely right. I need to lighten up and maybe even play with fire a little." I grin. "I have a feeling things could get wild with my new living arrangements. And I plan to enjoy every minute of it."

Beck and Sarah exchange an excited squeal.

"That's our girl!" Sarah crows. "Go get 'em!"

I laugh, feeling emboldened. I have a sudden vision of myself walking into the apartment, my three roommates' heads swiveling in unison to take me in.

Oh yes, this could definitely be fun.

I make a mental note to pick up some new lingerie on the way home.

No sense in not being prepared.

CHAPTER 23

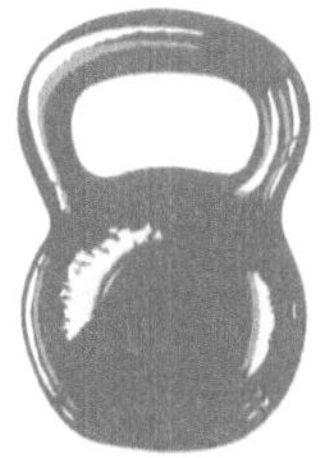

Noah

I t's early morning, and I'm leaning against the granite island as Jayden fires up the blender, whipping up his usual kale-apple juice protein concoction.

"You know she's into us? It's obvious," I say with a smirk as I watch Jayden work.

Jayden pours out the thick green juice into glasses. "You really think so? She's so hellbent on her feminist soapbox. It's like she thinks every single comment we make is a dig at women's sports, or at her personally. I literally was talking about a study on the link between high levels of testosterone and dominance on the rugby field, and she decided I was saying rugby was an all-men's sport and women should be relegated to the kitchen."

I chuckle, taking a sip of the tart juice. "Nothing wrong with having strong views. Makes her even more interesting, if you ask me."

We all appreciate Dylan's fiery spirit, even when we don't quite understand her perspectives.

I'm genuinely interested in getting to know the real Dylan, beneath the surface. What motivates her? What are her secret passions? There's an intriguing tension between us as we navigate living together. A sensual energy I'd love to explore.

But for now, I'll take it slowly, showing my respect on her terms. Our verbal sparring is exhilarating, and I sense she's starting to enjoy it too. Perhaps an invitation to work out together would break the ice. A chance to connect athlete to athlete, pushing each other's limits.

I mentally draft a message to Dylan, pitching the idea. I feel a spark of excitement at the thought of our bodies glistening with sweat, hearts pounding in rhythm, endorphins flooding our systems.

I want to discover the unguarded Dylan, stripped of pretense and politics. Based on the times she's let her guard down and we've had a laugh together, I think we could have some real fun.

Killian joins us and leans against the counter, his arms crossed over his muscular chest, his tattoos so closely packed they form two sleeves where each tattoo seems to be jostling for space. "What about inviting her to work out? It could show her we respect her as an athlete and a person."

I nod, rinsing out my glass and watching the thick green residue swirl down the drain. "I'm game for that. I've been thinking along those same lines, getting to know her on her terms, respecting her space and views." It's a solid idea—we definitely all have common ground in sports.

Jayden grins, a mischievous glint in his eyes. "Alright, how about a friendly bet, then? Who can impress her the most, but with a catch—it has to be by genuinely getting to know her, no shortcuts." He glances at Killian and gives him a knowing look. "And no bringing out the signature moves."

Typical Jayden, always wanting to turn everything into a competition. But I have to admit, the challenge intrigues me.

"Alright, I'll take the lead because I saw her first," I say, clapping Jayden on the back. "But it's not about winning a bet. It's about breaking the ice properly."

Jayden snorts. "Dude, we literally met her at exactly the same time. But okay, you can have the first try."

As we finish our juice, the conversation turns towards brainstorming potential activities Dylan might enjoy. We do actually want to get to know her. The bet is just playful banter.

I type out a message:

Noah:

Hey Dylan, some of us are going for a trail run Saturday morning and then grabbing coffee after. Wanted to see if you're interested in joining. No pressure if you have other plans, just let me know!

I read over the message, hoping it strikes the right tone—friendly but not pushy. I even add a few emojis because I know girls like that type of stuff.

As I hit send, I feel a blend of nerves and excitement. Dylan challenges me in ways I haven't experienced before. Beyond her obvious physical appeal, her sharp mind and bold views intrigue me. I feel optimistic that getting out of the house and onto a topic other than rugby gives us the chance to form some type of bond.

I want to connect on a deeper level. To understand her perspective and experiences. To find common ground. And yeah, if I'm being totally honest, to eventually get her into bed for some mind-blowing sex.

She's absolutely gorgeous and the possibility of something more excites me, but I know if it's meant to be, it'll happen naturally in its own time.

For now, I just want to see her smile and be comfortable around us.

"Okay, you know what? I think you're right. She *is* into us. It's obvious now that I think about it, if I ignore the massive chip on her shoulder about women's sports," Jayden says with a smirk as he rinses out the blender.

"Oh, you agree now?" I quirk a brow. "In that case, my plan is going to work superbly. More than five minutes around you two and she'll quickly work out what dickheads you both are, and she'll be all mine."

CHAPTER 24

Dylan

When I get home after an action-packed practice game, my body is aching for some sort of release.

I flick the switch on my vibrator, letting out a soft moan as the familiar buzz fills my room.

My mind swims with thoughts of the team's victory today, how I proved my worth in that final play. It may only have been a practice, but I know the coach and team management are still scrutinizing our every move, and the fact I was able to showcase some of my signature moves was an important part of cementing my place on the team.

My hips rock to meet the vibrations, chasing the building pleasure. I think of Coach's praise, the awe in my teammates' faces.

For once, I felt seen. Valued for my skill, not my tits. And completely away from all the politics I endured at my last club.

The coil in my belly winds tighter, my breath coming faster as thoughts of the practice match dissipate and are gradually replaced by images of hot male rugby players. But instead of faces, I just see colorful swirls atop muscular bodies with rippling thighs and bulging biceps.

I imagine strong, calloused hands on my thighs, parting my legs.

A hot mouth kissing up my inner thigh, teasing me.

My free hand finds my breast, pinching a nipple. "Please," I whimper, so close.

There's a chuckle in my ear, a deep rumble that makes me shiver. "Come for me, love."

The fantasy voice undoes me. My back arches as waves of bliss crash over me, rippling out from my core.

I cry out wordlessly, lost in the throes of ecstasy.

When I come back to myself, I'm panting and flushed. And despite the sensations of pleasure that just coursed through my body, the familiar ache lingers where I need to be filled.

I sigh, turning off my vibrator. Looks like I'll be dreaming of faceless lovers again tonight.

The buzz of my vibrator still echoes in my ears as I bask in the afterglow. My limbs feel pleasantly heavy, muscles lax.

A knock at my door jerks me from my reverie. "Dylan? You in there?"

Shit, that's Noah.

Panic flares in my chest as I fumble to shove my vibrator under my pillow. "Uh, yeah. Just a second!" My voice comes out high and breathless.

I yank a blanket over my lap just as the door creaks open.

Noah pokes his head in, brows furrowed. "I thought I heard something, and then I thought Jonah might need to get out. Are you alri—"

His eyes land on my flushed face, the blanket barely hiding what I was up to. A slow, wicked grin spreads across his lips. "Well, well. Did I interrupt something?"

My face flames hotter than the sun. I clench my jaw, refusing to give him the satisfaction of a response.

Noah saunters into my room, closing the door behind him. He stops at the foot of my bed, crossing his massive arms. Muscles bulge under his shirt, threatening to rip the fabric.

My pussy, still sensitive from release, quivers at the sight of him. It's like one of the faceless figures from my fantasies has suddenly come to life, and he's standing right at the foot of my bed.

"You know, I could give you a hand with that." His heated gaze rakes over me, setting my blood aflame. "If you want."

I stare at him, my heart pounding so hard it threatens to leap out of my chest.

My first assumption is he thinks it's hilarious walking in on me like this, and that he's making fun of me.

But the look in his eyes is anything but teasing. It's predatory, filled with sinful promise.

My traitorous body responds, warmth pooling between my legs despite me coming just moments ago.

I swallow hard, torn between mortification and desire. "I don't need your help," I say, but it comes out weak. Unconvincing.

Noah tilts his head, a smug smile playing on his lips. "Are you sure about that?"

He hooks his fingers around the waistband of his gray shorts, and I'm paralyzed. I'm a sucker for gray sweatpants, gray shorts, anything. And who can blame me for admiring this stunning, tattooed man?

"Co-come here," I say, my words coming out in a whisper.

"Are you sure?" He quirks a brow as he yanks down his shorts, revealing he's just as turned on as I am.

"Ye-yes. Before I change my mind."

Without hesitating, Noah climbs onto the bed. He positions himself next to me and pulls the blanket away from where I was covering myself with it, revealing my nakedness.

Noah looks down at me, his gaze trailing over my body and landing on my bare, wet pussy.

"You're so incredibly beautiful, Dylan. My god, I can't keep my eyes off you. And look at your pussy. So wet and ready for me."

His words practically make me drip onto the mattress, and I throb in anticipation. But he doesn't make an immediate beeline for my pussy.

Instead, he places a muscular arm on the far side of me so he's basically pinning me to the bed. I feel helpless and vulnerable, but in the best way. Trapped willingly underneath this gorgeous man.

He leans in and captures my lips in a searing kiss, his tongue sliding through to meet mine.

It's hard to explain, because it's only a kiss, but the second our mouths touch I feel an almost supernatural connection. Some people are terrible kissers in general, or they can't quite make it work with a specific person, but Noah has none of those problems.

When a man just about makes you come from kissing you, that's a sign his kissing skills don't need work.

Noah gently trails his hand down my body as he continues to lock lips with mine in a deep kiss, his tongue continuing to explore as his hand finds the bottom of my T-shirt, sliding up underneath until his palm cups my ample breast.

He teasingly tweaks my nipple between his thumb and forefinger, sending a zap of electricity straight to my core.

I feel my wetness continuing to increase at his touch, and my body threatens to come apart again just by him touching my breast and kissing me.

His hand continues its journey down my body, little butterflies jumping around as his fingers skim my belly He pauses there for a moment, letting out a soft moan as he seems to enjoy his hand cresting the gentle swell of my belly. I'd normally be self-conscious if someone touched me there, but it's as if he's turned on by my womanly curves.

His hand continues its descent until it reaches the apex of my thighs, and he cups my pussy in his giant hand.

He moans as he feels the heat and wetness that are pooling there.

"My god, Dylan," he says, groaning. "You're so warm and wet."

His hand continues to slide until his fingers reach my entrance. Slowly, teasingly, he rubs his fingers against my wetness and slides two of them inside me.

I moan under his touch, enjoying the way his calloused fingers feel as they glide against my walls.

My hand slides down and very quickly finds his rock hard cock. And Jesus Christ, it's massive. Girthy and long, I wrap my palm around it, enjoying the feeling of its ample size that fits perfectly in my hand. I feel the familiar texture of pre-cum as my palm brushes over his tip.

He angles his thumb so it brushes against my clit and I cry out. "Noah, yes," I gasp. I swore that any type of fraternization with my roommates was a strict no-go, but there's no way I would stop this now.

The train has well and truly left the station.

My resolve has gone out the window, and there's no going back.

His thumb gently caresses my swollen clit as his fingers continue to slide in and out of my wet pussy, and the coil within me tightens further.

"Fuck, Noah," I cry out as the sensations of pleasure take over.

I'd be embarrassed by how quickly he's making me come, but my body needs the release even though it just had one.

My back arches and my hips buck against his hand and he intensifies our kiss as I come all over his fingers.

Well, so much for not screwing the crew.

We lock eyes, and suddenly Noah removes his hand. He pushes himself away from me and I let go of his cock, even though my hand was quite happy to stay wrapped around it. He stands up, yanks up his shorts and leaves without a word.

My breathing is ragged as I stare at the ceiling, aftershocks still rolling through my body. Noah worked me over until I saw stars, then just up and left. What the hell just happened?

I sit up on shaking arms, dragging a hand through my tangled hair. My muscles feel like jelly, a pleasant ache settling into my bones. But my mind is spinning.

Noah has pushed my buttons from the day I moved in here, but I never expected him to push them like this. We're supposed to be roommates, not fuck buddies, for God's sake.

So why did that feel so good?

If he'd walked in at any other time, I would have been fine. I would have felt equipped to reject him. But in the throes of giving myself pleasure, thoughts of him and the others and various other smoking hot rugby players were racing through my mind. And then suddenly he was here, real, offering to help me.

With his gray pants of seduction and his muscles and tattoos, it was impossible to refuse.

Heat creeps into my cheeks as I remember the way he watched me come apart under his hands.

The possessive look in his eyes and the rough tone of his voice as he whispered filthy things against my skin.

I flop back onto the bed with a groan. What have I done? I've just crossed a massive line, and this can only end in disaster.

Noah is dangerous in more ways than one, and if I'm not careful, he might destroy me and my aspirations for a long and enjoyable rugby career.

But some traitorous part of me wants to play with fire. Wants to give in to this twisted attraction and see where it leads, consequences be damned.

I'm so screwed.

CHAPTER 25

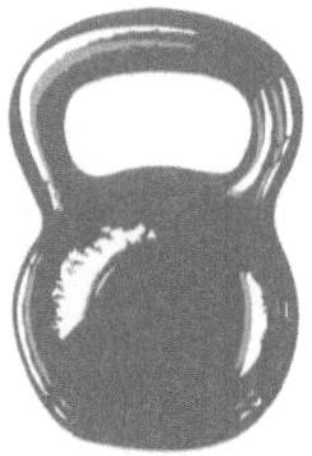

Noah

The muted rumble of traffic drifts up through the open window as I pace the confines of my sparsely furnished room. Functional, pragmatic—that's how I've always been. But now these blank walls feel almost oppressive, like they're closing in all around me.

I sink onto the edge of the bed, my hands clasped, my mind racing over the evening's events.

I truly intended to start off slowly and get to know Dylan on a friendship level. It was complete coincidence that I thought her cat was trapped in her room and opened the door to make sure he was okay... and there she was, lying there all sexy and flushed.

If the other guys knew I'd just fingered her to orgasm, there would be a consensus that I won our little wager.

But the victory leaves a bitter aftertaste. It's not why I made my way into her room and finger fucked her. I didn't do that because of a bet. I did that because she looked so gorgeous lying there, her eyes hazy with desire. But that would be hard to explain.

And if she ever finds out…it won't just be her trust I've betrayed.

It'll be her whole perception of me, of us.

"I won, but at what cost?" The words slip out in a tortured whisper.

It was just a harmless bet, or so I told myself. But now? Now there are lines blurred, boundaries pushed too far.

My pulse quickens as I picture her face. That infectious laughter, her defiant spirit. She's like a fucking magnet and I'm a tiny piece of shrapnel.

It started as physical attraction, sure. But now? Now it's more. She stirs things in me I thought long buried. Makes me feel…alive.

I sink back on the bed, staring at the ceiling.

Why did I go along with Jayden's idea for that stupid bet, anyway? I know why. It wasn't about winning.

It was about her. About Dylan. An excuse to get closer to her. I'd do it again in a heartbeat, just to be near her.

And that's the problem. I've crossed a line.

I pace the room, glancing at the trophies lining the shelves. Symbols of achievement, of my relentless competitive drive. But now they seem to mock me, shining reminders of the very trait that's brought me to this point.

My eyes land on a photo from the leadership course, Dylan's face alight with laughter. Her spirit is magnetic, drawing me in. There's an undeniable connection between us that goes beyond the superficial.

I sink into the desk chair, my head in my hands. "What have I done?" The question echoes through my mind.

In pursuing a reckless bet, I've jeopardized so much more. The possibility of what we could become.

My pulse races as I picture her again. I joined this team to prove myself, but with Dylan, I don't need trophies or accolades. I want to know the real her. To peel back the layers and connect on a deeper level.

I rise and move to the window, looking out at the city lights. The glimmering landscape once filled me with purpose and drive. But now it all seems hollow. Meaningless without someone to share it with.

There's not a shortage of women who would drop what they're doing to be with me, but I don't just want anybody just to say I have someone. Just to avoid being lonely.

My shoulders slump as realization settles over me. This isn't just attraction or infatuation. It's more. "I think I'm falling for her," I whisper into the night. The admission fills me with equal parts exhilaration and dread. The wager was dumb, but I know now there are some compromises I'd be willing to make for Dylan.

I only hope I haven't shattered everything beyond repair.

I run a hand through my hair and let out a frustrated sigh. "I never meant for it to get this far," I mutter. But even as I say it, I know it's a lie.

Deep down, some part of me wanted exactly this—to break through her walls and discover the real Dylan underneath. The vibrant, passionate woman who makes me question everything I thought I wanted.

I lean back in my chair, eyes fixed on Dylan's image, unable to look away. Her smile tugs at my heart, reminding me of all the little moments we've shared over the past few weeks. The late night talks after practice, her teasing jabs when I miss a pass, the way she cheers the loudest when any of us score.

She's become so much more than just a teammate. More than a conquest or a prize to be won.

She's...everything.

Staring into her frozen smile, I can't deny the truth any longer. This stopped being about a bet the moment I saw past the surface. Now winning means nothing if it costs me a chance with her.

I made a mistake, but I'll find a way to make this right. For her, I'm willing to swallow my pride. Dylan's worth crossing every line for.

My fingers brush over her face, and I sigh. "What are you doing to me, Dylan?"

I've never let my guard down or opened up this way before. Never let someone sneak beneath my armor. But Dylan's different. With her, I find myself wanting to share things I've never told another soul.

It terrifies me even as it thrills me. I've never felt this vulnerable or exposed.

My eyes drift to the trophy shelf, symbols of a different life and different priorities. Being the best meant closing myself off, but Dylan makes me want to tear down those walls.

With her, I feel free to just be me.

"No more games," I whisper.

This connection between us—it's real. I have to tell Dylan how I feel, no matter the cost. I can't hold back any longer.

One way or another, she needs to know the truth.

And she needs to find out how I feel before she finds out about the bet, or I risk her leaving my life for good.

CHAPTER 26

Dylan

I take a deep breath as I step onto the field, trying to clear my head. I can't be distracted out here. The whistle blows and we're off, running drills up and down the pitch. Jessamine falls into stride next to me, her ponytail bouncing in a way that mimics her frenetic energy.

"How's it going?" I ask.

She grimaces. "Not great. I can't seem to get the spin move down."

I nod. "Here, watch me." I execute a perfect spin, faking left before whipping the ball to the right.

Jessamine frowns. "You make it look so easy."

"Don't worry, you'll get it. It just takes practice." We repeat the drill and I give her tips, telling her to shift her weight and use her hips more. By the fifth rep, she's starting to get it.

"Yes! That was perfect!" I high five her and she grins, flushed with accomplishment. We continue running plays and I lose myself in the rhythm of the practice, the physical exertion wiping my mind blissfully blank.

Towards the end, I glance up at the stands and freeze. Is that...? No, just my imagination playing tricks.

I shake my head and focus on the final drill. The whistle blows, signaling the end of practice, and I jog off the field with Jessamine.

"Thanks for the help today," she says. "I really appreciate you taking the time."

"No problem. That's what teammates are for." I smile and head to the locker room, feeling centered again.

Rugby and this team are my purpose now. The rest will work itself out.

I hit the showers, letting the hot water soothe my aching muscles. The steam fills the locker room as I reflect on practice. Jessamine picked things up so quickly—she's got real talent, and I can see this being a momentary stop on a long and illustrious rugby career. I rinse off and get dressed, ready to head home.

As I'm leaving, I spot Jessamine in the parking lot. "Hey, wait up!" I call out.

She turns. "Oh, hey Dylan."

"Just wanted to say again, you did awesome today. You're gonna do big things on this team... and beyond!"

Jessamine smiles shyly. "You really think so?"

"Absolutely. I saw myself in you out there. That drive to keep improving. You've got a bright future ahead."

"That means a lot, especially coming from you. You're, like, my rugby idol."

I laugh, feeling myself blush. It's humbling to realize from time to time that junior players have been tracking my career from afar. "Well, I'm happy to help anytime. See you at the next practice!"

We part ways, and I walk to my car with a smile. It feels good to encourage the next generation. My sour mood from this morning has lifted. Time to focus on the game, and nothing else.

I start my car and head for home, music blasting. The rush of practice still thrums through me.

As I cruise along, I think back to that moment I thought I saw Jayden in the stands. I shake my head and laugh at myself. Wishful thinking, obviously. I must be delirious if I'm imagining my roommates showing up at practice now.

Still, a tiny part of me wonders...was he really there?

No, impossible. He's made his feelings clear. This living situation is temporary for him. Once the season ends, he'll be off to his glamorous TV world or whatever. Filming ads for pizza or undies, most likely, while women hang off his shoulder, like all the other guys.

I crank up the music louder, drowning out my thoughts. The women's team is my focus.

I downshift as I take a corner, tires squealing. The roar of the engine and the speed clear my head.

Pulling into the driveway, my adrenaline is still pumping.

As I hop out, the front door opens. Jayden steps out, looking irritable. "There you are," he snaps. "Your damn car music is shaking the whole house."

I bite my tongue and head inside without responding. So much for wishful thinking.

Jayden

The crunch of leaves under my boots marks my usual path to practice. But today isn't usual at all. There she is—Dylan, warming up on the women's field, her short ponytail swishing as she moves. Curiosity pulls me from my route, leading me to a secluded spot at the back of the bleachers.

I settle into the shadows, intrigued by the contrast between the two teams. The women laugh and shout spirited encouragement while my teammates grunt and growl aggressively. But damn, Dylan is impressive—her athleticism and leadership obvious as she patiently coaches a junior player.

"She's good. Damn good. Not just at playing, but leading too," I think. "Reminds me of..." No. Don't go there. Dylan deserves more than unfair comparisons.

As practice ends, Dylan lingers to offer extra tips. She's not playing a part—she's living it. My view shifts subtly. Why do I feel like she could be...genuine? But I guess everyone deserves a chance to prove themselves—even me.

With a deep breath, I step from the shadows, moving beyond past hurts. Next time we talk, I'll make it right. Or at least try.

I emerge from the shadows and start across the field, my steps slow and uncertain. What will I even say to her? "Hey Dylan, sorry for being a jerk but you remind me of my cheating ex" or "hey Dylan, I have insurmountable trust issues because of my abusive stepfather and that's why I'm such a moody asshole"? Yeah, that'll go over real well.

My palms sweat as I near where she's still working with the junior player. Her voice carries on the crisp autumn air as she demonstrates a side-step technique, patient and focused.

I pause, lingering at the edge of the field unseen. She's so at ease here, in her element. This is where she belongs. I have no right to disrupt this moment for her.

Dylan glances my way and I freeze. Our eyes almost meet for a brief moment before I look away, pulse quickening. Does she recognize me? Has she noticed me watching her?

I suddenly feel a wave of awkwardness wash over me. I shouldn't be here. It feels like I'm violating her space, lurking here on the sidelines like some kind of demented stalker.

I shuffle away awkwardly, hoping she hasn't seen me retreating into the safety of the adjacent parking lot.

CHAPTER 27

Dylan

I stretch out on the grass, my muscles aching after a tough practice. The field empties as the sun sinks lower, shadows stretching across the turf.

Jayden's been acting weird lately. Instead of his usual scowl, today he gave me a half-smile. What's that about? I'm trying to figure him out.

I call Liv, needing her perspective on my roommate drama.

"Hey, got a minute? I need a sanity check on Jayden."

She sighs. "Is that jackass still hassling you?"

"Actually, he was nice today. But he was yelling at me about music just before. It's weirding me out."

"Don't let Mr. Mood Swing distract you," Liv says. "Keep your eye on the prize. But hey, no harm in enjoying the view if it makes life easier."

"Yeah, I've really got to stop letting him get under my skin. Which would be easier if he wasn't so goddamn attractive."

She laughs. "Aren't there a bunch of rugby guys? If you're so worried about it, pick one who doesn't live with you. Roommate hookups rarely end well. I know I was encouraging you to have some fun, but maybe that'd be less messy. But then again, you're clearly attracted to these guys."

Liv's right to remind me about focusing on my goals, but she's clearly as convicted with her advice as I am. It would be easier to find another rugby player who doesn't live with me. But, despite my best attempts, I can't seem to ignore the temptation right under my own roof.

As I walk home across campus, the sidewalks are crowded with laughing students headed to parties and bars, and laughter and music float from nearby apartment complexes. I smile, cautiously optimistic.

Who knows? Maybe this will be an interesting season after all. As long as we respect each other, a few blurred lines won't hurt.

I nod slowly to myself as Liv's advice sinks in. She's right—I came here to play rugby, not get caught up in apartment drama. I need to keep my priorities straight.

But I can't deny the appeal of my roommates. Their athletic physiques and charming smiles are hard to ignore.

God, this is hard.

My mind wanders to the possibility of late night encounters, flirtatious winks over breakfast, steamy showers together after practice. It wouldn't take much for those professional boundaries to blur into something more intimate.

I shake my head, trying to clear those thoughts. The carefree energy of those around me contrasts my pensive mood.

I remind myself of Liv's warning. "Don't piss where you eat." It's wise advice in most cases. But when your daily life is filled with enticing distractions, lines get blurry.

As I reach the apartment door, I take a deep breath. This living situation is complicated, but if we respect each other, things should be fine. I just need to keep my wits and not do anything rash.

Keys in hand, I enter the apartment. Thumping music and raucous laughter float down the hall. Who knows what possibilities this season holds? For now, I'll take it one day at a time and see where things lead.

The sounds of my roommates' laughter are a reminder that while my feelings are conflicted, life here goes on as normal.

I round the corner to find them sprawled on the couches, chatting and listening to music. For a moment, I observe them unnoticed—Jayden's strong arms as he gestures animatedly, Noah's playful smirk, Killian's wild and tousled hair falling just so.

Jayden spots me first, flashing that crooked half-smile that makes my knees weak. "Hey Dylan, we saved you some pizza if you're hungry."

"Thanks," I reply, grabbing a slice as I squeeze onto the couch. Their banter picks back up, and I find myself laughing along, the earlier tension fading away.

In this moment, things feels easy and light. No complicated entanglements or blurred lines, just friends enjoying each other's company. Okay, maybe more than friends in some cases, not that I've told anybody about Noah's and my little... slip-up. I just didn't expect to feel so at home here, but maybe this mismatched group is coming together after all.

As I glance around at their smiling faces, I feel a swell of cautious optimism. This season holds endless possibilities—for my rugby career, for new friendships, and maybe even for steamy romance if I play my cards right.

But I'm getting ahead of myself. For now, I'll take it one moment at a time and see where this unpredictable journey leads. Wherever it goes, at least it won't be boring.

"So Dylan, how was practice today?" Noah asks, his gaze lingering on me in a way that makes my pulse quicken.

"Good. Really good, actually," I reply. "I think the team is starting to gel. We might actually stand a chance this season."

"With you leading the forward pack, I don't doubt it," Jayden says. "I saw you out there today. You were a force to be reckoned with."

His compliment catches me off guard. "Oh, thanks. I'm just trying to do my part."

"She's being modest," Killian chimes in. "I have a few friends on the team, and I heard Dylan was schooling everyone out there. They said we should have seen the look on Coach's face when she scored that try—he was impressed."

I feel a blush spreading across my cheeks at their praise. I'm not used to having my talents acknowledged so openly.

"Well, I guess I'm just motivated this season," I say, tucking a strand of hair behind my ear self-consciously. "I really want to prove I deserve to be here."

"We know, and you do," Jayden says softly, his hazel eyes boring into mine. I feel a spark of electricity between us, and I know he senses it, too. I quickly avert my gaze before I do something reckless, like grabbing him by one of his bulging biceps and kissing him senseless. Get it together, Dylan. Platonic roommates, just friends. For now, at least...

The conversation moves on, but the charged moment lingers. As we joke and banter, I feel myself relaxing. Maybe this will work after all.

These tempting guys don't have to be off limits—with some friendly flirting and a little self-control, we can enjoy each other's company without crossing the line, more than we already have.

At least not yet...

CHAPTER 28

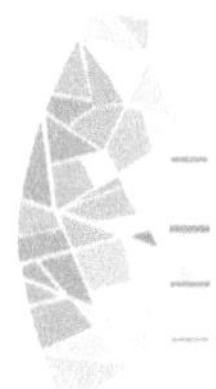

Dylan

The sun is high in the sky, hovering over the sports field. Shouts punctuate the air as athletes run drills, rugby balls spiraling, boots scuffing.

I weave through the crowds, eyes scanning for my team, when they catch on him.

Kai. Surrounded as usual by an enthusiastic group of beautiful women, their laughter too loud, their touches too casual. What is a group of women like that called, anyway? A bevy of beautiful Beckys? An army of attractive Amys? A harem of hot Hannahs?

But despite their enthusiasm, his easy smile doesn't reach his eyes, and they instead find mine. A jolt rushes through me as memories of our night together flash in my mind—the brush of his lips on my neck, his hands roaming my body.

I force my gaze away. Focus, Dylan. You're here for rugby, not some schoolgirl fantasy. Still, my eyes drift back to him, to the tattoos snaking down his arms, the muscles flexing as he stretches.

As I watch, he extracts himself from the women with an effortless excuse and starts towards me. My heart pounds. His walk is languid, yet purposeful.

"Fancy seeing you here," he says, his full lips quirking and revealing straight, white teeth that make my body respond with quivers and tingles. I'm a sucker for great teeth, muscles and tattoos, and this man checks all the boxes.

I laugh, a bit too high-pitched, and I inwardly wince as the sounds I'm making remind me of the gaggle of women that were just hanging off him. That's the right terminology. A gaggle of gorgeousness. "Rescuing me from my own thoughts, maybe." I shake my head ruefully. "You're trouble, Kai."

His eyes soften. "I know things have been...awkward. What do you say we reset, for the club's sake?"

"So you do remember me?" I'm beyond confused. The way he looked blankly at me by the bar made me feel so insignificant, so irrelevant to him.

"How could I possibly forget you, Dylan?" His words are smooth but his eyes contain something genuine. Remorse, maybe? A hint of embarrassment?

I quirk a brow and frown. "Then why did you pretend not to—"

"Look, I'm sorry," he frowns. "I was just so surprised to see you, and there were so many people around. I'd had a few beers. I know that's not an excuse, but I didn't know what to do, so I reverted to my neutral stare."

"Your... neutral stare?"

"Yeah. It's how I deal with complicated situations when I can't think of words."

"I see," I press my lips together in a firm line. "You called me by the wrong name."

He nods and sighs. "Sorry about that, too. I realized as soon as I said it. I'm terrible with names. Dylan. Dylan Dylan Dylan. I know your name. and I won't fuck it up again. I promise."

I nod, exhaling the breath I'd apparently been holding. "Okay then. You had me very confused. But I guess that makes sense? It's not like we were dating or anything."

He looks relieved. "So... clean slate?"

My eyes meet his one more time, and he still seems genuine. I take a deep breath. "Okay. Reset. Clean slate." We share a tentative smile, a truce, and solidify it with a handshake.

The touch of his hand against mine sends an enjoyable shockwave up my arm, and my fingers tingle as he pulls away. As we head in opposite directions, promise of friendship rather than fire lingers. My steps feel lighter as I head to practice, my mind clearing.

Glancing over my shoulder, I watch Kai return to his entourage, the women surrounding him with coy smiles and flirtatious touches.

A pang of jealousy twists in my gut before I tamp it down. Focus on the game, Dylan. You literally just convinced yourself that he was nothing more than a friend.

As I turn to leave the field, I replay the conversation in my head. Kai's proposition to reset things between us makes sense. Still, the simmering tension pulses just below the surface, like a live wire.

Being near him is playing with fire. But I meant what I said—a clean slate is exactly what we need. As hot as our one night stand was, there can be no repeat. For now, I'll douse the flames. Channel that energy into leading this team, proving my worth.

My steps feel lighter crossing the field. The sun's warmth soothes my skin. Around me, the sounds of sport fill the air—whistles, shouts, and the unmistakable thwacks of bodies colliding.

This is my element. Rugby courses through my veins. And I'll be damned if I let anything jeopardize my shot to finally lead. Kai's charm won't divert me from my goals now.

I'm playing the long game.

As I reach the door to the locker room, resolve settles in my gut. Time to focus on what matters—becoming the assistant captain this team needs. Proving my talent surpasses politics or petty drama, and it most definitely leaves guy problems out of the picture.

I push open the door and enter the locker room, the smell of sweat and rubber greeting me. My teammates' voices echo off the concrete walls as they joke and chat before practice.

But a hush falls over the group when I walk up to the whiteboard, marker in hand. Their eyes follow me, rapt with attention.

"Alright team, gather round," I say, authority ringing through my voice.

The other women gravitate toward me, forming a semicircle. I make eye contact with each one, seeing focus and trust shining back.

"I know tensions have been high lately. There's been uncertainty about leadership." Murmurs ripple through the group.

"But now, we move forward united. No more infighting or politics. We are one team with one goal."

The group nods and murmurs sounds of assent. The mood shifts, an electric current of motivation sparking to life.

"We have what it takes to go all the way this season. All the way to finals. We are strong enough. We are smart enough. And we sure as hell are stubborn enough."

Laughter and cheers erupt. I feel their energy feeding mine, fueling the fire within.

"Now let's get out on that field and show everyone what we're made of!" I shout.

The team whoops and hollers, thundering out of the locker room with purpose. As I follow, confidence surges through me.

This is exactly where I'm meant to be.

CHAPTER 29

Dylan

The stadium is electric. Cheers and chants echo through the stands as we make our way to our seats, fans decked out in the club colors shaking banners and flags. Nothing like the modest crowds at our women's games. A full band blasts energetic fight songs while cheerleaders down on the field prance and flip, hyping up the crowd.

"Get a load of this madness!" I nudge my teammate Jess as we settle into our seats. "We're lucky to get a smattering of other players and the odd loyal supporter at our matches."

"I know, right?" Jess laughs. "We definitely need to step up our game if we want even a slice of this kind of energy."

The fans around us are amped, their faces painted and voices already growing hoarse from bellowing. If only we could get even a fraction of this love and attention.

I've always felt like I had something to prove on the pitch, but seeing this—the pure passion these fans have—makes me ache to show what I can really do. To feel that roar of the crowd and know it's for me.

Maybe someday our team will get a similar level of recognition. But for now, I'm here as a fan like everyone else, determined to show my support and soak up the electric atmosphere. I'll be taking notes on what it takes to ignite a crowd like this. It's going to happen for us, too. And I plan to lead the charge.

The whistle blows, and the match kicks off with a flurry of activity. My eyes lock onto Noah, Killian, and Jayden—each unstoppable in their positions. I'm impressed by how in sync they are, executing plays through subtle cues and gestures.

"Check out that lineout signal from Jayden," I say to Jess. "Barely a flick of the wrist, but they all know exactly what to do. It's like they can read each other's minds."

The scrum battles are intense, neither side giving an inch. But soon the home team's backs get possession. The ball moves swiftly down the line before landing in Kai's hands.

He's off like a shot, deftly sidestepping a slew of defenders.

My breath catches as I watch the muscles in his thighs flex with each powerful stride. "Go on Kai!" I whisper under my breath.

He breaks through the last line of defense and dives over the try line in a blur of limbs.

The stadium erupts in celebration. Jess and I are on our feet, swept up in the exhilaration.

Kai pops up, pumping his fist as his teammates mob him.

"He's incredible," I marvel aloud. "With athleticism and charisma like that, no wonder he's a fan favorite."

I force myself to look away from his muscular frame glistening under the lights. Focus, Dylan! I remind myself. I'm here to support the team and maybe update some plays of my own, not ogle the players.

But still...a small part of me imagines what it might be like if I was down there on the pitch with him—with all of them—instead of up in the stands. Could we have that effortless chemistry? I quickly shake the thought from my head. That's a dangerous line of thinking that will only lead to trouble.

For now, I'm content to be a spectator...even if I can't tear my eyes away from the alluring athleticism on display.

The game winds down and the men emerge victorious. The crowd's energy simmers to a low buzz as people begin filing out of the stadium.

Jess and I linger in our seats, watching the players revel in their win. They look like warriors basking in the glow of the field lights, triumphant grins on their faces.

I let out a wistful sigh. "Is it them I'm attracted to, Jess, or just the thrill of the game?"

"Maybe a bit of both?" Jess suggests, laughing. "The game is exhilarating, and the players are fine as hell... there's no reason you have to choose! Take it all!"

I laugh too, knowing she's probably right. There's an undeniable magnetism that comes from watching talented athletes in their element. Still, I can't deny that the handsome players themselves hold some appeal, too.

"Well, ready to head out?" Jess asks, standing up and stretching. "We could grab a bite and decompress from the intensity of the match."

"Good idea," I agree, tearing my eyes away from the celebrating players. I need to get out of this charged atmosphere and back to reality.

As we make our way out of the rows of seats, I take one last glance at the field. Under the glow of the lights, it almost seems magical.

But it's just a game, I remind myself.

And like all games, the spell ends when the final whistle blows.

CHAPTER 30

Dylan

The sun beats down on my neck as I step onto the rugby pitch, the screams and grunts of the men's team practice assaulting my ears. The noises they make are a far cry from the much quieter women's team. We definitely yell, but it's nothing compared to this. It's as if they're frat bros at the gym, purposely trying to pick up the heaviest weight and doing exaggerated grunting in a 'pick me' move.

The grass is vibrant green and freshly cut, the scent mingling with the musk of sweat and effort. Across the field, a junior women's team whoops and hollers as they practice rucks and mauls, while the steady thwack of baseballs echoes from the nearby diamond.

The sun beats down on my neck as I make my way across the manicured pitch. The thick scent of freshly cut grass fills my nose while shouts from coaches and the thud of colliding bodies echo in the distance.

I clutch my notepad tightly, glancing around, momentarily over-stimulated by everything going on around me. Why am I here again? Oh right, coach wanted me to study tactics and teamwork. As if I don't know how to tackle. But it's more than that, she said. There's always more to learn.

I find a spot on the sidelines, and settle in to observe. The team is mid-scrimmage, intensity etched on their faces. This isn't just practice to them—it's everything.

Noah catches my eye as he charges down the pitch, the ball tucked tightly under his arm. There's a ruthless determination about him, a singular focus. The others fall into his wake, but no one quite matches his drive.

He crosses the try line and slams the ball down, breathing hard.

As the others congratulate him, I notice his expression. It's not triumph I see, but discontent. He's already critiquing his own performance, replaying each moment for flaws.

A leader who thinks he has to carry the team alone. Does he know they're there to carry him too? I guess that's why I'm here—to learn about balance. Mine and theirs.

I turn my attention back to the field as they reset for another drill, scribbling notes. What more can I discover by just watching and listening? What lessons lie beneath the surface, if you know where to look?

The sun inches lower as I study, pondering teamwork with fresh eyes. Maybe I'll get something out of this after all.

I continue watching as the team runs drill after drill. Noah continues to be a commanding presence, directing his teammates with confidence. But there's a wall around him so thick it's almost visible—he holds himself apart even as he leads.

"He's so intense out there," I comment to the woman next to me.

"Oh, that's just Noah," she says with a knowing smile. "Puts a ton of pressure on himself. Wants to be the best so badly it's like he forgets there are others on his team."

I nod, seeing it now. How he brushes off encouragement and focuses on each mistake. The weight on his shoulders—self-imposed but almost debilitatingly heavy nonetheless.

"Why doesn't he let the others help more?" I ask. "Isn't that what a team is for?"

The woman shrugs. "Guess he's not used to relying on others. Noah likes to be in control."

I watch him prowl the field, demanding precision. His teammates are eager to please but also wary, like animals who know they haven't yet gained their alpha's full trust.

Leadership through fear and intimidation rather than inspiration. It may work for a while, but is it sustainable?

I want to tell Noah he doesn't have to do it all alone. That sometimes surrendering control is the only way to gain strength. But some lessons have to be learned firsthand. Plus, he's been playing rugby for longer than me, and his illustrious career leaves mine in the rear-view mirror, so who am I to coach someone like him?

The whistle blows as practice winds down. Maybe someday Noah will see he can't just lead others—he has to let them lead him, too. But for now, all I can do is watch and learn myself.

The players head to the sidelines, grabbing water bottles and towels. Noah lingers on the field, hands braced on his knees, his chest heaving. For a moment, his invincible façade cracks. He looks less like a superhero and more like a younger man carrying the world's weight.

I approach slowly, not wanting to startle him. "Hey Noah."

He glances up, surprise flashing across his face before he rearranges it back to neutral. "Oh hey, Dylan. Just running some drills. Didn't expect to see you here. I thought I imagined you sitting over there. What brings you by?"

"Picking up some tips from the best," I say lightly.

His mouth quirks. "Appreciate that. But go easy on the praise...I've got a long way to go."

I shake my head. "You're too hard on yourself. It's okay to ease up sometimes, you know. And I'm not creeping on you, I promise. Coach sent me over here to observe how you run drills."

He smiles wryly. "Easier said than done, but thanks for looking out. And you're welcome to come watch any time."

We chat a few more minutes about innocuous topics like weather and schedules. But my mind is churning. Noah's strength is a shield, but also a prison. One he doesn't yet know how to leave.

I want to show him he doesn't have to be Atlas, carrying this team alone. Even superheroes need allies. But it's a lesson that has to come from within.

As I walk away, I sigh, glancing back at the field.

Someday, I hope Noah learns he can rely on others' strength. Until then, all I can do is be there when he's ready.

With patience and understanding, barriers crack and bridges form.

Even between awkward roommates like us.

CHAPTER 31

Jayden

Dylan saunters into the living room, and every pair of eyes lock onto her. She's wearing a little black dress that hugs her curves like a second skin, showing off miles of tanned legs and just a hint of cleavage. I try to keep my jaw from dropping. That dress should be illegal.

Damn, she looks hot.

But that's not new news. This woman looks hot in her cute little pyjamas. In a tank top and shorts. She was wearing a fucking cat onesie earlier today, of all things, and she was adorable. In her rugby gear she makes me swoon, even with her scrum cap on. Especially with her scrum cap on. Ugh, I have issues. She has me sucked in.

But tonight, there's an air about her. She's radiating some kind of sensual energy that I can't quite put my finger on. It goes beyond the way she's done her makeup, with her smoky eyes and her glossy red lips that I can imagine wrapped around my cock... in fact, there's nothing I'd like more than to see that red tint smeared all over it. It's not just her outfit that's leaving me weak. Or the heels, which I haven't seen her in before, tilting her calves in a way that makes my cock twitch.

My mouth goes dry as she spins on her heel, giving us a slow, tantalizing view of her body. The urge to peel that dress off her and run my hands over every inch of her smooth skin is almost overwhelming.

"Well?" She arches a brow, her plump lips curving into a teasing smirk. "Are we going or what?"

"Going where?" Noah croaks out, his eyes glued to the sway of her hips, as if he's forgotten the evening's plans. I can't really blame him for this onset of amnesia.

Dylan laughs, the sound like velvet and sin. "Weren't you boys taking me out for drinks tonight?"

Oh right, drinks. How could I forget? We'd suggested a workout, but Dylan had other plans which involved getting us to show her one of the latest cocktail spots.

Dylan sidles up to me, her perfume invading my senses, and slides a hand down my chest. "You're not getting cold feet now, are you, Jayden?"

My heart kicks into overdrive as her fingers brush over my abdomen, making my muscles twitch. "Never."

Our gazes lock, and the heat in her eyes promises that tonight will be a night to remember.

My body tightens in anticipation.

Dylan smiles, slow and predatory, fully aware of the effect she has on me. "Good. Then take me out for a night on the town, boys."

She spins on her heel again, grabbing her clutch from the table, and strides out the front door.

The rest of us scramble to follow, tripping over ourselves in our haste.

Tonight is going to be fun.

We pile into Noah's SUV, Dylan sliding into the middle seat between me and Killian. As Noah starts the engine and pulls out onto the road, she rests a hand on my thigh, her fingers dancing teasingly over the inseam of my jeans.

My muscles tense, heat pooling low in my gut.

Her touch is casual, almost innocent, but the glint in her eyes tells me she knows exactly what she's doing.

Dylan leans in close, her breath warm against my ear. "You look tense, Jayden. Do I make you nervous?"

A shudder runs down my spine at the husky note in her voice. I turn my head to find her gaze locked on my mouth, her pink tongue darting out to wet her already glossy lips.

"Should I be nervous?" My own voice comes out rough with want.

"Not yet." She winks. "The night is still young."

Dylan shifts closer until our thighs are pressed together, and her hand slides higher up my leg.

My hips jerk in response, my cock straining against the zipper of my jeans.

Noah glances over his shoulder, his eyes narrowing at the intimate position we're in. "Hey, no touching until we get to the bar. I don't want you two distracting me while I'm driving."

Dylan pouts but removes her hand, much to my disappointment. "You're no fun at all, Noah."

"The fun hasn't even started yet," he retorts with a smirk. "But we'll get there faster if you keep your hands to yourself for the next ten minutes."

Dylan huffs but settles back into her seat, the warmth of her body still seeping into mine. The anticipation for what's to come buzzes through my veins, setting my blood on fire.

Tonight is definitely going to be a night to remember.

The other guys chat and joke around, but I can't focus on anything but the warmth radiating from Dylan's body. Her perfume envelops me, something floral and light that makes me want to bury my nose in her neck. Normally, it annoys me when girls wear perfume—it's usually cloying and sickly and makes me want to aggressively scrub myself in the shower. But I feel like Dylan could bathe in toilet water right after I took a dump and I'd be into it. Fuck, I really do have issues.

When we arrive at the club, Dylan steps out of the car. The slit in her dress parts to reveal a glimpse of black lace panties.

I swallow hard, my pants suddenly feeling way too tight. I discreetly adjust myself. This is going to be a long night. Dylan wants to prove she's one of the guys? In that outfit, she's proving she's very much *not*. And at this rate, she'll get a lot more than she bargained for.

Tonight, I'm going to mess with her until she's desperate for release. And when I finally give it to her, she'll be screaming my name.

Dylan has no idea what's coming for her. But she will soon.

We walk into the club, the pounding music vibrating through my chest. The moment we enter, I feel eyes on us. I'm sure we stand out—three massive rugby players and the hottest woman who has ever set foot in this establishment, no doubt about it.

I'm instantly overwhelmed by a sense of protectiveness, and maybe a hint of jealousy, as I notice men's gazes roving all over Dylan's curvy, athletic body.

Noah and Killian immediately head to the bar.

Dylan starts to follow them, but I grab her wrist, tugging her back against me.

She stumbles, her ass pressing into my crotch.

I grit my teeth as my cock strains against my jeans. "Where do you think you're going?" I growl into her ear.

She whirls around, her eyes flashing. "What are you doing? Let go of me."

"I don't think so." I pull her closer, grinding my hips into hers. She sucks in a sharp breath, and I feel the tremor that runs through her body. "You've been teasing me all night. Did you really think I wasn't going to do something about it?"

"I haven't been teasing you, and it's only the start of the night," she protests, but her voice is breathy. She licks her lips, and I zero in on the glimpse of pink tongue again. What I'd give to feel that swirling around the tip of my hungry cock.

"Liar." I fist my hand in her hair and crush my mouth to hers. She gasps, and I take advantage, thrusting my tongue into her mouth.

She kisses me back hungrily, her hands sliding up my chest to loop around my neck.

I lead her across the room to a secluded corner and walk her backwards until she's pressed against the wall, my body pinning hers in place.

One of my hands slides down to grip her ass, kneading the firm muscle. The other slips between our bodies, trailing up the slit in her dress until I reach the edge of her panties.

She jerks as my fingers brush her clit through the thin fabric, a strangled moan escaping her.

I rub slow, teasing circles, feeling her slick heat through the lace. Her head falls back, her lips parting, as her hips rock into my touch.

I grin against her neck. "Still want to pretend you don't want this?"

"Please," she gasps out. "Jayden... we just got here. We're in public..."

"Tell me what you want," I demand hoarsely. My own need is raging, my cock straining against my zipper, but I won't give in until she begs.

I glance around to make sure my massive frame is completely hiding hers from view. Once I confirm we're all clear, I reach down and slide a finger under her panties, dipping into her wetness.

She cries out, her inner walls clenching around me.

"Tell me," I repeat, "or I'll stop right now."

Dylan glares at me, her cheeks flushed, but surrender flickers in her eyes. She licks her lips again and takes a shuddering breath. "I want you to fuck me."

I chuckle, withdrawing my hand to grab her hips and grind against her. "Not good enough."

She growls in frustration, nails biting into my shoulders. "Dammit, Jayden, I want your cock inside me right now!"

"There, was that so hard?" I tease.

I take her by the hand and head in the direction of the restroom. She deserves a million times better than the bathroom stall of an upscale club, but now's not the time to be choosy.

The electricity between us has overtaken us both.

My cock springs free and I shove her panties aside, sliding into her slick heat in one hard thrust.

We both groan at the sensation.

She's scorching and wet, gripping me like a velvet vice. I pause for a moment, savoring the feel of her, before starting up a punishing rhythm.

Our moans mingle as I pound into her, the sound of skin slapping against skin echoing in the empty hall.

Her head falls back again, her lips parted in a silent scream.

I duck my head to close my teeth over the cord of muscle in her neck, sucking hard.

She clenches around me, her inner walls rippling.

I grip her hips tighter, angling to hit that sweet spot deep inside. "Come for me, Dylan." My voice is rough, strained. "I want to feel you come all over my cock."

With a cry, she shatters around me. I thrust wildly a few more times before joining her, spilling deep inside her warmth.

We stay there for a long moment, panting harshly against each other.

Finally I lift my head, meeting her gaze.

Her eyes are hooded, her lips swollen from my kisses. She licks those lips. "Still think this was a mistake?"

I smirk. "I never said that." Then I swoop in for another searing kiss. Eventually, I pull back, still buried deep inside her.

Our ragged breaths mingle in the scant space between us.

Dylan's eyes are shut, her face flushed with lingering pleasure. She's beautiful like this, her lips parted and wanting.

I can't resist ducking my head to capture that mouth again, teasing her with light brushes of my lips.

She makes a sound of protest, but her hands come up to grip my shoulders, keeping me close.

I chuckle against her mouth. "Thought you were annoyed with me."

One eye opens to glare at me. "I still am, you infuriating man." Her hips lift, taking me deeper. We both groan. "But I also want you again. Now."

Heat flares in my gut at the lust in her tone. "Bossy." I nip at her jaw, hands sliding down to grip her ass. "I like it."

Without warning, I pull out of her, ignoring her cry of protest, and spin her around to face the wall. I kick her feet apart and thrust back inside her, setting a punishing pace.

She cries out, bracing her hands against the wall.

I lean over her, blanketing her body with mine.

Our harsh breaths echo through the hall along with the slap of skin.

We ignore the knocking that suddenly starts from the outside. "Is this occupied?" A voice calls out from the door.

"Yep, and it will be for a while. Find somewhere else," I yell in a warning tone.

The knocks stop.

"Is this what you wanted?" I growl against her ear. My hips piston wildly, chasing the tight coil of pleasure in my gut. "To be fucked like this, hard and fast against the wall in a club, you dirty little slut?"

"Yes," she gasps. Her fingernails scrape against the wall, her hips rocking back to meet my every thrust. "God yes, Jayden. Just like that."

The coil snaps and I come with a shout, pumping into her depths once again.

She follows after a few more thrusts, her inner walls clenching like a vice around my cock.

We stay there a long moment, trembling against each other as we catch our breath.

I press a kiss to the nape of her neck and straighten, pulling out of her warmth.

She turns around, her eyes hooded and lips swollen. Reaching out, she hooks a finger through my belt loop and tugs me close. "I'm still annoyed with you," she says, but there's no heat behind the words.

I smirk, brushing a stray hair back from her face. "Duly noted."

I kiss her once again, and we adjust our clothes. She looks just as hot as before. In fact, her slightly tousled appearance and the afterglow of our spontaneous fuck have left her hotter than ever. I'm going to really have to keep an eye on her for the rest of the evening.

Without another word, I take her by the hand and guide her out of the bathroom, past a line of impatient people, some of whose jaws drop as they see us both leaving the room.

CHAPTER 32

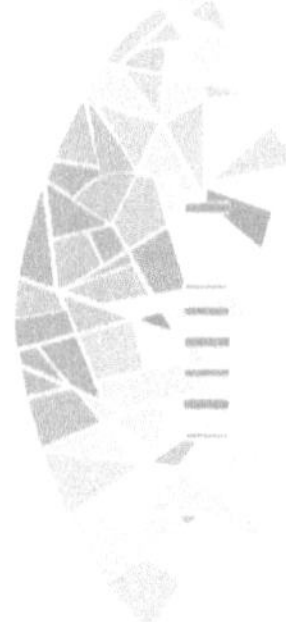

Dylan

The pulsing beat vibrates through my body as we step back into the main room of the crowded club. Neon lights flash in time with the music, illuminating the sleek minimalist decor and packed dance floor. My senses are overwhelmed by the sights, sounds and smells—gyrating bodies, the DJ's booming playlist, cloying perfume mixing with the tart sting of alcohol in the air.

My body is a combination of tingly and numb, and I still can't quite believe what we just did right there in the club.

"Welcome—officially—to our usual haunt. It's new, but it has the best cocktails in town," Jayden leans in close to be heard over the din. "Looks like you're the star tonight."

I glance around self-consciously as heads turn our way, drawn like magnets to Jayden and the other guys beside me. Their athletic physiques and casual confidence attract female attention wherever we go. Jayden smirks, confident in our clandestine knowledge of what just took place between us.

"Seems like everyone knows you guys," I reply, still not used to being in their orbit. Back home, I was the odd one out, the jock girl in a family of academics. But with this club and my team, I finally feel seen, appreciated for my talents on the field. The female rugby player in a room full of sharks part is totally new, however.

As we weave deeper into the club, women approach with flirtatious smiles and sultry looks. But the guys deftly angle their bodies around me, a subtle message that I'm their focus tonight.

The attention is equal parts thrilling and nerve-wracking. I don't want a repeat of what happened with my old team, pushed aside due to petty club politics. This time has to be different.

I was so focused on my roommates—Jayden in particular—that I didn't really notice the other women watching us when we first got here. But now, it's hard to miss their made-up faces that tighten into envious scowls as the guys fawn over me.

"Isn't she that rugby chick?" one says loudly. "Kind of bulky for a dress like that, don't you think?"

Her friend smirks. "Maybe she should've worn a jersey instead. More her style."

I clench my fists, the dig at my athletic build stinging. Great, not only do I have to navigate this new club, but also dodge catty comments. Just what I needed.

Before I can respond, a drunk girl staggers up and deliberately spills her cocktail all over me. I gasp as the cold liquid splashes down my front.

"Oops, did I do that?" she snickers. "Clumsy me. Maybe this will cool you down, honey."

I bite my tongue, willing myself to stay calm. "Real mature. Accidents happen, but you should watch where you're going next time."

My hands tremble with anger and embarrassment. But I won't let their petty jealousy ruin this night. The guys want me here, and value me for exactly who I am. I may not be the skinniest person in the room, but since when has that been my goal? I have curves and I'm strong.

This body of a club-level rugby hooker didn't just happen overnight. It took a lot of tenacity and persistence, and long mornings of strength training.

I straighten my back and lift my chin. We're just getting started.

Noah steps forward, his eyes flashing. "That's enough," he says in a low, firm voice to the woman who spilled her drink. "We're here to have a good time, not start trouble. You should leave before this gets worse for you."

Killian and Jayden close ranks around me, blocking the spiteful girls from view.

"Here, take my jacket," Killian says gently, draping it over my shoulders to cover the stain. "Don't let her ruin your night. She's not worth it."

Jayden grins, lightening the mood with his infectious charm. "Yeah, let's show these drama queens how we really enjoy ourselves!"

I smile back, the guys' support washing away my anger. We won't let petty drama distract us from having an amazing time together.

"Thanks, I needed that reminder," I say.

Noah loops his arm through mine. "Come on, let's head to the VIP section. Drinks are on me."

I let him guide me away, the others trailing behind. In the more exclusive area, the atmosphere is elevated but cozy.

We claim a plush booth and the guys insist I relax while they grab the first round.

When they return, Noah passes me my favorite cocktail—a Naked and Famous. It's a gorgeous orange color, and a potent mix of smoky mezcal, bitter aperol, herbaceous chartreuse and lime. I don't drink often because... well, rugby... but when I do, this is my drink of choice. "To our unshakeable team," he toasts.

"Sláinte!" the others chorus. Everyone gets a little more Irish when they're drinking, I reckon.

The drinks and lively company lift my spirits. We chat and joke easily, the earlier confrontation already fading.

On the dance floor, Noah pulls me close. Our bodies sway in sync as the music pulses through us. Under the swirling lights, I meet his intense gaze. In this moment, I've never felt more wanted or more protected.

After a few songs, Jayden cuts in, twirling me theatrically. "No hogging our star player!" he winks, the other guys oblivious to what transpired earlier between us.

I laugh, intoxicated by the attention. With these guys, I finally feel seen—not just for my athletic skills, but for me. As the night winds down, their fierce loyalty and support fill me with joy.

This is exactly where I'm meant to be.

The remainder of the evening flies by in a blur of dancing, drinking, and easy camaraderie. Before I know it, the lights are coming up and last call is announced.

"I guess that's our cue," Noah says, helping me to my feet. The effects of one too many cocktails make me unsteady, and he grips my waist to support me. But I'm not worried about loosened inhibitions—with these guys, it's like having three gigantic bodyguards ready to fend off anyone unsavory.

"Let's roll out, team," Jayden calls.

We gather our things and head for the exit. The cold night air hits my flushed cheeks. Noah keeps his arm around me as we walk to the car.

"That was epic," Killian grins. "We definitely owned that club tonight."

"All thanks to our secret weapon," Jayden winks at me.

I smile, warmed by their praise. "I should be thanking you guys. For having my back in there."

"Anytime," Noah reassures me. "We look out for our own."

Their words kindle a glow in my chest. With these fierce, loyal men by my side, I feel I can handle anything thrown my way.

We pile into the car, trading laughs and stories from the crazy night. The earlier drama is long forgotten, erased by the bonds we've strengthened.

As I glance at each of them, my heart swells with gratitude and maybe something more. This isn't just the alcohol talking.

Right now, I'm more certain than ever that this is where I belong.

CHAPTER 33

Dylan

The guys crowd into the tiny entryway of our apartment, shucking off their coats and boots.

"Dylan, you're soaked through," Killian says, reaching for the hem of my dress. "Why didn't you say something? I didn't realize she emptied the whole bloody glass all over you!"

"I'm fine," I insist, but three pairs of hands are already peeling the clingy fabric over my head.

"Look at you," Noah murmurs, tracing a finger down my collarbone. "So beautiful. So perfect."

Heat pools low in my belly at the praise, at their hungry eyes roving over my bare skin. I cross my arms over my chest, suddenly shy.

"Don't hide from us, sweetheart," Noah says softly. "You have nothing to be ashamed of."

"Quite the opposite." Jayden's hands encircle my wrists, gently prying my arms away from my body. "You're exquisite."

Killian's lips brush the curve of my neck, his breath hot against my skin. "And we can help make you even stickier, if you'd like."

A flush creeps up my chest at the implication in his words. "Killian!" I protest, but it comes out breathy and wanting.

He chuckles, the sound rumbling through me. "Just a suggestion, sexy. We're here to worship you tonight, in whatever way you desire."

"You're too good to me," I whisper, trembling under their heated gazes and seeking hands. After years of striving to prove my worth, to show I'm more than just a pretty face, it's both thrilling and terrifying to be desired so completely.

"Nonsense." Noah captures my mouth in a searing kiss, effectively silencing my doubts. "You deserve the world, Dylan, and we aim to give it to you."

I melt into Noah's embrace, surrendering to the delicious sensations flooding my senses.

The heady scent of sandalwood and spice, the silk of his lips moving against mine, the warmth of his hands skimming down my sides to cup my ass.

I moan into his mouth, desire pooling hot and urgent between my thighs.

When Noah finally releases me, I'm breathless and aching, clinging to his shoulders to remain standing. The other men crowd closer, a wall of solid heat and muscle, hands roving over my sensitized skin.

"Bath time," Killian declares, scooping me into his arms before I can protest. He carries me into the spacious ensuite bathroom and lowers me into a sea of frothy bubbles in the enormous sunken tub.

I sigh in bliss, the hot water soothing my pleasantly throbbing body.

Jayden settles in behind me, pulling me back against the hard plane of his chest. His hands glide over my shoulders and collarbone, kneading away the remaining tension.

Killian climbs into the tub in front of me, facing me, his massive cock pressing into my upper thigh as he leans forward to kiss me.

Noah picks up a loofah and squeezes a dollop of shower gel onto it. "Lean forward, princess."

He begins to wash my back in slow, sweeping strokes, occasionally dipping lower to squeeze my ass.

I whimper, rocking my hips back into his touch and then forward against the hard length of Killian's cock.

"Minx," Jayden growls from behind me, nipping at the curve of my neck in reprimand. His hands slide down to cup my breasts, rolling my nipples between his thumbs and forefingers until they peak.

Noah sits on the edge of the tub, a book in hand. "Shall I read to you, sweetheart?"

I nod, beyond words as Jayden's hands drift around to tease my breasts and Killian's slip lower still. The water sloshes over the side of the tub as they maneuver me further onto Jayden's lap, his hard cock nestling between my thighs.

"Comfortable?" Noah asks with a wicked grin, flipping open the book. I can only moan in response, writhing helplessly between them as Noah begins to read in a silken tone and their hands roam freely over my fevered skin.

I emerge from the bath on trembling legs, skin flushed and sensitive from their ministrations.

Killian scoops me into his massive arms with a smug grin, carrying me into the living room and depositing me onto the plush couch.

"So beautiful," Noah murmurs, pushing my knees apart to settle between them. He drags his tongue through my folds, circling my clit until I cry out. "The sweetest little pussy."

Jayden captures my mouth in a searing kiss, muffling my moans as Noah's clever tongue works its magic. He pulls back with a nip at my lower lip, dragging my gaze to where Jayden is stroking his thick cock. "Can't wait to be inside you, darling. You're going to be so tight and wet for us."

Heat coils in my belly at his words, the promise of being filled and fucked by them. Noah sucks hard on my clit and I shatter with a wail, vision whiting out as pleasure crashes over me in waves.

They trade places before I've even caught my breath, Jayden and Killian lavishing attention on my sensitive cunt as Noah claims my mouth. I clutch at his shoulders, whimpering into the kiss that tastes like me. It's too much, the ache inside growing impossibly deeper with each pass of their tongues and stroke of their hands.

"That's it, sweetheart. Come for us again." Killian's voice is a dark purr against my thigh. He seals his lips around my clit and sucks, pushing two fingers deep inside me.

The coil snaps and I scream into Noah's mouth, my back arching off the couch as a second, more powerful orgasm rips through me.

I'm only half-aware of them maneuvering me upstairs and tucking me into bed, drifting off to the feeling of their hands stroking over my skin and soft words of praise in my ear.

CHAPTER 34

Dylan

The early morning sun streams through the windows as I move around the well-equipped kitchen. The aroma of simmering tomatoes and peppers fills the air as I prepare the shakshuka, poaching the eggs gently in the spicy sauce. Next to it bubbles the golden khachapuri, its melted cheese releasing an irresistible scent.

I smile to myself, feeling a new lightness after last night. The guys really came through, treating me like a teammate, maybe even a friend... and then definitely something more.

This breakfast is my way of saying thanks, and of acknowledging the way we've progressed to the next level, whatever that means.

As I chop parsley for garnish, I hear shuffling behind me. I glance back to see Jayden yawning, his hair endearingly mussed from sleep.

"Morning, sleepyhead. I'm just finishing up a special breakfast as a token of appreciation." I say, unable to keep the grin off my face.

"Wow, Dylan, you didn't have to go through all this trouble." Jayden looks touched, his eyes widening as he takes in the spread.

"It was no trouble at all. You guys are... well, you're all great."

I plate the shakshuka and khachapuri with pride.

As we sit down to eat, the conversation flows easily. It's so freeing finally feeling like I'm able to completely be myself. The lingering hurt and doubt of my past fade with each laugh we share.

I smile as Killian wanders in, his hair sticking up every which way.

"Rise and shine! I hope you're hungry," I say, sliding a piping hot plate of shakshuka in front of him.

He inhales deeply, eyes still bleary with sleep. "Mmm, smells amazing. Is today my birthday or something?"

I laugh. "Nope, just wanted to say thanks for being so amazing yesterday."

His eyes soften. "Of course."

Noah shuffles in next, equally disheveled and adorable. He perks up at the sight of food.

"Dang, Dylan! You trying to fatten us up or what?" He jokes, piling his plate high. "I wondered what that was. It smells divine."

"Maybe! Gotta keep my guys well-fed," I quip back, thrilled they're enjoying my cooking.

The conversation flows easily as we eat, laughter and steaming mugs of coffee warming the kitchen. I truly feel like I fit in here—that I'm actually wanted—and it makes me more than a bit giddy.

As I clear the empty plates, Killian claps a hand on my shoulder. "You're alright, Dylan. I'm glad you're here."

My heart swells. With food and friendship, we're building something special.

I smile to myself as I start washing the dishes, the chatter and laughter of my teammates warming my heart. This feels right.

A knock at the door interrupts my musings. Noah jumps up to answer it.

"Hey Kai, what's up?"

My heart just about stops at the mention of his name.

Kai steps inside, gym bag in hand. "Just dropping off that equipment you needed. Sorry to barge in on you guys."

"No problem! We're just finishing up breakfast. Care to join? Dylan made a mean feast. Shakshuka and… what was it again? Khacha-something?" Noah gestures to the remnants of food spread across the table.

"Khachaphuri," I say, pressing my lips together, afraid of what else might come out of my mouth if I don't hold back.

Kai glances at me hesitantly. I give him an encouraging nod. "Yeah man, plenty left over."

"Well, in that case, don't mind if I do!" He grabs a plate and digs in eagerly.

I find myself watching him, struck by his muscular frame and the intensity of his focus as he eats. He glances up, catching me staring, and grins.

"This is insane, Dylan. You can cook for me anytime."

A warmth spreads through me at his praise. "It's nothing, really. Just a little something I whipped up."

"Are you kidding? This is restaurant-quality," Kai insists.

The conversation drifts to rugby as we finish up.

"So, Dylan, tell us about your experience so far playing at this level. It's intense, right?" Kai asks.

I nod. "Definitely. The training is grueling, the competition fierce. But it's rewarding, you know? Like cooking, but with full contact and more tackling," I joke.

The guys chuckle, but their eyes shine with interest.

I find myself opening up, sharing stories of tough coaches, early morning practices, and the thrill of playing in front of huge crowds.

For the first time, I feel my passion for rugby being matched by those around me. The bonds between us grow stronger with each shared experience.

Killian leans forward, his expression intent. "Seeing you play ...it's clear you're not just going through the motions. You're making really innovative plays. Mad respect."

A swell of pride rises in me at his words. "Thanks, that means a lot coming from you guys."

We fall into an animated discussion about the similarities and differences between men's and women's rugby—training regimes, game strategies, team dynamics. The guys listen raptly, chiming in with thoughtful questions and observations.

I feel a heady rush, being taken so seriously for both my cooking and rugby skills.

These men aren't just teammates or roommates. They're becoming true friends, maybe even like the brothers I never had. Well, not brothers because... they don't do things to you like these men did last night. I blush as the memories come flooding back.

As the meal winds down, the mood remains lively, but a deeper sense of connection hums between us.

Jayden grins at me. "You know, Dylan, you're pretty cool for a roommate. Glad you ended up here with us."

I return his smile. "Right back at ya. And if any of you ever want to learn how not to burn water, I'm your girl."

We share a laugh as I start clearing dishes. A feeling of contentment settles over me. I hadn't expected to find this—not just a place to live, but the beginnings of a real family.

In the warmth of this kitchen, surrounded by raucous laughter and the lingering scents of breakfast, I know I've found where I belong.

CHAPTER 35

Dylan

I retreat to my room after our lively breakfast, the laughter fading as I close the door. My little sanctuary, a blend of cozy and functional. Rugby gear is piled in the corner, and posters and photos from home are plastered on the walls alongside my various trophies and inspirational quotes. It's lived-in yet tidy, reflecting my journey both on and off the pitch.

Jonah is snuggled comfortably in his cozy cat bed, one of his front paws adorably covering his face to shield it from the ray of sunshine that angles in from the large window.

I plop down on my quilt-covered bed and stare out the window, watching the leaves flutter in the breeze.

My mind drifts to the guys—Noah, Jayden, Killian. Each so unique, bringing their own strengths.

Noah's leadership and sensitivity.

Jayden's humor and protectiveness.

Killian's intellect and thoughtfulness.

And Kai... he came out of left field, to say the least. A quiet leader, a star player... so different from any man I've met before.

They all have something attractive to offer. But together, as one unit? "That's just fantasy..." I mutter.

I wrestle with my feelings, considering the social expectations about relationships.

Could it actually work, the five of us together? There's no doubt we each have strong personalities. And then there's my own insecurities to contend with.

I shake my head and laugh softly. Don't get ahead of yourself, Dylan. That's crazy talk.

They could each have an army of women if they wanted. Why in hell would they all settle for sharing someone? Especially me.

Yet even as I dismiss the thought, a new curiosity takes root.

I continue staring out at the fluttering leaves, symbolizing the ideas swirling in my mind.

Could I really do it—be with all four of them? It sounds insane, but... maybe it could work. If we communicated openly and built trust.

I make a mental note to do some research on polyamory later, intent on understanding how these dynamics play out. It always sounded like something other people did, that I'd read about or seen in movies, so it's not something I'd spent a lot of time thinking about. I had a friend who briefly dated someone she referred to as 'Mr. Ethical

Non-Manogamy', and learned a bit about it from her. That's really the extent of my knowledge on the topic.

But for now, I just watch the leaves dance on the breeze, letting the "what ifs" swirl freely.

No need to rush into anything. I'll just see what happens... consider the possibilities.

Absentmindedly, I find Liv's number in my phone and hit the call button. Her voice rings out from my phone speaker after a couple of rings, pulling me from my thoughts.

"Hey Liv, got a minute? I need to sort through some crazy thoughts," I say.

"Shoot, what's stirring in that wild head of yours?"

I hesitate. "It's the guys. I'm drawn to each of them, but it seems like a no-win situation. I can't think there's anything beyond friendship, right? I mean... I guess we fooled around last night, but we'd been drinking and I'm beyond sure it didn't mean anything to any of them."

"Why limit yourself, Dyl? You've got so much to offer. Who says you have to pick just one?" Liv counters.

My eyes widen. "You mean...all of them together? That can't actually work, can it?"

"Why not? My cousin's been in a polyamorous relationship for years. It's all about communication and honesty," she explains casually.

I'm quiet for a moment, intrigued yet uncertain. "I guess I've never pictured myself in that kind of setup. But the idea doesn't sound...h orrible?"

Liv laughs warmly. "Trust the lesbian with a childhood sweetheart to school you on managing multiple men. Especially one raised by two moms in a house full of sisters."

I have to laugh too. "Okay, fair. You may know jack about dudes, but you know people."

"Exactly. If they care and you all communicate, what's to stop you from exploring it?" Liv reasons. "It's the 2020s, not the Middle Ages."

I ponder her perspective, realizing she's opened my mind to possibilities I'd never considered. "Let's just see what happens," I conclude. "No rush, no expectations. I'm just...considering the options."

"There you go. Embrace those crazy thoughts," Liv encourages.

I smile softly, watching the leaves dance again. Maybe I could embrace more than I realized... like... four hot men.

"Thanks Liv, you've given me a lot to think about," I say, ending the call.

I stare out my window, watching the leaves flutter as new ideas take root in my mind. Could I really do it—be with Noah, Jayden, Killian and Kai all together? It sounds insane, but maybe it could work. It would definitely require tons of communication and trust, though.

I spend the next hour reading various articles and personal accounts. There are definitely challenges, but with openness and agreed upon boundaries, some make it work smoothly.

Setting aside my phone, my mind now swirls with questions and hypothetical situations. I don't want to assume anything or make impulsive choices.

For now, I'll just observe how things unfold naturally with the guys.

No pressure, no expectations, just possibilities.

I shake my head and laugh softly. "Let's see where this crazy thought experiment goes..."

Despite the unconventional notion, a part of me is undeniably intrigued and hopeful.

CHAPTER 36

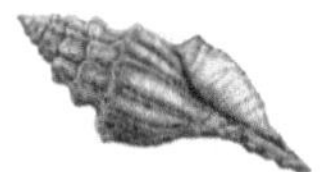

Killian

The morning sun casts a soft light across my tidy room. There's something about keeping everything in its place, especially when the rest of my life is feeling a little out of control.

I sit at my desk, coffee mug in hand, staring out the window but not really seeing anything. The apartment is quiet, a calm settling after the chaos of last night.

I think back to the laughter and easy banter from the evening before, and how effortlessly Dylan fit into our little group. Her smile lit up the room as we shared stories and inside jokes. It was different than our usual nights out together.

And then when we got home, most definitely different from our usual nights in as roommates.

More than just fun—it was genuinely enjoyable.

Dylan clicked with us so naturally, it was like she'd always been here. Could there be something more than just... whatever last night was?

I remember how she teased Jayden when he tried showing off during our rugby scrimmage, matching his competitiveness with her own feisty spirit.

The way she made Noah laugh heartily with that ridiculous impression of our coach, the way I hadn't seen him laugh in years.

And when we locked eyes across the living room, sharing a private smile at the guys' antics, some kind of circuit in my mind that had blown long ago seemed to fuse back together, making me feel all was right with the world.

Dylan is unlike anyone we've ever known. She challenges me—challenges us—in new ways. Makes me think about taking risks I've never considered. Exploring something extraordinary.

Because maybe there's a chance we could all care for her, in our own way.

And maybe, if we're brave enough, she could care for each of us, too.

I grab my journal, scribbling down these swirling thoughts and feelings. If we're all on the same page, we need to talk openly and honestly. Figure out if trying for something real with Dylan is a leap worth taking. A relationship like we've never had before, but could build together.

As I close my journal, resolve settles within me. Along with a spark of anticipation.

It's time to find the guys. No more wondering about what if—we need to look our future in the eye. A future that might just include Dylan as our shared love, if we're willing to embrace the unexpected. To ask the right questions rather than just regurgitate all the conventional answers that have been hammered into us relentlessly by our parents, teachers, the media, and whoever else has an opinion on what a relationship should look like.

Because maybe Dylan herself is the best thing we could have ever imagined would enter our lives. She's abundance personified, and if there's someone with enough generosity and kindness and spirit to go around, it would be her.

And maybe, just maybe, we're ready to explore the possibilities she represents. For all of us.

I find Noah in the kitchen, sipping his morning coffee. His broad shoulders are tense, his forehead creased in thought. But when I enter, he glances up with a smile.

"Morning. Sleep okay after last night?" His voice is light, but there's an undercurrent of something else.

I pour my own coffee. "Honestly? I was up thinking."

Noah raises an eyebrow. "About Dylan?"

"Yeah, what else?" I chuckle wryly. "It's a little hard to focus on rugby at the moment. She's not like anyone we've met before."

Noah nods. "She's one of a kind. Tough yet so damn vibrant." Affection warms his tone.

"Exactly. And it got me thinking..." I hesitate. Noah's protectiveness could make this conversation tricky. "Wondering if we should talk about...possibilities."

Noah stills. "Possibilities," he repeats carefully.

I forge ahead. "Look, we all care about her. And she fits here, with us, so easily. Almost like..."

"Like she belongs," Noah finishes quietly. "And when I say 'belongs'... there's something she brings to each of us individually, and then collectively as a group as well."

I'm relieved he understands my meaning. "Right. So do we just ignore that? Or actually discuss it?"

Noah is silent, mulling it over. Then he meets my gaze, resolve in his eyes. "Yeah. Let's talk."

Just then, Jayden wanders in, yawning. His hair is mussed from sleep, his eyes bleary.

Noah clears his throat. "We were just talking about Dylan."

Jayden perks up instantly. "Yeah? What about her?"

I exchange a look with Noah. No going back now.

"About exploring something real. The three of us, with Dylan." I watch Jayden closely. "If that's something we all want."

Jayden glances between us, then grins slowly. "Hell yes, let's talk."

Relief floods through me, along with a hum of anticipation. This conversation won't be easy, but now we're facing our future head-on. Embracing the unexpected with brave hearts and open minds.

A future that just might include Dylan. In a way we never imagined, but are willing to build together.

I take a deep breath as Noah and Jayden settle in at the table, mugs of coffee in hand. This is uncharted territory for us all.

"So..." I begin slowly. "I think we need to lay everything on the table here. Talk through how each of us feels, and what we want. Really figure this out. To see if this could actually work, or if it's just a silly idea that could never really happen in practice."

Noah nods. "You're right. No assumptions." He meets my gaze. "I'll start. Dylan is special. Strong, passionate, beautiful. Being with her just feels...right. But it's more than that." His voice softens. "She makes me want to be better. For her, and for us. I admire her strength and tenacity—the way she's overcome hardships in her real life and faced some pretty tough challenges head-on. But she hasn't lost her softer side, her generous side. She's already taught me so much about balance and not letting the shit stuff that happens harden us forever."

I'm touched by his candor. Now it's my turn. "Since she got here, it feels like everything has changed. In the best way. With her, it's easy, comfortable, but also challenging... and if I'm honest, which we need to be here, at times, even infuriating. There's a richness in our lives that didn't exist before. Forget all the fangirls and the nights out on the town making poor decisions that feel good for a fleeting moment. I can't imagine her not being here." I take a breath. "And I don't want to."

We turn to Jayden. He rakes a hand through his hair. "You know me. Not one for talking about feelings and all that." His mouth quirks up. "But yeah, she's got under my skin, too. In a big way... I tried and tried to hate her, and to push her away. But she kept coming back and now I'm the one who can't stay away."

I lean forward intently. "So we're all on the same page here. We care about her, a lot. We all want this to work." I meet each of their gazes. "But we have to be smart. Talk through the challenges. This doesn't sound simple just talking about it, and it's only going to get more complicated in practice."

Noah frowns. "Well, I'll admit I'm pretty protective of her. Just like I am with all of my things. Not sure I'm cut out for sharing."

"Same here," Jayden grunts. "I don't like thinking of her with any-one else."

I nod slowly. Their territorial instincts could be an issue. "Right. But this only works if we're all equal partners. No jealousy, no possessiveness. Dylan deserves better than that."

Jayden exhales sharply. "Yeah, you're right. It's just...new. But we can figure it out. For her, I would make this type of exception. Especially if you guys were the ones I had to share her with."

Noah murmurs his agreement.

"And me?" I prompt them. "What are your worries there?"

Noah considers me. "That your desire for monogamy might make this difficult. Sharing intimacy, affection. I've never even seen you rotate between short-term flings. You have a shitty reputation for being a player, but you're actually a really loyal guy, and this type of arrangement is going to challenge your sense of which way is up."

I rake a hand through my hair, uneasy but knowing he's right. "I'll admit, it won't be easy at first. But Dylan..." I trail off, then continue resolutely. "She's worth challenging myself for. Worth trying for."

Jayden nods firmly. "Yeah. She's worth everything."

A new sense of possibility settles over us. This won't be simple, but together, we can build something extraordinary.

I meet their eyes, voice steady. "So we do this. Together."

Noah's mouth curves. "Together."

Jayden grins crookedly. "Together."

"Okay," I say, convinced we at least need her to hear us out. "Let's continue to talk this through. To really think about it. We might be open-minded now, but I have a sense that feelings might change if and when things start to get real. Plus, we should really involve Dylan in any future conversations about this. I know I was the one to bring it up, but I'm starting to feel like we're talking about her as if she has no say in any of this. When really, she's the person who matters most."

The others nod.

It's time to bring Dylan on board, and to hold her up like the queen she is.

CHAPTER 37

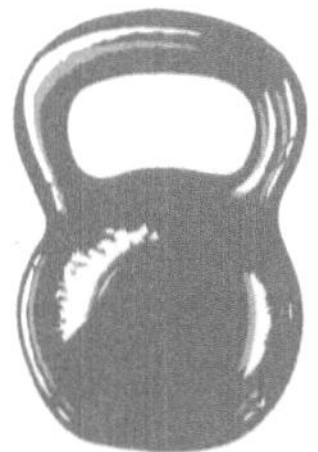

Noah

I glance up from my sports magazine, watching as Dylan laughs while cooking dinner in the kitchen. Her smile lights up the whole apartment. Lately, I can't take my eyes off her whenever she's around.

Who am I kidding? From the moment I first laid eyes on her, they may as well have been slathered in gorilla glue and stuck to her permanently.

The way we've all let her take over the kitchen so frequently—and definitely not because she's a woman, but because cooking for other people clearly brings her genuine joy—is a testament to how she's started breaking down each of our walls.

Before, occasionally, Killian would wow us with some new vegetarian dish, or I'd whip up a Laotian meal from time to time. Jayden would nip into the kitchen to stuff some protein down and then quickly exit. But she's changed all that.

Seeing how relaxed she is joking with Killian and Jayden makes me twitch with jealousy. I want her all to myself, but that selfish urge goes against how we've always done things.

I know I said I was open-minded, but the more time I've had to think about it, the more I realize that words are very different from reality. Even the idea of what we talked about is starting to dig at me like needles under my skin.

"It's different with Dylan," I mutter under my breath. I can't shake this feeling that I want her all to myself. But it's looking more and more like if any of us are going to get to be with her, we're all going to have to be with her. And that's just not how we've ever done things around here.

It's not how the entire world works, either.

We're not some fucking harem.

My eyes trace over her body as she moves gracefully through the kitchen. I imagine pulling her into my arms, feeling her soft skin pressed against me, hearing her moan my name...

I shift in my seat, forcing myself to look away before my thoughts wander too far. Dylan's not just some random hookup—she could be something real. Something lasting.

And, the more I think about it, I realize I'll be damned if I'm going to share her the way I would any other girl.

She's too important for that.

If she were just anyone, someone who didn't make me feel like this, I might be more open. But she is perfection in a tank top—not just her body but her personality and her mind... I'd go as far as to say her *soul*... and that makes me feel possessive.

Mine.

I know pursuing her exclusively could jeopardize everything between the four of us. But I need clarity, even if it means risking it all.

I've made up my mind. I know what I said to the guys, but in the clear light of day it's time to get real.

I'm going to tell Dylan how I feel. Let her choose me and only me. It's the only way forward, no matter how messy it gets. I just hope I don't end up pushing her away for good.

I take a deep breath, steeling myself for the conversation ahead.

Killian closes his laptop and walks over, his expression serious.

"So..." he says, his eyes darting between me and Jayden. "Are you guys ready to tell Dylan she doesn't have to pick just one of us?"

I let out a short laugh, shaking my head. "Come on, man. I know we talked about it conceptually, but you know that's not how things work. Dylan's not just some girl we met at a club. This is different."

Killian frowns. "Is it though? Some of us have shared before. Why would this be any different?"

My jaw clenches. "Because I want more than just a fling. Dylan could be something real for me. For us."

Jayden mutes the TV and looks over, raising an eyebrow. "So you do want to force her to choose, despite everything we talked about? That's a risky game, Noah. What if we end up pushing her away completely?"

I meet his gaze steadily. "Then that's a risk we have to take. Better than living in some limbo where we all end up hurt."

Killian sighs, raking a hand through his hair. "I don't know, man. I think you're playing with fire here. And I couldn't bear to lose her just because one of us is being selfish."

"It's about clarity," I say firmly. "Either we know where we stand, or we don't stand at all."

Jayden and Killian exchange uncertain glances. The tension in the room is palpable.

I stand, resolute in my decision. "I'll talk to Dylan. It's better if it comes from me. We'll set up some dates, make it fair. But I need to know where I'm at with her. Who she wants. I'm not prepared to share her, even with you guys."

Killian shakes his head slowly. "Just...be careful, Noah. We don't want to lose her, not over this. And I'm pretty sure she's not going to like your ultimatum."

My heart pounds as I walk toward the kitchen. I know I'm steering us into rough waters, but it's the only way I can see clearly.

I just hope we make it through the storm.

CHAPTER 38

Dylan

I drop my rugby bag on the floor with a thud, rotating my sore shoulder right as Jonah sprints past, rubbing against my leg in a warm welcome. Practice was intense, and I seem to have aggravated an old injury that I haven't had to deal with in a while.

The guys are already sitting around the dining table, shifting glances between each other.

Something's up. Their body language screams serious conversation ahead. My stomach knots. What have we done? Are we getting evicted already?

Noah clears his throat as I grab a plate. "So, Dylan. We've been thinking..."

He pauses as if unable to speak any more words, and Killian jumps in. "Maybe you should go on individual dates with each of us. You know, to see who you really vibe with."

My fork halts halfway to my mouth. "You want me to date all of you? Like some bachelor-style competition?" I narrow my eyes at Noah. "So I was right... you're trying to force me to pick. But you're doing it in some weird way that feels like a dating game show."

Jayden fidgets with his napkin. "Not a competition exactly. More like... helping you figure out the best fit."

I set my fork down, my appetite almost vanishing. After the drama at my old club, being forced to choose sides nearly crushed me. And here it is, happening again, albeit in entirely different circumstances.

Don't they get it? This will only drive me away, not pull me closer.

But I'm tired of always making compromises. If they want to play this game, fine. Time to raise the stakes.

I force a sweet smile. "Sure, I'll go out with each of you." I pause. "Oh, and Kai, too. Just to keep my options really open."

Killian's eyes widen in surprise. Noah looks like he just chugged sour milk.

They glance at each other.

"Well, that's one way to do it," Killian finally says with an awkward chuckle.

Noah grimaces. "If that's what you need."

I poke at my food, my appetite now fully gone. My show of nonchalance masks the turmoil twisting inside. The thought of losing any of them makes my chest ache. My shoulder pain intensifies, as if to punctuate the emotions swirling around me.

What have I gotten myself into? Why did I ever think I could make it work with more than one of these testosterone-fueled men? I could never be enough for all of them. Hell, I might not even be enough for one of them.

I stare blankly at my half-eaten dinner, the clinking of silverware and awkward glances bouncing around the tense silence.

Part of me wants to take it back, to say I was just kidding about Kai. But why should I be the only one compromising here? If they want to put me through some twisted dating game, why not make them squirm a little too?

"So...dates. This should be interesting," Killian says, trying to cut through the discomfort.

"Yeah, interesting," Noah mutters.

I clear my throat. "Look, it doesn't have to be weird. We're friends first, right? So really, these are just...friend dates."

Jayden nods slowly. "Right, just hanging out. Getting to know each other better."

"Exactly. Keep it casual," I say with false confidence. Inside, my thoughts churn while my stomach flip-flops.

Did I just make a huge mistake? What if this backfires and I end up losing them all? But I couldn't just let them corner me into choosing one because they're in some possessive alpha male delusion.

The more I think about it, the more I'm certain this was Noah's idea. He's the one I thought would be the most reluctant to share. And once one person isn't okay with an arrangement like the one that was starting to emerge, it kind of fucks it for everyone else involved.

I push back my chair and grab my plate. "Well, I'm beat. Gonna call it a night. Thanks for the food."

As I rinse off my dish, Jayden approaches tentatively. "Dyl, about all this..."

I cut him off. "We'll figure it out. Goodnight."

Before he can respond, I slip away to my bedroom, closing the door firmly behind me.

Flopping onto my bed, I let out a long breath. What a mess. But maybe this is the only way to really know. Or to show them how it feels to be put in this position.

I just hope we don't destroy everything in the process.

I stare out my bedroom window at the twinkling city lights, feeling conflicted.

Part of me is thrilled by the idea of intimate dates with each of the guys. A chance to connect one-on-one and see if a deeper bond emerges.

But another part aches, knowing this could drive a wedge between us.

The easy camaraderie we've built as roommates and teammates hangs delicately in the balance. What would happen if I realized two of us clicked better than the others? Given what's happened already, would it be possible to have a relationship with just one of them? Or is this all just fucked from the start?

I take out my journal, hoping to make sense of my tangled thoughts.

No matter what happens, I need to stay true to myself, I write. *Even if it means risking everything. Love shouldn't be about losing yourself, but finding where you truly belong.*

As scary as it feels, this is the only way forward. For all of us to be honest about what we really want.

And for me to listen to my heart, even if it doesn't follow the expected path.

I take a deep breath and close my journal. Whatever comes next, I know I can handle it. As long as I stay grounded in who I am.

With the guys, with rugby, with love—I need to trust my instincts. That's when I'm at my best.

When I leap without overthinking. When I play from the heart.

That's when magic happens.

This is just another kind of game.

And I don't intend to lose.

CHAPTER 39

Dylan

The first rays of sunlight creep through my blinds, stirring me from a restless sleep. I roll over with a groan, the knot in my stomach tighter than ever.

My rugby gear sits ready and waiting, but my mind is far from prepared for practice.

This is exactly what I was trying to avoid, coming here. My plan was to focus on rugby and only on rugby, maybe make some good platonic friends along the way.

It certainly wasn't to come here to be distracted by men who will take me further away from my dreams, the ones I've worked so hard for. Still, right now my roommates—and Kai—are all I can think about.

I drag myself out of bed, my thoughts swirling. "Why should I have to choose one? They all bring something unique to my life. Isn't there a way to have it all without hurting anyone?"

Maybe some one-on-one time would help clear the air. But it feels less like getting clarity and more like being forced into a choice I don't want to make.

But the empty room offers no answers. With a sigh, I haul myself out of bed. Time to face the day.

The dewy grass crunches under my cleats as I join the team on the pitch. My teammates chatter and laugh as they loosen up, but I feel detached, going through the motions on autopilot.

Coach blows the whistle, signaling the start of drills. I take my position, but my focus is shot. The complicated situation with my roommates invades my thoughts once again.

"Maybe spending individual time isn't such a bad idea," I think, passing the ball half-heartedly. "It could clear things up... But why does it feel like I'm being cornered into choosing?"

My inner turmoil must show on my face, because Coach pulls me aside after practice. "Get your head in the game, Dylan. I can't have my star player distracted."

His choice of words is flattering, and the gravity of them is embarrassing. How could I take this level of an opportunity and squander it over the promise of some good dick? Really good dick, but dick nonetheless.

I nod, promising to leave my personal drama off the pitch.

But as I hit the showers, my thoughts drift once more.

Spending one-on-one time with each of the guys could help provide clarity, yet the pressure to choose between them feels suffocating.

I still can't shake the feeling that Noah is behind this, but Jayden and Killian have chosen to go along with it, and now I've brought Kai into the mix—not that he knows it yet.

If I'm honest, despite the uncertainty of everything, that last part still gives me a lingering sense of satisfaction. Throwing Kai into the mix really shook things up, disrupting Noah, Killian, and Jayden's expectations. It made me feel like, for one precious moment, I was in control.

I can't help but smile to myself.

At least that made them think, I muse internally. Maybe now they'll see how ridiculous this whole 'choose one' thing is. It's all fun and games making people choose until they add in a few options of their own.

After toweling off, I stare at my reflection in the locker room mirror. Dark circles underline my eyes, evidence of another sleepless night. At this rate, none of them are going to want me. I'm a complete mess. With a sigh, I throw on fresh clothes and grab my gear bag.

Stepping outside, the morning sun momentarily blinds me. I blink against the glare, resolved to push aside my worries for now. Practice is over, but the day has just begun.

Time to tackle things one step at a time.

As I walk to my car, I repeat Coach's advice like a mantra: "Get your head in the game." Easier said than done when my heart is so conflicted. On the pitch, I'm in control. It's the one place where the ball is mine to command. Except for today, where I sucked.

For now, rugby will be my escape and my anchor amidst the storm. Eyes on the prize, Dylan. One match at a time.

Whatever happens with the men happens. But it can't distract me from the main reason—the only reason—I'm here.

After changing, I head out to the usual post-practice social spot. Kai is surrounded by his usual entourage, including that one annoying bitchy girl who's always trash-talking me.

Fueled by defiance and the need to add my fourth choice into this impossible decision I'm faced with, I steel my nerves and stride right up to him.

"Hey Kai," I interrupt, "want to go out with me sometime soon?"

He looks surprised, but smiles. "Yeah, sure. I'd like that."

The bitchy woman snorts derisively. "Really, Kai? You're going out with *her*?" She crinkles her nose up in disgust as her gaze trails over my freshly showered body, which is now adorned in comfy shorts and a clean racerback practice shirt.

Normally, that type of gaze would have me shriveling into myself, but in the face of everything I'm dealing with, it has the opposite effect.

I puff myself up, internally and physically, jutting out my chest and keeping my shoulders high and proud. I allow my gaze to trail over her, this vapid cookie cutter who only cares about the title of being a rugby player's girlfriend, and about how much he can spend on her.

Kai meets my eyes, his expression firm. "Yes, really. I'm looking forward to it, Dylan."

I can feel his gaze on me as I walk away, a new sense of empowerment rising in my chest. The bitchy woman's glare just about burns holes in my back.

"Take that," I say to myself. "I'm not just some pawn in their game. I make my own moves."

What comes next, I'm not sure. But I stood my ground, and that's what matters.

Now to get ready for these ridiculous dates and see where things go from here.

Whatever happens next, I'm ready.

CHAPTER 40

Dylan

The amber glow of my bedside lamp casts shadows that match my mood—confused and disoriented.

A gentle knock startles me from my thoughts. I open the door to find Jayden, his usual scowl replaced with a look of concern.

"Mind if I join you for a bit?" he asks. "Thought maybe you could use a friend."

I'm surprised by his uncharacteristic softness, but nod. "Yeah, I'd like that. Thanks, Jayden."

He sits beside me on the bed, not pushing for conversation, just offering silent support. I appreciate him giving me space while still making me feel less isolated.

Maybe he's not the callous jerk he pretends to be. Could he actually care? I don't know what to make of this vulnerable side of him.

"Rough day, huh?" Jayden finally says. "Don't let it get to you. I know that there's a lot going on, and a lot for you to think about. But no matter what happens, we're here for you, Dylan."

His sincerity catches me off guard. I've spent so long fighting for respect and worrying that my new team, my new friends, would betray me like my old one. But Jayden's compassion gives me hope—hope that I've found people in my life who truly see me for more than just athletic ability and what purpose I can serve them.

"Thank you, Jayden," I reply, managing a small smile. "I didn't expect this from you, but...I'm glad you're here."

For the first time today, the weight on my shoulders feels a little lighter. Maybe I don't have to prove myself to them. Maybe these guys, this whole situation, will truly be different.

I take a shaky breath, trying to hold back the emotions bubbling up inside me. But it's no use—the stress of everything catches up and I feel hot tears spill down my cheeks.

Jayden wordlessly hands me a tissue. "It's okay, let it out," he says gently. "We're all just figuring this out as we go."

"I just hate that all of you want me to choose sides, and I know Noah is the one in the driver's seat with this," I sob. "It reminds me of my old team's politics and mind games. I feel like I'm right back where I started. It's like my rugby situation from back then repeating, but with relationships this time."

Jayden nods thoughtfully. "Noah can be stubborn, always thinks he has to fix everything. He has a need to call the shots. This might not actually be about you choosing—it could be his way of regaining some control. Of making sure he's looked at every angle before confirming that something less conventional than any of us ever expected could actually be the best option for everyone involved."

I dab at my eyes, sniffling. "I don't know. It feels like he's pushing me away. That I'm being forced into something that doesn't feel good for anyone. I don't know if I can do this."

"He's not perfect, that's for sure," Jayden says. "But I know he cares about you a lot, Dylan. We all do, in our own ways."

His words are a balm, easing my hurt.

Jayden looks at me earnestly. "Just remember, you're not alone in this."

I meet his gaze, sincerely touched. "Thank you, Jayden. That means a lot."

He gives my shoulder a supportive squeeze. "We're more than just roommates now. You're one of us. Whatever happens."

I feel a glimmer of hope. If we stick together, perhaps we can weather any storm. I smile for the first time all night, comforted by Jayden's support.

Maybe he's right, and there's a solution where no one has to lose, I think, new hope rising within me. One where we can all stay together... but first, we just need to do this whole date thing. For Noah.

"Try to get some rest," Jayden says gently. "Tomorrow's a new day. We'll figure this out—together." He squeezes my shoulder with a massive hand, his touch both comforting me and turning me on.

Still, now's not the time to get all sexy. There's too much on my mind.

"Yeah...thanks again, Jayden. I really needed this."

He smiles and rises from the bed. At the door, he pauses. "You know where to find me if you need anything. Hang in there."

With a final reassuring look, he closes the door behind him.

Alone again, I feel lighter somehow. Jayden's kindness has given me a new perspective.

I'm not solo in this—we're a team. And together, we can find an answer that works for all of us.

I snuggle under the covers, a tentative smile on my face. The future seems less daunting now.

As I drift off, my last thoughts are of gratitude...and hope.

And curiosity about what Killian has planned for our date.

CHAPTER 41

Dylan

The shelter is a chorus of yips, meows, and purrs, a symphony of new life seeking love. I spot Killian sitting cross-legged on the floor, a pile of puppies tumbling over his lap. He laughs as they lick his face, pure joy lighting up his features.

"Dylan! Come meet the gang," he says, beckoning me over.

I plop down next to him and immediately have an armful of wriggling fur. "They're adorable!" I bury my face in their soft coats as a tiny tongue licks my nose.

Killian grins. "It's the best part of my week, coming here. Hard to feel down with this much cuteness."

I nod, letting a pup gnaw on my fingers. "They just need a little love. We all do."

A knowing look passes between us. I don't have to explain—Killian understands. My heart swells, full of new hope.

After an hour or so of playing with an army of the most gorgeous animals I've ever seen, Killian drives us to the beach. He rolls the windows down as we make our way along the main strip, and I close my eyes, savoring the wind in my hair and the sun's glow on my face.

When I open my eyes, I catch him looking at me.

Some looks need no words. This man really cares about me.

The afternoon sun beats down on the sand as we join the crowd of volunteers at the beach. Styrofoam cups, food wrappers, and cigarette butts litter the once pristine shore. It makes me infuriated that people seem to bring whatever they feel like down to a gorgeous place like this and use it as their personal trash can. It's not something I've really thought about, but right here, right now, it's all up in my face.

Killian hands me a bag, and we get to work, clearing piece after piece.

As we clean, we chat about ways to curb pollution and keep our oceans healthy. Killian points out pieces of coral washed ashore, damaged but still pulsing with life. He's like a walking trivia book about conservation and recycling, and about the risks humans pose to sea life.

I listen with interest. It's not a topic I know much about, or that I expected him to be an expert in, but his enthusiasm is as contagious as his adorable smile.

At one point, Killian excuses himself and walks to a rocky part of the shore where a pretty woman is standing. I feel a pang of jealousy as I watch their easy interaction, her body angled into his as he envelops her in a hug. I see her pointing at something on the shoreline, and he walks over to check it out, bending over to pick something up. But my jealousy is short-lived when he returns and retrieves something from his pocket.

He presents me with the most beautiful shell I've ever seen, textured and patterned in a way that makes me marvel at the power of nature to create the most beautiful things.

"That was my friend Shelley... I'm not joking. That's her actual name. She's the shell expert around here. We grew up next door to each other actually, and I'm good friends with her wife."

A surge of relief washes over me. Maybe Noah and I aren't so different with our possessive qualities, after all.

Killian interrupts my deep thoughts, gesturing at the shell. "You know, if you listen to it, you can always hear the ocean, no matter how far away you are."

"So I can always find my home?"

"Yes, exactly. You can always find your home."

Our bags grow heavy as the sun dips low. Just in time, we join the group releasing baby sea turtles.

I gasp as the tiny creatures paddle furiously towards the lapping waves. Freedom, at last. So brave as they willingly wade into the unknown. I have the urge to follow them into the ocean and swim to some deserted island. To start a new life afresh, free of the stress of everyday life or the need to choose between four devastatingly hot men who would burn down the world if it made me happy... as long as they don't need to share me, apparently.

Killian squeezes my hand. "Every bit helps. We'll keep fighting the good fight."

I squeeze back, my once-jaded heart now brimming with hope. "With you, I believe we can."

As the sun sets, I think we might be done with our date, and I would have left happy with the time we spent together. Honestly, I'm going to remember today for the rest of my life.

And I know it's because of Killian, and the way he made me feel while he introduced me to some of his favorite activities.

Whether I choose him or not, there are definitely going to be more animal shelter snuggles and turtle releases in my life.

But we're far from done, as it turns out.

Next stop, he announces, is one of his favorite restaurants of all time.

The scent of simmering spices wafts through the cozy restaurant as we're led to an intimate table. Local artwork adorns the walls, and the warm lighting makes me feel at home.

A lanky teenager greets us, barely suppressing his grin. "Hey there, folks! I'm D! I'll be your server as well as cooking some of the items, and we've got a really awesome menu for you tonight."

Killian smiles. "I think we'll let you decide, Chef D. Surprise us."

The teen's eyes widen before he rushes back to the kitchen. Killian chuckles. "This place takes kids from rough neighborhoods and trains them to be chefs. Gives them skills and confidence."

"That's amazing," I say. My respect for him deepens.

D returns, balancing two steaming plates. "Ok, we've got a chickpea curry and some naan bread. I made the curry sauce from scratch, loosely based on my grandmother's recipe. Let me know if you need anything!"

We dig in. The flavors explode in my mouth, complex yet comforting.

D hovers anxiously until we both give him a thumbs up. He almost bursts with pride as I ask for a to-go container for an extra helping to share with our roommates.

Between bites, Killian talks more about the restaurant's impact. At-risk youth finding meaning through food. My heart swells.

"You were right. This place is perfect," I tell him. "It's inspiring. Makes me want to do more."

Killian's eyes shine. "That's exactly why I wanted to bring you here. To show you the good we can do together."

Under the candlelight, I find myself leaning closer. The food, the company, the purpose—everything feels right.

After dinner, Killian leads me down the beach to a secluded cove. The sun has long since set, leaving behind hues of purple and orange. He spreads a blanket on the sand and lights a few candles.

"I wanted to end tonight somewhere peaceful, just the two of us," he says, his voice low.

My heart flutters as I join him on the blanket. The sound of waves crashing fills the comfortable silence between us. I meet his gaze, darker now in the candlelight.

Slowly, he reaches out and brushes his fingers against my cheek. I shiver at his touch.

"Dylan," he whispers. "You are so beautiful."

I feel my cheeks flush. No one has ever looked at me quite the way Killian does now, with a mix of desire and tenderness.

He leans in, his eyes flickering to my lips in a silent question.

I answer by closing the distance between us.

The kiss is soft at first, almost reverent. I run my hands through his hair as he pulls me against him.

We melt into each other under the starry sky, the rest of the world fading away.

When we finally break for air, he rests his forehead against mine.

"I want to make you feel good, Dylan," he murmurs. "But only if you want me to."

My heart pounds. I know this is uncharted territory for us, but in this moment, I trust Killian completely.

"Yes," I whisper. "I want that."

He smiles and kisses me again, deeper this time. His hands roam my body, leaving heat in their wake.

I arch into his touch, craving more.

Killian's hands are reverent as he undresses me, his eyes never leaving mine.

I feel bare, but not exposed. Cherished.

He lays me back against the blanket, kissing every inch of newly revealed skin. My breath catches when he reaches the inside of my thigh.

"You're exquisite," he murmurs against me.

I'm already slick with want for him.

His mouth descends, and I cry out, tangling my hands in his hair. No one has ever made me feel quite like this—so cared for, so seen. This man is passionate about everything he does, and the way he's worshipping me right now is no exception.

Killian's hands glide over my bare skin, leaving a trail of goose-bumps in their wake.

The white sand is soft under my cheek as the waves lap at the shore, a soothing rhythm to match Killian's kneading fingers.

My muscles melt under his skillful touch. He finds each knot and works it out until I'm putty in his hands.

When his fingers trace the edge of my pussy, heat blossoms low in my belly. My breath catches as he slides his hand further around, grazing the curve of my ass.

"Relax," he murmurs. His breath ghosts over my neck, sending a shiver down my spine.

I swallow hard, forcing my body to loosen under his ministrations. It's impossible to stay tense as his hands map every inch of my skin.

When his fingers dip between my legs, I gasp. My eyes fly open to take in the glittering stars overhead. The roar of the waves can't drown out the rush of pleasure spiraling through me.

My hips rock into his touch as a moan slips free. He chuckles, the sound rumbling through his chest against my back.

"That's it, baby. Let go."

His fingers work magic, pushing me higher and higher. The coil of heat in my core winds tighter and tighter until it snaps.

Pleasure washes over me in waves to rival the ocean, stealing my breath and thoughts alike.

I sag into the sand, boneless and sated.

Killian peppers kisses over my shoulder, his hands resuming their lazy exploration of my body.

The massage may be over, but the night is still young.

I tilt my head back to catch Killian's gaze, heat simmering in his emerald eyes.

"Your turn," I purr, rolling onto my side to face him fully. My hands skim down his chest, relishing the way his muscles jump under my touch.

A chuckle rumbles in his chest as I pull on the drawstring of his shorts. "Eager, are we?"

I quirk a brow, slipping my hand into his shorts to wrap around his length.

His breath hitches, his blue eyes darkening another shade. "You have no idea."

He surges forward, capturing my lips in a searing kiss that steals my breath.

I meet him stroke for stroke, my free hand tangling in his hair to hold him close.

By the time we break apart, we're both panting. I give him a light squeeze, grinning at the groan that slips out. "Less talking, more action."

Killian growls, shucking his shorts and flipping us over in one smooth motion. I find myself on my back in the sand, caged under the hard lines of his body.

"Careful what you wish for," he rasps, sliding into me in one deep thrust.

Pleasure ricochets through me, tearing a moan from my lips. My nails bite into his shoulders as I rock my hips up to meet his.

He sets a hard, fast pace, his hips pistoning against mine.

I wrap my legs around his waist, pulling him deeper with each thrust.

The coil of heat in my core winds tighter and tighter, ready to snap at any moment.

Killian shifts, hitting that sweet spot inside me.

Stars burst behind my eyes as I tumble over the edge with a cry. My inner walls clamp down on him, sending him over with me.

We cling to each other as the aftershocks fade, hearts pounding in tandem. A lazy smile curves my lips as I run my fingers through his hair.

I stretch out on the blanket, humming in content as the waves crash softly on the shore, a cool evening breeze rustling the trees behind us.

Killian pulls me into his arms, peppering kisses over my shoulders.

"Round two?" he murmurs, one hand sliding down to cup my ass.

Heat pools low in my belly at the promise in his voice.

I wiggle back against him with a grin. "What did you have in mind?"

His grip tightens, and I find myself flipped onto my hands and knees. Anticipation thrums through me as his hand wraps around my throat, tilting my head to the side.

"I want to watch you come undone again," he rasps, nudging my entrance.

I gasp as he slides in, inch by inch, until he's seated to the hilt.

Killian sets a punishing pace, his hips slamming into me from behind. His fingers tighten around my throat with each thrust, cutting off my air and intensifying the pleasure.

I rock back to meet him, chasing that sweet spot within.

Stars burst behind my eyes as he hits it. The coil of heat in my core snaps, sending me tumbling into bliss. I clench down on him, dragging Killian over with me.

He collapses on top of me from behind, both of us panting.

I wiggle beneath him, grinning at his groan.

"Best...night...ever," I manage between breaths.

Killian huffs a laugh, pressing a kiss to the back of my neck. "It's only just begun, love."

And with that promise, round three begins as he flips me over and slides back into me, instantly ready to go. I've never experienced anything like it.

After, we lie tangled together under the stars, the sounds of the crashing waves a soothing lullaby. I rest my head on Killian's chest, listening to the steady thump of his heart.

His fingers trail up and down my spine, raising goosebumps in their wake. "You're very beautiful, you know that?"

Heat floods my cheeks at the compliment. "You're not so bad yourself," I quip.

Killian chuckles, the sound rumbling through me. "I'm being serious. You're strong, smart, kind—you light up the room just by walking in. I don't know how I got so lucky."

Tears prick at my eyes at his words. My throat tightens—no one's ever said such kind things to me before. "You really think that?"

He tilts my chin up, gazing into my eyes. The adoration and honesty in his has my breath catching. "With all my heart. You're amazing, Dylan. Never doubt that."

I surge up to capture his lips in a deep kiss, trying to convey all the emotions swirling through me. He returns it with equal fervor, his hands tangling in my hair to hold me close.

We break apart, resting our foreheads together.

I take a deep breath, steeling my nerves. "I think I'm falling for you," I whisper.

The smile that spreads across Killian's face is breathtaking. "That's perfect, because I'm already in love with you."

My heart swells to bursting at his confession. Joy and wonder and love fill me until I'm glowing from the inside out.

I brush another kiss across his lips. "Best night ever," I repeat.

This time, though, I don't just mean the sex.

"You mean that, love?" he asks, pressing a kiss to my temple.

"Yes, it was incredible," I breathe. "I feel...free. Like I can fully be myself with you."

He smiles, pleased. "That's all I want. For you to feel safe and appreciated."

After basking in the afterglow for a few more moments, we slowly gather our belongings and pack up our little sanctuary on the beach. I'm almost reluctant to leave this private oasis we've created.

As we fold the blankets, Killian turns to me with a soft smile. "I'm glad we could share this day together. There's so much more I want to show you, so much more we can do."

His words warm me. "I'd really like that," I reply. "Today opened my eyes in more ways than one."

He takes my hand as we walk back to the car, a comforting, steadying presence.

I reflect on everything we did today—volunteering at the animal shelter, cleaning the beach, releasing the sea turtles. Taking me to a little-known restaurant with exquisite food that lifts up young people and gives them a chance to thrive.

It was more meaningful than I could have imagined.

And of course, there was the intimacy we shared. The care and trust behind it.

I glance at Killian as he drives, his handsome profile bathed in moonlight. There's so much depth to him that I'm only just discovering.

Back at our place, we linger in a close embrace. "Let's keep making a difference, together," I murmur.

He smiles and kisses me tenderly.

My heart feels full.

Tonight, with Killian, I literally saw stars, both in the sky and in the heights of passion we reached. But it's clear I have much more to learn about this intriguing man.

The thought fills me with anticipation for what comes next.

It's going to be hard for any of the guys to top this night.

I can't wait to see what Jayden has up his sleeve.

CHAPTER 42

Dylan

The intoxicating and unmistakable scent of aging paper fills my nose as I trail my fingers along the spines of books, their leather bindings smooth beneath my touch.

Jayden's voice floats back to me as he regales some tale of a prolific romance author, his enthusiasm evident.

I can't help but smile, enjoying this glimpse into his interests.

"And here we are," he announces, sweeping his arm towards a cozy nook tucked away in the back. "The romance section. Take your pick of any that catch your eye."

Feeling like a kid in a candy store, I excitedly scour the shelves. There's so much to choose from, each book holding an entire universe of plot and characters... entire worlds between the pages.

While I'm looking, Jayden excuses himself and comes back armed with two coffees.

"You spoil me!" I say as he hands me one, and I inhale the heady scent of roasted beans before taking a long, satisfying sip.

"Don't let me distract you," he says, gesturing back at the books with his muscular, tattooed arm.

My god. Between the vast collection of books—the sight, the smell, the possibilities, this delicious cup of coffee, and this delicious tattooed rugby player who is spoiling me, I'm just about melting on the floor.

I pick out a couple of books I've been hearing good things about, as well as a few from authors I've never heard of before. I let the covers and the blurbs on the back guide me. The common theme is strong female characters, and men who would burn the world down for them just because they asked them to. A bit of spice and a happily ever after never go astray, either.

Jayden looks on with amusement, seeming to enjoy my facial expressions when I flick through a book and find the odd bit of smut.

I scan the titles, my gaze landing on one that makes me smirk. "How about this one?" I say, plucking out a book featuring a scantily clad woman gripped in the arms of multiple men. "Mafia Menage," the title reads.

Jayden raises an eyebrow, a grin playing on his lips. "Well now, looks like someone's ready to dive into the deep end. Should I be worried...or intrigued?"

I let out a laugh. "Maybe a bit of both. I suppose it depends on how well you handle a little competition." I flash him a coy look, enjoying our flirtatious banter.

He steps closer, his voice lowered to a husky whisper. "Competition gets my blood pumping. But when it comes to you..." His fingers brush my wrist, sending a shiver through me. "I don't like to share you with mafia men."

My breath hitches, heat rising to my cheeks. Oh, the promises in those words. I have a feeling things are about to get very interesting between us. And I can't wait to see where this adventure leads.

I'm drawn from my thoughts as Jayden gently takes the book from my hands, sliding it back onto the shelf.

"I think that's enough adventure for now," he says with a playful grin. "Wouldn't want to get too carried away before dinner. Speaking of which... let's pay up and get out of here."

Jayden leads me to the front of the store, where the bookseller looks surprised and pleased by the tower of books we place on the counter. He wraps them with care, pointing a couple out as new favorites.

Jayden discreetly produces a credit card, and the bookseller hands me two large bags. My TBR just got a whole lot longer, and I can't wait to work my way through it.

"To our next destination?" Jayden asks after thanking the bookseller.

"Lead the way!" I say, excited about what the rest of the night will bring.

Hey, even if it totally sucks, which I doubt it will, my reading is sorted for the next few weeks at least.

Jayden takes one of the bags and offers his other arm to me.

I loop mine through it, letting him lead me out of the cozy bookstore and onto the streets. The sun is just starting to set, casting a warm orange glow over the city.

We walk a few blocks before arriving at an art museum. It's quite famous, and on my list of things I've been meaning to do since arriving in the city.

Jayden guides me through the grand arched doorway.

Inside, the space has been transformed into something straight out of a romance novel. Soft lighting and candles create a warm, intimate ambience. A small table for two sits nestled between stunning works of modern art. The soaring ceilings and open floor plan make it feel lavish yet cozy.

"Jayden, this is incredible," I breathe, taking it all in. "Did you really have this arranged especially for us?"

"Only the best for you," he says, pulling out my chair.

I sit, marveling at the perfectly set table. Crystal glasses, fresh flowers, fine china—he clearly went all out.

As we eat, Jayden tells me about the ingredients, many of which have been picked for their symbolic meanings in romance. "A love story on a plate," he says with a smile. The food is delicious, but his company is even more so.

We talk for hours, the conversation flowing easily.

After dessert, he retrieves a guitar and serenades me with a song he wrote just for me. His voice is like honey as he sings of adventure, new beginnings and a heart finally feeling whole. I didn't even know he could play a musical instrument. Like Killian, too, this man is full of surprises and unexpected depth.

My own heart swells listening to his beautiful words. When the song ends, I take his hand, our eyes meeting. "Jayden...you make me feel seen. And valued. I've never had this before, where someone's seen me for more than my rugby skills or my appearance. It's obvious that you value my intellect as much as anything else. It's... it's just really nice." Tears threaten to spring forth, but I manage to blink them back.

He squeezes my hand gently. "You make me feel the same way, Dylan."

In this moment, with Jayden, I know I've found someone special. Someone who truly understands this lesser-known part of me. I can't stop smiling, to the point my jaw is starting to hurt.

After dinner, Jayden leads me to a more secluded part of the museum exhibit. Candles flicker softly around an ornate rug laid out under the installation's dazzling centerpiece.

"Shall we create our own work of art?" he asks playfully, pulling me close.

I grin, matching his flirtatious tone. "I'm ready to be your masterpiece."

He kisses me deeply as we sink down onto the luxurious rug. My skin tingles everywhere his hands explore. Each caress is deliberate, honoring my every curve and contour.

We undress each other slowly, the modern art surrounding us adding to the sensuality.

As the passion builds, Jayden pauses, meeting my eyes. "Tell me what you want, Dylan. I'm here for your pleasure tonight."

His words make me feel respected, valued. Seen as more than just a body.

"Touch me like this," I whisper, guiding his hand. I lose myself in the ecstasy of his intimate care, my mind blurring into a haze of lust.

Jayden retrieves a rope from beneath the rug and binds my wrists above my head, securing them to the cold metal pillar with rough rope.

"Keep your eyes open," he growls into my ear before trailing hot, wet kisses down my neck.

My breath hitches as his lips graze the swell of my breasts. I force my gaze forward, taking in the erotic art display in front of me. Nude bodies intertwine, a tangle of limbs and lust.

Jayden kneels before me, running his hands up my thighs. "So beautiful. All of you."

He places a kiss on my hip, another lower on my abdomen. I squirm against my restraints, aching for more. Needing his touch.

Finally, his mouth is on me. Worshipping. Devouring.

I cry out, struggling to keep my eyes on the art. To obey.

It's exquisite torture. The rasp of his tongue and beard on my sensitive flesh. The coil of desire winding tighter and tighter within me.

Through half-lidded eyes, I watch the lovers on the canvas, imagining us in their place. Jayden's strong body pressed to mine, joined as one.

A moan escapes my lips. I'm so close.

He slides two fingers inside me, crooking them in a beckoning motion.

My orgasm crashes over me in waves, intense and all-consuming. I throw my head back, my wrists straining against the rope.

"Eyes open," Jayden growls, nipping at my thigh.

I blink, refocusing on the painting. On the lovers and their dance of flesh. Just as Jayden wants.

Always just as Jayden wants. Because he knows exactly what I need.

Jayden stands, trailing his fingers up my body as he rises and loosens the rope slightly.

I meet his gaze, my cheeks flushed and my heart pounding.

"On your knees," he commands softly.

I sink to my knees, the rope around my wrists slackening. He reties them, binding my hands behind my back.

"Open." He taps my lower lip with his thumb.

I part my lips, eyes locked on his. On the bulge straining against his jeans.

He frees himself, his thick cock springing free. Precum glistens on the tip.

"Suck."

I lean in eagerly as he comes closer, flicking my tongue over his sensitive head. Teasing. Tasting.

A growl rumbles in his chest. He fists a hand in my hair, guiding himself between my lips.

I relax my throat, taking him deeper. Choking. Gagging. Spit trailing down my chin.

The sounds grow wet and vulgar. I work him with lips and tongue, hollowing my cheeks. My throat contracting around his length.

"Fuck, just like that," Jayden groans, his hips bucking.

He's close. I can feel it. Can taste it on my eager tongue.

I redouble my efforts, moaning around his cock, the vibrations shooting straight to his balls.

With a shout, he spills down my throat. Hot and bitter and perfect.

I swallow greedily, not stopping until he pulls away.

Chest heaving, Jayden stares down at me. His pupils are wide with desire.

"Good girl," he rasps, tucking himself away.

Pride blooms in my chest at the praise. I remain on my knees, his release clinging to my lips.

Waiting. Wanting. Needing whatever comes next.

He spreads out another fur blanket and lights more candles, then unties me from the pillar and takes me by the hand, leading me to to it and getting me to lie down.

The blanket is soft against my back, the fur tickling my sensitive flesh.

Jayden straddles my hips, candle in hand. "Ready?"

I nod, pulse racing in anticipation.

He tilts the candle, hot wax spilling onto my collarbone. It stings, then cools, solidifying into a shell.

He drips more wax over my breasts and down my body, blowing to accelerate the cooling, and leaving goosebumps across my skin.

My nipples pebble as the wax creeps lower, coating my breasts in a lacework of red.

Each drop is followed by Jayden's breath, cooling the burns and leaving a trail of goosebumps in its wake.

I squirm beneath him, arousal dampening my thighs. The mix of pain and pleasure is addictive.

"More," I breathe.

Obliging, he moves lower, circling my navel with scarlet droplets before wandering south.

The insides of my thighs are slicked with wax and desire. I'm writhing uncontrollably now, chasing release.

Mercifully, Jayden sets the candle aside, his eyes dark with lust as he surveys his handiwork. I'm drizzled with hardened wax from collar to knee, every inch sensitized and wanting.

"Please," I sob, too far gone for pride.

A wicked grin. "Please what?"

"I need to come."

"Not yet." .

Jayden kneels between my legs, his grip bruising my hips, holding me in place.

His mouth descends. Hot and wet and perfect.

I cry out at the first swipe of his tongue through my lips. The wax amplifies each sensation tenfold.

He works me slowly, methodically. His tongue flicks against my clit before spearing into my entrance, fucking me with his mouth.

The coil in my belly winds tighter and tighter. I'm writhing against his grip, my incoherent pleas falling from kiss-swollen lips.

Sucking hard on my clit, Jayden slips two fingers into my cunt, crooking them just so.

Stars explode behind my eyes as I come apart. I shout his name at the top of my lungs, my every muscle locked in ecstasy.

He works me through the aftershocks, only relenting when I go limp, breathless and sated.

"My good girl," Jayden murmurs again, his gorgeous lips brushing my thigh.

I can only hum in response, floating in a sea of endorphins.

But we're not done yet. He uses one of the large cushions to prop up my hips and fucks me hard, and I enjoy watching his cock sliding in and out of my pussy as he plows me.

I'm boneless as a rag doll as Jayden manhandles me onto my hands and knees.

The blunt head of his cock teases my entrance, even more wet and ready for him than before.

I rock back, trying to take him in, but he pulls away with a dark chuckle.

"So impatient." A sharp smack on my ass that makes me gasp. "Ask nicely."

I swallow my pride again and beg. "Please, Jayden. I need your cock. I need you to fill me up and fuck me again."

He growls, gripping my hips to hold me in place as he sinks into me. Slow and deep until I can feel the weight of his balls against my clit.

I moan, my eyes rolling back in my head at the delicious stretch and burn. I can still feel where the ropes cut into my wrists, and it only heightens the experience.

"Look at me," Jayden commands, stilling inside me. Waiting.

I meet his gaze over one shoulder, my pupils blown wide with lust and possession. A gold-framed mirror to the side of us lets me see even more.

"I want you to watch," he says, withdrawing until just the tip remains inside. "Watch as I fuck you. As I claim what's mine."

He slams back in, setting a brutal pace. Skin slapping against skin as he pistons into me. Hard and fast and everything I need.

I can't look away from the reflection in the mirror. Transfixed by the sight of his cock disappearing inside me again and again. By the ecstasy etched into the lines of his face.

The coil in my belly winds tighter and tighter. Building towards another shattering climax.

"Come for me," Jayden growls. "Now."

My vision whites out as I tumble over the edge, my cunt spasming around his cock, milking his own release.

We collapse in a tangle of sated limbs. His weight is a welcome anchor, pinning me in place. I've never felt so owned. So cherished.

Jayden kisses the nape of my neck, lips curving into a smile against my skin.

"Mine," he whispers.

"Yours," I agree, and mean it with all my heart.

His girl.

Afterwards, Jayden wraps me in a blanket, holding me close as we catch our breath.

"You're incredible, Dylan. Tonight was about more than the physical for me. It was about truly connecting with you."

I snuggle into his strong chest. "I've never felt more connected to someone in quite this way, either. Thank you for this perfect night."

Under the shimmering installation, I feel profoundly close to Jayden—in body, mind and spirit.

As we lay together, the flickering candlelight casts dancing shadows across our skin. Jayden's fingers trace delicate patterns down my arm, raising goosebumps.

"I know it's only been a short time, but I feel like I've known you forever," he says softly. "Like our souls recognize each other."

His words resonate deeply within me. "I was just thinking the same thing. With you, I feel at home."

We share a tender kiss, a promise of more to come. As the night winds down, it's clear that neither of us wants it to end.

Reluctantly, we gather our clothes and make our way outside, hand-in-hand. The cool night air is refreshing against our warm skin.

My heart is full as we walk to the car. This evening was unexpected in the best possible way.

With Jayden, it's not just about feeling desired. It's about feeling truly seen, valued, understood. As if he's attracted to my mind just as much as my body, perhaps even more.

I can't stop smiling, possibilities dancing in my mind. This could be the beginning of something life-changing.

"Thank you for tonight," I say, squeezing Jayden's hand. "It was perfect. You showed me a part of myself I've never shared before."

He smiles back. "The magic has only just begun."

CHAPTER 43

Dylan

I spend half an hour perfecting my makeup and choosing an outfit that's casual yet elegant: fitted black jeans, sky-high heels, and a silky top that shows a hint of cleavage.

When I check my phone for the address Noah texted and pull it up on my phone's map, my heart skips a beat. A professional kitchen? What is he planning now?

I arrive at the industrial space, inhaling the aroma of spices and garlic.

Noah turns from a counter laden with vegetables and grins at me, holding up two chef's aprons. "I bet you were expecting roses and champagne from me. But surprise! We're making dinner tonight."

"Cooking, huh?" I laugh, warmth flooding my cheeks. I'm actually shocked by this turn of events. Noah comes across as the more predictable one of the group, and I definitely pictured him arranging some more conventional champagne and roses kind of date. "You're surprisingly full of surprises."

"And you're overdressed," he says, his eyes dancing over my outfit. "Absolutely stunning, but overdressed nonetheless."

I shrug out of my jacket, acutely aware of his gaze following my every move. "But we can fix that very soon."

He knots an apron around my waist, his fingers brushing against my hips.

I suck in a breath, heat pooling low in my belly.

When his hands linger, I look up to find his eyes dark with desire.

"Are we really here to cook?" I ask softly.

"We'll get to the food eventually." Noah pulls me close, one hand tangling in my hair. "But first, I owe you an apology for how I acted about this whole dating thing. I didn't mean to upset you, or to make you feel pressured." He runs a hand down my arm, causing goosebumps to appear.

I go still, stunned by his admission. An apology is the last thing I expected. "It's okay," I say automatically. "We're all trying to figure this out. It's... complicated. I never expected to feel this way either."

"It's not okay." Noah cups my face, forcing me to meet his gaze. "You're the most amazing person I've ever met. And I don't want you to feel like I'm forcing you into something you don't want. I'd never wish that upon you. Because I know how that feels, and you deserve better."

My throat tightens at the earnestness in his voice. After years of struggling to fit in, to be accepted, his words mean everything. "Thank you," I whisper.

Noah's eyes soften. "You're welcome. That all said, I'm stoked to spend some one-on-one time with you tonight. Now, are you ready to cook something unforgettable with me?"

I smile, warmth flooding my cheeks for an entirely different reason. "Absolutely."

Maybe tonight will hold more surprises than I ever imagined. And maybe, just maybe, Noah and I are cooking up something far more lasting than dinner.

Noah pulls out ingredients for larb and sticky rice, launching into an explanation of Laotian cuisine as we get to work. He tells fascinating stories about his visit to the country, including a crazy tale where he tubed down a river lined with bars where you could pull up in your tube to grab another beer, and then continue on.

His passion for cooking rivals his intensity on the pitch, and I find myself caught up in his enthusiasm.

We chop and stir, trading playful banter and laughs along the way.

When Noah challenges me to a chopping contest, competitiveness flares. "Think you've got the skills to beat me?" he asks with a cocky grin.

I grab a knife, determination burning in my veins. After years of striving to prove myself, I never back down from a challenge. "I grew up watching *Yan Can Cook* and ads for Ginsu knives on TV. Chopping is my jam. You're about to be schooled, pretty boy."

We race to chop vegetables, Noah nudging me with his hip and bumping up the tempo of Laotian pop music blasting from his phone.

In the end, I win by a hair, both of us breathless with laughter.

"I demand a rematch," Noah says, catching my hand as I reach for more cabbage. His touch ignites sparks, and I still, my pulse racing for an entirely different reason.

"Next time, I'll destroy you," I say, hoping my voice sounds steady.

Noah steps closer, heat shimmering in his eyes. "Is that a promise?" His other hand comes to rest on my hip, his touch searing even through my clothes.

I swallow hard, caught between the urge to close the distance between us and flee before I do something I regret. "If you think you can handle losing again," I challenge weakly.

Noah grins. "Losing has its benefits." And then his mouth descends on mine in a kiss that steals my breath away.

My hands come up to grip his shoulders as Noah deepens the kiss, hunger and heat rolling off him in waves.

I respond in kind, pent-up desire crashing over me in a tidal wave of sensation.

We break apart, our chests heaving.

Noah rests his forehead on mine, eyes dark with want. "To be continued?" he asks in a rough whisper.

I nod, heart pounding. "Definitely."

After all, we have a date with some larb and sticky rice.

We pull apart reluctantly, the tension between us simmering.

Clearing my throat, I bend to scoop up bits of cabbage and meat and sticky rice.

Noah does the same, though his gaze keeps straying to me, heat flickering in his eyes.

My cheeks flush under his gaze as we enjoy our meal. The flavors are intense, potent, and in a way they remind me a lot of Noah. But they're also exotic, sexy and dangerous... a side to Noah that he seems to keep hidden but is clearly very much part of him.

Finally, Noah speaks, his voice casual though his words are anything but. "So, you think you can handle me in the bedroom as well as you do on the pitch?"

I nearly drop the bowl I'm holding. "Is that a challenge?" I ask, aiming for nonchalance and missing by a mile.

Noah's grin is slow and predatory. "If you think you can keep up."

My breath catches at the images those words conjure. I set the bowl down before I really do drop it. "Don't make promises you can't keep."

Noah steps closer, and I back into the counter, heart pounding. He braces his hands on either side of me, leaning in until his breath feathers over my lips. "I never make promises I can't deliver on."

The simmering tension ignites into an inferno. I surge forward, claiming Noah's mouth in another searing kiss. Noah groans, pulling me flush against him, and desire pools low in my belly.

His massive hand moves to my throat, wrapping around me and gently squeezing as our mouths mash together.

I feel drunk on his power as he holds my mouth to his, claiming me. We break apart, our chests heaving.

"Fuck me. Now," I demand, surprised at my own boldness.

Noah's eyes darken. "Your wish is my command."

He takes my hand and leads me out of the kitchen and toward a room off to the side, desire burning in his every step.

The promise of what's to come sets my blood aflame, and I quicken my pace to match his.

He's set up a little romantic space for us, complete with blankets and cushions, a little laptop set up so we can watch a movie after our meal. Although to be honest, watching a movie is the last thing on my mind right now.

Tonight, Noah is going to learn I always deliver on my promises, too.

Noah closes the door behind us with a soft click.

I turn to face him, my heart pounding in anticipation.

Noah stalks toward me, stripping off his shirt as he goes.

I swallow hard at the sight of his muscular, tattooed chest, my pussy clenching hard as desire continues to pool low in my belly.

"On the blankets," he orders, his voice rough with need.

I scramble to comply, situating myself in the center of the air mattress.

Noah joins me, caging me in with his enormous body. His hands slide under my shirt, his calloused fingers skimming up my sides.

I arch into his touch with a gasp.

"So responsive," Noah murmurs. He slides my shirt over my head, discarding it on the floor.

I reach for his waistband, fumbling with the drawstring in my haste.

Noah swats my hands away. "Patience." He unclasps my bra, baring my breasts to his heated gaze.

I squirm under the intensity of it, desperate for his touch.

"Please," I whimper.

Noah grins, slow and predatory, tracing a finger down between my breasts. "Not yet." He slides down my body, trailing kisses along my stomach as he goes.

My back arches off the mattress when he reaches the waist of my pants.

Noah pops the button open and drags the zipper down with agonizing slowness. He hooks his fingers under the waistband of my pants and lacy black underwear, dragging them down and off in one smooth motion.

"So beautiful," he murmurs, running a hand up my inner thigh.

I spread my legs wider, trembling in anticipation. "And all mine."

Noah dips his head, and pleasure explodes through me at the first touch of his mouth.

I cry out, fisting my hands in his hair to keep him right where he is.

Tonight is going to be unforgettable.

Still in the afterglow of my orgasm, Noah suddenly pulls me to my feet. He slams me against the nearby wall, his fist twisting in my hair as his mouth finds my neck.

A sharp sting and sucking heat blossom over my pulse and I gasp. My thighs clench around his waist as he hauls me up, pinning me in place.

"You're mine now, kitten," he growls against my skin.

Every inch of me tingles, igniting like wildfire under his hands and voice.

After weeks of circling each other, months of tension and longing looks across the pitch, he's finally fully claimed me.

And I'm more than ready to be taken.

I arch into him, nails biting into his shoulders. "Prove it."

A low chuckle rumbles through his chest. "With pleasure."

His mouth crashes over mine, devouring and demanding.

I meet him stroke for stroke, pouring months of pent-up passion into the kiss.

By the time he releases me, we're both breathless.

Noah's eyes gleam, pupils blown wide with lust and possession. "You asked for this."

Before I can reply, he lifts me higher, guiding me onto him inch by inch. A strangled moan escapes me as I'm filled so exquisitely full by his magnificent pierced cock.

"Ride me," he orders, his grip tightening on my hips. "Show me how much you want this. How much you want me."

I do as commanded, rolling my hips in a slow grind. Sparks flash behind my eyelids and a cry spills from my lips. He's right where I've always wanted him—deep inside me, surrounding me, claiming me as thoroughly as any man can claim a woman.

And I'm never letting go.

I set a punishing pace, using my back as leverage against the wall to lift myself almost all the way off his cock and slam back down.

Noah meets each thrust with a snap of his hips, driving me higher and higher.

The chill from the concrete seeps into my overheated skin, but I hardly notice. All I can feel is Noah—his hands, his mouth, his cock possessing me so completely I'll never be the same.

"That's it," he rasps. "Take it. Take all of me."

I clench around him and he growls, surging forward to capture one nipple between his teeth. Sharp sensation spears through me and I shatter, coming apart around him.

Noah fucks me through the aftershocks, relentless as the tides.

I'm limp as a rag doll in his arms, held aloft by the strength of his grip alone.

"I'm not done with you yet," he warns, and spins us around.

The floor rushes up to meet me, barely breaking my fall before Noah is there, forcing my legs apart. His mouth descends, hot and hungry, tracing the path his cock just took.

I whimper, my over-sensitized flesh protesting even as my need builds again. "Please," I beg, not even sure what I'm asking for. More, less, everything he'll give me.

"Patience," he says, and spreads my cheeks, baring me completely.

The first swipe of his tongue over that tightly furled ring of muscle shreds the last of my restraint.

I keen, bucking back into the delirious mix of pleasure and discomfort.

Noah holds me in place, alternately sucking and spearing his tongue into that most intimate place.

I fist helplessly at the floor, sobbing with need.

Just when I think I can't take any more, he rises over me, nudging my entrance with the thick head of his cock.

"Ready for more?"

I nod frantically, beyond words. Noah sheaths himself to the hilt with one smooth stroke.

"That's my girl."

He takes me then, hard and deep, wringing every ounce of pleasure from my willing body.

I come again and again, awash in sensation, belonging, love.

By the time Noah follows me over the edge with a shout, I have no doubt.

I'm his. And he's mine.

I'm limp as a rag doll when Noah lifts me, arranging us so I'm draped across his lap.

His fingers trace idle patterns over my back and butt, a soothing counterpoint to the lingering ache between my legs.

"You were amazing," he murmurs, dropping a kiss on my shoulder. "So responsive, so passionate. You make me crazy, you know that?"

Heat stains my cheeks at the praise even as warmth blossoms in my chest. I never dreamed I could be this for someone, a source of desire and delight.

"You're one to talk," I retort, craning my neck to meet his gaze. Mischief glints in his eyes, softening the intensity of his regard. "The way you were looking at me...the things you did..." I shudder at the memory, desire stirring again.

Noah's hand stills on my lower back, his eyes darkening. "Is that so? And what exactly did I do?" His voice drops into the smoky register that never fails to make me squirm.

I lick my lips, watching his gaze track the movement. "You—you held me down and took your pleasure." The words emerge breathy and wanting, an invitation I hope he won't refuse.

"Did I?" Noah's hand resumes its path, drifting lower to cup one cheek, squeezing lightly. "And did you like it, me using your body for my pleasure?"

"Yes." It's barely more than a whimper. I'm melting under his touch, needing more. Needing him. Again.

"Mmm, good." His fingers slide between my legs, finding me wet and wanting. "Because I fully intend to do it again."

I gasp as Noah's fingers plunge deep, my hips jerking towards his hand of their own accord.

"You like that, don't you?" His voice is a rough growl against my ear. "You love me filling your greedy little cunt."

"Yes, yes, please," I babble, beyond caring about how thirsty I sound. All that matters is his hands on me, in me, his cock pounding me into oblivion.

Noah chuckles, the sound dark and delighted. "So impatient." He withdraws his fingers and I whine at the loss, trying to chase them.

A sharp smack on my ass stills my movements. "Ah ah, be good now, kitten. I'll give you what you need."

I force myself to remain still, watching through hooded eyes as Noah settles between my legs. He grips my hips, dragging me onto his cock in one rough thrust.

A cry tears from my throat at the sensation of being so filled, so perfectly, utterly possessed. Noah gives me no time to adjust, setting a brutal pace as he slams into me again and again.

It's everything I crave, his hands and cock claiming me as his own. I come with a sob, pulsing around him, and Noah follows soon after with a groan.

He collapses beside me, pulling me into his arms.

I nestle against his chest, basking in the warmth and scent of him, a deep contentment settling into my bones.

Noah presses a soft kiss to the top of my head. "Thank you for today. For...for everything." His voice is rough with emotion, and I glance up to see a wealth of tenderness in his eyes.

My heart swells, overflowing with affection for this man who sees me, all of me, and loves me still. "I love you," I whisper, meaning it with all that I am.

Noah's arms tighten around me, his smile like the sun breaking through the clouds. "I love you too, Dylan. So damn much."

After what seems like forever, Noah finally allows my release, intensifying our connection. He pulls me close and whispers in my ear. "Imagine what phenomenal little rugby players we would make."

I smile, not quite sure what he means. But little rugby players sound cute.

"I told you tonight would be unforgettable," he says, brushing the hair back from my face. I can only laugh, still catching my breath.

"You were right." I tug him down for a kiss, tasting myself on his lips. "And what was that about little rugby players?"

"Just thinking ahead." Noah's eyes gleam with mischief. "We'd have some powerhouse kids, don't you think?"

I smack his shoulder, unable to contain my smile. "Let's work on the first part before we get to babymaking, huh?"

Noah ducks his head, chuckling. "Point taken." His gaze softens as he looks at me. "Are you okay?"

"More than." I run my hands over his chest, marveling at the play of muscle under warm skin. "That was incredible, Noah. I didn't know this side of you."

"What can I say, you bring it out in me." Noah kisses me slow and deep, erasing any remaining doubts I might have had.

Tonight has changed everything. With Noah, I might just get the future I never dared to dream of.

He holds me close, his touch tender, as if he wants to make me feel both cared for and safe. "Are you okay? I've got you."

"More than okay," I say as I nestle closer to his massive body.

As I drift off to sleep in Noah's protective arms, a mix of exhilaration and deep affection washes over me. Tonight has changed my perception of him, revealing depths I had only glimpsed before.

Who knew a night of cooking could lead to such fireworks? He might just be the surprise I didn't know I needed.

With him, I feel like a true equal on the rugby field and off. Like I can be all of myself, multidimensional. The driven athlete, the woman who craves intimacy, the woman who sloths around the house in sweatpants but who can also rock a pair of ridiculously high heels—and all without judgement.

Noah knows me, really knows me, imperfections and all. And he likes me a lot for who I am. Maybe even more.

I curl into his warmth, a smile playing on my lips. The future is ours to explore, filled with passion and partnership and play.

Together, we could be unstoppable.

I can't wait to see what's in store for us next.

But first, there's a date with Kai calling my name.

CHAPTER 44

Kai

I walk up to the apartment, eager to hang with the guys while Dylan is out on her date with Noah.

As soon as I walk in, Jayden snaps his head towards me. "There he is! The man with the master plan for his upcoming date with our girl." Jayden grins and fist bumps me in greeting.

Killian gives me a nod from where he lays sprawled out on the couch. "We figured you'd want to strategize about how to sweep Dylan off her feet after Noah kept her out way past curfew last night. They're still out. Would you believe it?"

I scoff as I plop down in the overstuffed recliner. "That wasn't part of the rules we all agreed on... it's meant to be an evening date only, right?"

Jayden nods. "Of course he would force her to choose between us and then make his own rules. Typical Noah bullshit. It's like he thinks he's better than the rest of us."

"Yeah, he's always been a sneaky one when it comes to getting his way." I shake my head.

Killian sits up, rubbing his chin thoughtfully. "But who knows... maybe this extra time with Dylan will make Noah realize that sharing her is better than losing her for good."

"I hope so, because I'm not ready to give her up yet, not when things are just getting interesting between all of us." I crack my knuckles, gearing up mentally for planning the perfect date. "So, what do you guys think I should do to sweep Dylan off her feet tomorrow night?"

Jayden launches into an elaborate plan involving a hot-air balloon ride, while Killian advocates for a more relaxed picnic in the park approach. I listen to their suggestions with amusement, already having crafted a night that Dylan will never forget. Noah may have gotten extra time last night and this morning, but tomorrow night is my turn to show Dylan just how much I care about her. I can't wait to surprise her and watch her melt in my arms.

I nod along as Jayden and Killian bounce ideas back and forth, only half listening as I mull over my own plans for the date.

"So, what do you think they're doing? Where do you think he took her?" Killian asks. It's a question we're all thinking about.

"Knowing Noah, he probably took her to that new fancy French place downtown," Jayden says. "All tiny portions and snobby waiters."

Killian chuckles. "Yeah, I can just imagine him trying to impress her by ordering fancy shit like escargot and foie gras, but mispronouncing all the menu items."

Their joking eases the tension that has been building while we wait for their return. I knew Killian and Jayden are both just as anxious as I am to find out what's happened between the two of them. There is still a risk that Noah has a diabolical plan to sweep her off her feet without the rest of us being a factor in his plans.

"There's definitely more to Noah than his serious, stoic exterior," I chime in. "He has a playful side too, from what I can tell... it's just... obscured by his alpha male act."

Jayden and Killian turn to me in surprise.

"No way, you've seen that side of him, too?" Jayden asks incredulously. "I thought he just saved it for us roommates."

I nod. "Yeah, I have. Occasionally, at practice, he'll let the shield down. Only ever for a moment, and then he's back to the Mr. Alphahole act. But when it comes to Dylan, it happens more often. I've seen the way he looks at her sometimes when he thinks no one's watching. There's a heat there that suggests there are some...skills he keeps hidden."

"Huh," Killian raises an eyebrow. "Maybe he does have some tricks up his sleeve."

"No matter what tricks Noah might have, I've got plenty of my own to make Dylan forget all about her date with him," I say with a grin.

Jayden and Killian laugh, the mood lightening as we speculate on the passion Noah likely unleashed on Dylan the night before. But tomorrow night she's mine, and if all goes my way, Noah will be nothing but a distant memory.

Killian claps me on the back. "That's the spirit, Kai. Bring your A-game tomorrow." He pauses, then continues. "You know, this is just so weird. But with you guys, I don't feel threatened... not because I don't think either of you has just as good of a chance of stealing her away as I would. I just... know you care about her as much as I do, and that makes me happy."

Jayden and I both nod in unspoken understanding.

I smile, envisioning the romantic surprises I have planned for Dylan. "I just hope she's not too worn out from whatever Noah did to her last night and this morning. I'd hate for my plans to fall flat if she's already satisfied."

"Doubtful," Jayden says, rolling his eyes. "Noah may have stamina, but he doesn't have a ton of creativity. I'm sure you'll blow her mind."

"I hope so." I laugh. "She deserves to be swept off her feet. And I intend to do just that."

Just then, the apartment door swings open and Dylan stumbles in, her hair mussed and lips swollen. Noah follows close behind, a strange dominant energy emanating from him.

"Well, well, look who finally decided to come home," Jayden says sarcastically.

Dylan flushes. "Sorry, we just lost track of time and..." she pauses and glances at Noah shyly, "he had some special things planned that took a little longer than expected." Her cheeks flush.

"I bet you did," Killian mutters under his breath.

Noah shoots him a glare before turning to Dylan. "I should get ready for practice. I'm going to go shower. But I'll see you soon." He pulls her in for a searing kiss before leaving abruptly.

Dylan stares after him, touching her fingers to her lips. I feel a flare of jealousy, but also anticipation of our date. I'm more determined than ever to make her forget all about Noah.

"So," I say lightly. "How was it?"

Dylan turns to me, her eyes shining. "Incredible. He's full of surprises. Not at all what I expected..."

I grin. "Well, I'm glad you like surprises. Because I've got a few of my own..."

CHAPTER 45

Dylan

The fragrant aroma of garlic, coconut milk and spices wafts down the narrow alleyway, and my stomach grumbles in anticipation.

"Ready to try some real Polynesian flavors?" Kai asks, squeezing my hand. "This is going to be just like what my mom would make, or at least close to it."

My heart flutters at the mention of his family. I'm desperate to learn more about his culture, his upbringing, all the things that made him into the fascinating man walking beside me.

We duck under a faded awning into a small, bustling restaurant.

Kai greets the woman behind the counter in a language I don't understand, but the warmth in his tone is unmistakable. She waves us over to a small table in the corner, already laden with colorful dishes.

I slide into the seat across from Kai, barely containing a gasp. The food looks like nothing I've seen before, vibrant and aromatic. My mouth waters.

Kai grins, clearly pleased with my reaction. "Go on, dig in. Try a bit of everything."

I reach for something unidentifiable but delicious smelling, realizing I have no idea what I'm about to put in my mouth. My stomach clenches nervously. What if I don't like it? I don't want Kai to think I'm uncultured. But one look at his expectant face and my anxiety fades. I trust him.

Taking a bite, an explosion of flavors dance across my tongue. "Wow," I breathe around my mouthful. "This is amazing!"

"I'm glad you like it," Kai says.

"What do I say if I love something in your language?"

"Say, 'Chur'!'" he teaches me. "It's like saying 'Oh sweet!' but with more excitement."

"Chur!" I repeat enthusiastically, the unfamiliar syllables tumbling awkwardly from my lips.

"You can also say, 'Faaaaaa!'"

"Faaaaaaaa...?"

Kai throws back his head and laughs, the sound rich and vibrant. A blush steals across my cheeks, but I can't help laughing along with him.

When his laughter fades, he fixes me with a heated look. "With the right inflection, that can also mean something else entirely."

My blush deepens as I register the desire in his gaze. The food is momentarily forgotten. I clear my throat, fighting to regain my composure. "I guess I'm learning fast, huh?"

"Faster than you know," he says softly.

A delicious shiver runs down my spine. This date is turning out to be more enlightening than I ever could have imagined.

Our food crawl continues down the street, Kai teaching me more phrases as we go. Some are humorous, others flirtatious, which we use playfully.

"Not even, ow!" he exclaims.

"Not even... ow?" I quirk a brow.

"That's the one!"

"What does it mean, though?" I ask. "Like... it doesn't hurt or something!"

"It's more like 'no way'. But...if you really want to impress," Kai says, leaning close to whisper in my ear, "say 'you're hardout skux!' It means 'You're handsome'... not that you need to use it on anyone but me tonight."

Heat blossoms across my cheeks at his proximity, his breath warm against my skin. I swallow hard, meeting his gaze. "You're... hardout skux, Kai," I say softly. "Am I saying it right?"

The smile that curves his lips is slow and sinful. "Better than I could have hoped."

We continue down the street, the banter and casual touches coming more easily. I find myself relaxing into the flow of conversation, no longer overthinking my responses. With Kai, I can just be. It's freeing and intoxicating all at once.

I steal a glance at him as he speaks animatedly about the history of his tribe, noticing the passion that lights his eyes. He's sharing parts of himself that most people never get to see. I feel impossibly lucky in this moment.

This date is turning into an education of the best possible kind. I'm learning not just about Polynesian culture, but about the complexity of the man beside me. And with every new discovery, I find myself falling deeper under his spell.

After dinner, we arrive at a sleek cocktail bar, dimly lit and filled with the murmur of conversation. Kai leads me inside, where he's instantly approached by several people, and he comfortably greets patrons and staff alike by name. There's an ease to his manner that speaks of familiarity and frequent patronage.

"Everyone knows you here. It's like you're a celebrity!"

He looks at me and laughs, and although the lighting is dim, I swear a blush passes over his cheeks.

As we settle onto bar stools, he admits, "I may have failed to mention that I co-own this place."

I stare at him, stunned. "You what?"

He grins, clearly enjoying my reaction. "Surprised?"

"You could have given a girl some warning!" I say, shaking my head even as I laugh. Trust Kai to spring something like this on me.

"Where's the fun in that?" he teases, signaling the bartender. "The usual for us, Luke."

As Luke mixes our cocktails, a couple of women sidle up to the bar on either side of Kai. They eye him appreciatively, their smiles turning predatory when they notice me. I see the way they look at him, like he's something to be conquered or possessed. It leaves a bitter taste in my mouth.

Don't they realize there's so much more to him than appearance? Beneath the charm and playboy façade is a depth of character I'm only just beginning to fathom. Kai is culture and contradiction, sensitivity and strength. He's everything they can't see.

I love the fact that his background is different from my own, but it's not why I'm with him. There are so many things I admire about him. I just get the vibe their interest in him is surface level, as if hanging on his arm in Instagram photos will make them more attractive by association.

My hands tighten around the stem of my glass, a surge of possessiveness washing over me. I want to shield this side of him from their gaze, to keep his complexity for myself alone. The depth of my emotions startles me. I'm in deeper than I realized. And if the look in Kai's eyes is any indication, he knows it, too.

The woman on Kai's right runs a hand down his arm, her gaze lingering on his tattoos. "I just love your tattoos, they're so...exotic. I bet you have a gorgeous accent as well. I've heard about people from where you're from... you're all so... gorgeous. I've longed to meet a man from there."

A flare of irritation sparks in me at her objectification. I move closer, sliding an arm around Kai's waist and meeting her look with a smile. "Aren't my husband's tattoos amazing? Each one has a story that's even more fascinating. Right, Kai?"

His arm wraps around me in turn, grin flashing. "That's right, wifey." The woman's smile falters at the implication, and Kai gives her a polite but dismissive nod. "Thanks for the compliment. Have a good night."

She stalks off in a huff, her ankle twisting awkwardly on her impossibly high heels and almost sending her careening to the floor, with her friend hurrying after her.

I let out a breath, the tension easing from my shoulders.

Kai's hand squeezes my hip, drawing me against his side. "My hero," he murmurs, humor glinting in his eyes. "How will I ever repay you?"

"I'm sure you'll think of something." I arch a brow and meet his gaze, unable to resist the flirtation. "Nice 'neutral stare', by the way." I grin.

A deep laugh rumbles in his chest. "Careful. I may take that as a challenge." His gaze turns molten, igniting a slow burn of heat low in my belly. "Ready to get out of here?"

I nod, my pulse leaping at the promise in his tone.

We drain our drinks and head out into the night, Kai's giant arm remaining comfortably snug around my waist. The cool air is a relief after the close warmth of the bar, sharpening my senses. Kai hails a cab, giving the driver an address I don't recognize.

"Where are we going?" I ask as we slide into the backseat.

"My place." He grins, eyes glinting. "I thought it was time I showed you where I live."

Anticipation thrills through me at the implication. I lean into him as the cab pulls away from the curb, my pulse racing with the unknown. What else will Kai reveal to me tonight? I can hardly wait to find out.

The cab rolls to a stop outside a stylish high-rise, all sharp angles and glittering glass. "This is me," Kai says, ushering me through the lobby. We take an elevator up to the penthouse, and the automatic doors open into a spacious loft with panoramic views of the city.

The space is modern but warm, decorated in a blend of sleek and rugged with artful nods to Polynesian influence. Kai gives me the tour, pointing out details of personal significance with casual intimacy, as if I've been here many times before.

It's a glimpse into a private world he rarely shares. I soak in each detail, piecing together a fuller picture of the man behind the charm. Here, in this place he calls home, I find Kai laid bare. It's a massive change from the last time we were together, in a neutral hotel room full of beige and other neutral tones. This is much more exciting, much more personal. And I want nothing more than to lose myself in every part of him.

When the tour ends in the bedroom, I turn to find Kai watching me with a smoldering look. Heart pounding, I close the distance between us and press my lips to his. There's no pretense, no suggestion of a nightcap that neither of us is remotely interested in.

Kai returns the kiss hungrily, his giant hands roaming my body. He lifts me onto the bed, leaning over me as our kisses grow more heated.

"I want this to be unforgettable for you," he murmurs against my skin. His lips trail down my neck, igniting sparks with each touch. "Let me show you how much you mean to me."

I arch into him with a gasp, desire flooding my senses. "With you, it's always more than I could have imagined."

Kai grins, his eyes darkening, and proceeds to prove my words true in the most pleasurable way. His hands and mouth move over me expertly, drawing out responses I never knew I was capable of. Before long I'm trembling at his mercy, my senses overloaded with bliss.

Kai guides me from the bed and presses me up against the floor to ceiling window, my palms pressed against the cool glass. Below us, the city is a sea of twinkling lights, a breathtaking view from up here in his penthouse.

His massive cock slams into me from behind and I gasp, seeing stars. So deep, so hard—it's almost too much.

"Look at that view, Dylan." His voice is a low rumble against my ear. "Gorgeous, isn't it?"

I can't speak, can only moan in response. He knows what he's doing to me, the bastard. Knows I'm helpless against the pleasure and the sight before me.

Another sharp thrust. "Isn't it?"

"Yes," I gasp. "Stunning."

"Not as stunning as you." His hands slide up to cup my breasts, rolling my nipples between his fingers. I clench around him and he groans. "So responsive. So fucking sexy."

He quickens his pace, slamming into me over and over, and I'm floating, weightless, nothing anchoring me to the earth but Kai's hands on my body and his cock inside me. The tension building and building, pleasure rippling out from where we're joined until I shatter around him with a cry.

Through the haze of my orgasm, I'm dimly aware of Kai following after, his hips stuttering against my ass as he empties himself inside me with a groan.

We stay there for a long moment, both catching our breath. The city glitters below us, but in this moment, I have eyes only for Kai.

Kai pulls out slowly, leaving me empty and aching. But before I can protest, he presses a button and a sex swing descends from the ceiling.

My breath catches. I've joked about these with my friends, fantasized about using one, but never tried it.

Kai grins at me, all wicked intent, and helps me into the swing. He secures my hands above my head so I'm unable to touch him. My legs are spread wide apart, leaving me completely exposed and vulnerable.

Helpless.

I whimper, desire flooding me anew. Kai runs a hand down my body, stopping just short of where I need him most.

"Look at you," he murmurs. "So wet and ready for me." His fingers dance across my inner thighs, my hips jerking towards his touch. "Patience, darling."

He turns and opens a box I hadn't noticed before, withdrawing one toy after another. A vibrator. A set of ben wa balls. A feather.

I swallow hard, watching with wide eyes as he approaches me, tools in hand. He's going to take me apart, piece by piece, and put me back together again.

The first touch of the vibrator against my clit has me gasping. He moves it in slow, maddening circles, bringing me to the edge again and again only to pull away. The ben wa balls fill me, the slight movements of my hips causing them to shift inside.

By the time he picks up the feather, I'm writhing in the swing, desperate for release. He drags it across my skin, my nipples, down between my legs. I'm sobbing with need, with pleasure, with—

"Come for me, Dylan."

The vibrator presses hard against my clit and I shatter, screaming his name. Wave after wave crashes over me and still he doesn't stop, drawing orgasm after orgasm from my trembling body until I'm limp in my restraints, boneless and sated.

Only then does Kai turn off the vibrator and remove the toys. He lifts me gently from the swing and carries me to the bed, curling around me and pressing soft kisses over my face and neck.

"You were exquisite," he whispers. "I know it's quick to say, but I think I love you."

I smile, utterly content in his arms. "I think I love you too," I whisper as I fall asleep.

I wake slowly, still nestled against Kai's chest. It's still dark outside, just a brief nap brought on by the afterglow of amazing sex. He's stroking my hair, his other arm wrapped securely around my waist.

"How do you feel?" he asks, pressing a kiss to the top of my head.

"Amazing." I tilt my head up for a proper kiss. "Thank you for that."

"My pleasure." He grins. "In more ways than one."

I laugh and swat his chest. "You're incorrigible."

"You love it." His expression softens. "I meant what I said earlier. You're exquisite, Dylan, and I love you with all my heart."

When Kai finally joins me in release, I cling to him breathlessly. We lie together as our heartbeats slow, the city lights casting a soft glow over his features. The night we spent together months ago went by in a drunken haze, enjoyable at the time, but the details were quickly forgotten. Tonight is different, a far more meaningful experience. From the way he holds me close to his perfectly sculpted body, I can tell he feels the same.

I trace the lines of his tattoos with a fingertip, mesmerized by the stories behind them. But what fascinates me most is the story of the man himself, one I'm only just beginning to discover.

Kai pulls me closer, pressing a kiss to my forehead. "I hope tonight showed you a side of my world," he says softly. "It sucks I have to go back home for a bit to deal with some family stuff, and I wish I could take you with me. I want to share even more with you, Dylan."

"I can't wait," I reply, and mean it with all my heart. I'm eager to see where this connection might lead, feeling more drawn to Kai than ever before.

My breath catches at the emotion in his eyes.

He kisses me again, slow and sweet, then pulls back with a sigh. "We should get up. We both have big games to prepare for, remember? We need to get you home so you can get ready."

I groan, burrowing into his chest. "Can't we just stay here forever instead?"

"Tempting." He strokes a hand down my back. "But if we don't get up now, I'm going to want to continue what we started. And we both know if that happens, we won't make it to the game at all."

He has a point. I lift my head again. "Fine. But after we win, we're coming straight back here."

"It's a deal." Kai presses a quick kiss to my nose before sliding out from under me. "Now come on, time for a shower."

He holds out a hand to help me up. I take it, lacing our fingers together, and follow him into the bathroom.

I turn on the shower and step under the warm spray, sighing as the water cascades over my body. Kai steps in behind me a moment later, wrapping his arms around my waist and pulling me back against his chest.

"That was amazing. You were amazing," he murmurs, dropping a kiss on my shoulder.

"It was." I tilt my head back, resting it on his shoulder as his hands glide up to cup my breasts. "You were incredible."

"So were you." His thumbs tease my nipples, sending sparks of pleasure down my spine. "The way you moved, the sounds you made...you're the sexiest thing I've ever seen."

Heat floods my cheeks at the praise even as my body responds to his touch. "Kai..."

He chuckles, giving my breasts one last squeeze before sliding his hands down to my hips. "Sorry, I got carried away. We do need to get our heads back onto the actual game."

I turn in his arms, looping my own around his neck. "After that, I'm definitely going to need a rematch."

"Definitely." Kai grins down at me, eyes dark with promise, before leaning in for a long, deep kiss full of desire and promises.

By the time we finally climb out of the shower, we're both breathless and flushed. After drying off and getting dressed, Kai pulls me in for one last kiss before I get ready to head out.

Insisting on walking rather than having him drive me home, I leave Kai's apartment with a rush of emotions—excitement, respect, and a growing infatuation. My skin still tingles from his touch, my mind replaying moments from our date on a loop.

Everything about tonight was perfect, from the authentic Polynesian cuisine to learning bits of Kai's native language. Most of all, I loved seeing him in his element, surrounded by people who appreciate him for who he really is.

Kai isn't just another pretty face or fantasy. He's depth, culture, passion—everything I didn't know I needed. I've always felt like the odd one out, never quite fitting in. But with Kai, as with the others, I can just be myself. He sees beyond the surface to the real Dylan underneath.

My phone buzzes as I stroll along the streets of the dimly lit neighborhood. A text from Kai lights up the screen: *Made it home safe? I'm already counting the hours until I see your face again.*

I grin, heart fluttering at his words. How is it possible to feel so deeply for someone I've only just met? All I know is that when I'm with Kai, the world feels brighter and more vibrant. And I want nothing more than to lose myself in his arms again.

I text him back: *Almost home safe, but wishing I was still with you. Tonight was amazing—thank you for sharing your world with me. I look forward to many more dates like this.*

His reply comes instantly: *As do I, Dylan. Sweet dreams, gorgeous—you're all I'll be thinking of.*

I practically float the rest of the way to the apartment. I feel dizzy, giddy, all of the things. Something tells me sleep will be elusive tonight, my mind too filled with thoughts of Kai and my dates with the other men to rest. But I can't bring myself to mind. Not when this feeling is so exhilarating.

Who knew that taking the time to get to know each of the men would only strengthen my feelings for all four of them? I have a feeling each of them will continue surprising me at every turn. And I wouldn't have it any other way.

Unfortunately, however, I'm not sure that Noah will change his mind, and I have a life-changing decision to make.

CHAPTER 46

Dylan

I t's early morning and I sit on my bed, surrounded by notes and trinkets—little mementos from each perfect date.

My fingers trace over the gorgeous shell Killian found for me on the beach. His thoughtfulness and compassion touched me, from the animal shelter to the beach cleanup, to the vegetarian meal prepared by underserved youth. Jonah noses around, interested in each of my finds.

I pick up a dark romance book and the bookmark bearing photos of the museum, recalling the intellectual date Jayden took me on. He'd revealed hidden depths that night, showing me his deeply romantic and thoughtful side. A smile tugs at my lips as I remember our initial meeting and how I thought he really didn't like me.

And then, in my phone, I bring up a candid photo of Noah and I. We're laughing, his arm slung playfully around my shoulders as we showed off our Laotian cooking skills. That spontaneous, fun-loving date had been such a pleasant surprise, not at all what I expected from the one who displays himself as a buttoned-up, serious type.

I lift the jade pendant Kai gave me that now sits against my chest, running my thumb over the smooth stone. He opened my eyes to his rich culture and passions.

Each man makes me feel alive in different ways. Each lights up a different part of my heart, my brain, my body and my soul.

How can I possibly choose just one path when my heart longs to explore them all? It's overwhelming, this longing for each of them. For the first time, I allow myself to imagine it—finding happiness together.

My mind races with possibilities as I pace my room. Being with one, being with all, wondering how we could possibly find a way. What would life look like if they were all in it as my partners?

I sit back down, pulling out my journal. It's time to lay all my cards on the table. Whatever happens tomorrow, I need to be true to myself and my heart.

Feeling overwhelmed, I pick up my phone and call Liv, my trusted friend and confidante.

"Liv, I'm torn. Each of them brings something special, something that makes me feel alive in different ways," I confess. "I though the dates would provide clarity, but they just showed me how much I care about all four of them."

"Sounds like you're really stuck," Liv says sympathetically. "Do you think they're really set on you picking just one of them? What if they had to choose between sharing you or not having you at all?"

I sigh. "I don't know...Noah seemed pretty adamant about me making a choice. I'm not sure if the dates changed anything for him or the other guys. But yeah, a girl can dream, right?"

"Well, you need to be honest—with yourself and them. Don't force yourself into something that doesn't bring you the joy you deserve."

After I hang up, I start pacing again, my mind racing even faster now. I visualize scenario after scenario—being with each man individually, then all together—wondering how we could possibly make it work.

What would life be like if I didn't have to choose? Could we find happiness together, or is it just a fantasy?

I know the only way to find out is to lay it all on the line. I sit back down and begin drafting a message to each of them, asking them to meet me tomorrow evening. It's time to discuss my thoughts openly and see what happens.

Dylan:

> *Hey, are you free tomorrow evening? There's something important I want to discuss with all of you together. Please come with an open mind. 7pm at the kitchen table. See you then.*

My heart pounds as I hit send.

I take a deep breath as I set my phone down, the message sent. The ball is in their court now.

I grab my journal and begin scribbling down my feelings, making a pros and cons list for each potential relationship. My mind spins as I try to envision what a polyamorous dynamic between the five of us could look like—how we would make it work logistically, what we'd need to consider emotionally, how it might feel.

Could I be the link that brings us all together? I wonder. Is there a way to make this work where everyone feels valued and loved? Or are they really going to make me choose?

My chest tightens at the thought. Because at this point, if I have to choose just one of them, I don't think I can choose any of them.

I know it's a lot to ask. Most people aren't open to this kind of relationship. But I also know what my heart wants—all of them, together. I don't want to have to let any of them go.

Finishing my journaling, I feel more confused, but also strangely hopeful. Now I just have to make it through the day until our meeting tomorrow. No matter what happens, I know I need to be true to myself. And I'm ready to lay all my cards on the table.

My stomach clenches as I think about the text I just sent to each of them—Killian the altruistic empath, Jayden the intellectual romantic, Noah the dominant alpha with a secret spontaneous and silly side, and Kai the sensitive and quiet leader with a spiritual depth like I've never seen. All of them, hot and sexy men with bulging biceps, tight curvy asses and enormous thighs that could crush my body in a heartbeat, not to mention washboard abs and tattoos that make me literally drool. But inside, so much that sets them apart from each other, and from anyone around them.

I spend the next few hours oscillating between nerves and excitement. Pacing my room, I psych myself up. Alright Dylan, tomorrow's the night. No more hiding, no more choices made out of fear. I'm ready to embrace whatever comes next.

I tidy up the apartment as I continue to think things through, planning snacks and refreshments to accompany tomorrow's discussions. I want them to feel comfortable even though this will be an intense conversation.

But first, a big practice for both the women's and men's teams tomorrow. It's at this moment I realize rugby hasn't even crossed my mind for several hours.

CHAPTER 47

Dylan

I take a deep breath of the crisp morning air as I step onto the field. My teammates are already running drills, their shouts and grunts mingling with the thuds of rugby balls. I try to focus, but my mind keeps wandering back to last night.

The scrum half's whistle pierces the noise. We line up for one of the most important drills—the scrum. As a hooker, I'm crucial to making this work. I bend down and brace myself against the opposing hooker's shoulder, my hands wrapped around my props' heads.

"Crouch, bind, set!" shouts the scrum half.

My mind flashes back to strong arms around me, soft lips on my neck. In my mind, all four of the men's faces blur into one. The ball shoots into the scrum but I'm too late engaging. Our scrum creaks and shifts as their prop surges forward.

"Dylan, get it together!" shouts my teammate. "We need you solid in here!"

I grit my teeth and push back, stabilizing the scrum. But it's too late—their scrum half has broken away with the ball. "Sorry," I mutter, shaking thoughts of last night from my head. I have to focus. My team is relying on me. No more distractions. Rugby comes first.

The assistant coach blows the whistle, calling a timeout. She gestures for me to come over. I jog to the sidelines, bracing myself for the inevitable lecture. "What's going on with you today, Morgan?" Coach asks, her voice stern. "You seem distracted. Your head's not in the game."

I open my mouth to explain, but she holds up a hand.

"Word is you've been spending a lot of time with the guys' team lately. In particular, there are rumors you're involved with several members of the men's team." She raises an eyebrow. "Now, I'm not here to judge how you spend your personal time, but you're a contracted professional rugby player and we have standards, rules and protocols. Dating around isn't why you're here. You need to figure out your priorities and right now, or there'll be someone waiting in the wings to immediately take your place. Do you understand?"

My cheeks burn with embarrassment. Is that really what people think of me?

"Sorry Coach," I say quietly. "It won't happen again."

She nods curtly. "See that it doesn't. Otherwise, you'll be on the bench or off the team for good."

As we return to the scrum drills, I catch the disappointed looks from my teammates. Their doubt stings more than the coach's words ever could.

Great. Now I'm the team distraction. This isn't who I am. I need to sort this out quickly.

I set my jaw with determination. No more distractions. For the rest of practice, rugby is my sole focus. It's time to show them what I'm really made of.

I'll figure out the guy situation later, because unlike rugby, that can wait.

I throw myself into the rest of practice with renewed intensity. During tackling drills, I drive into opponents with focused aggression, using perfect form to take them down. When it's my turn to be tackled, I twist and evade, refusing to go down easily.

In a one-on-one drill, I'm matched against Torres "Tornado" Helmswood, one of our biggest forwards. She charges toward me, her massive arms outstretched. At the last second, I feint left then dart right, leaving her grasping at air. Before she can recover, I tackle her around the thighs, driving her to the ground.

"Nice hit, Morgan!" Tornado laughs as she gets up. "Glad to have you back."

I grin, exhilarated. This is where I belong—on the field, giving it my all. No more distractions.

When practice ends, the others head to the locker rooms, chatting and joking around. I linger on the field, waiting for the coach.

"Hey Coach, got a minute?" I ask.

She turns, eyebrows raised.

"I just wanted to apologize for today," I say sincerely. "I let personal stuff get in the way of rugby. It was unprofessional and it won't happen again."

Coach regards me for a moment, then nods. "Apology accepted. Just remember why you're here, Morgan. You've got real talent—don't waste it over dicks. Trust me, I've been there, and it doesn't end well."

I thank her and head to the showers, feeling motivated. I'm ready to focus completely on rugby again. No more drama, no more distractions. It's time to show everyone—including myself—what I can really achieve.

After my talk with the coach, I decide to stay late and work on my scrum technique. A few teammates stick around to help.

We set up and I take my usual position as hooker. As the scrum half feeds the ball in, I drive forward with all my might, keeping my bind tight. We hold the scrum steady, no collapsing this time.

When we break apart, Nina grins. "That's the Dylan we know and love! Solid as a rock."

I smile back, feeling more confident. This is my element, where I excel. No one can take that away from me.

We run a few more scrums until I'm satisfied with my form. As I gather my things to leave, a sense of determination wells up inside me.

I may have gotten sidetracked, but my priorities are clear now. I'm here for one reason—to play top notch rugby. I can balance my personal life without letting it become a distraction. There's too much at stake.

From now on, any free time goes into training. No more staying out late or showing up bleary-eyed to practice. I'm going to prove I deserve to be here.

With renewed purpose, I head home. I'm ready to focus everything I've got into being the best player I can be.

This time, nothing will get in my way. Not even the four incredibly hot men anxiously waiting to hear my life-changing decision.

CHAPTER 48

Noah

The sun beats down on my shoulders as I sprint across the field, the ball tucked firmly under my arm. Jayden and Killian flank me, perfect mirrors of focus and determination. But my gaze keeps sliding to the sidelines, where Dylan watches us, her ponytail swinging every time she claps for us, which is often.

Why is she always staring at Kai? Doesn't she see how hard I'm working out here? How much I want her attention?

But no, all the girls go crazy over his appearance. I'm a decent enough looking guy, but I'm not that different in appearance than many of the other rugby players around. It's not too hard to find tall and muscly guys with short, dark hair around here. Sure, not everyone has tattoos, but that's hardly enough to keep me 'interesting' when next to someone like Kai.

It's infuriating. He's an exceptional player, sure, but everyone's just so obsessed with his accent and his... I don't know, charisma. His ability to score try after try, seemingly without effort, is just icing on the cake.

As if reading my mind, Kai suddenly has the ball, a blur of motion downfield. He dodges tackles like they're not even there, before diving over the try line. A perfect score.

Dylan leaps up, clapping and cheering. "Amazing run, Kai!" Her smile is huge, and I watch him glance over at her and give her a thumbs up accompanied by a massive grin.

I clench my jaw. Of course she's fawning over him. Mr. Hotshot with all the skills and the natural charm that makes ladies wet just by looking at him. Not me, sweating it out here every day. Trying to prove I deserve her.

Someday she'll see. Someday she'll be cheering for me.

The whistle blows and we're back at it, running drills at full tilt. The sun beats down, making the turf shimmer.

Maybe I'll get a chance to prove to her that I'm an excellent player too, that just because I don't stand out as much as him doesn't make me mediocre.

I see an opportunity to grab the ball and I charge toward it. But I underestimate the distance between me and it, and my fingers knock it forward. The ref blows the whistle for a knock-on, and I put my face in my hands and groan. Great, now she probably thinks I'm completely incompetent. I'm trying to impress her, but all I can manage is to make a complete fool of myself.

Kai snags the ball again, darting down the sideline. The same break-away run as before. My frustration boils over. Doesn't anyone see how hard I'm working? Can't she see how much she means to me?

We reset, returning to our positions on the field, and the opposing practice side gets possession of the ball again. As Kai nears the try zone, I charge, seeing red. I tackle high, my shoulder crashing into his torso. We both slam to the ground.

The ref's whistle screeches. "Noah! Off the field, now! That was dangerous play!"

I stare down at Kai, dazed in the grass. What did I just do?

Glancing up, I see Dylan, a hand over her mouth in horror. Tears brim in her eyes as she turns away.

Shame washes over me. I wanted her to see me out on the rugby field, but not like this. Never like this.

What have I done?

Before I can help Kai to his feet like I would any other player I'd taken to the ground, he jumps up on his own and storms off the pitch. Which is kind of nice of him, to be honest... most guys in his situation would have started a fight.

The team gathers around after practice, their faces stern. Jayden steps forward, his arms crossed. "What were you thinking out there, Noah?"

"Ugh, I don't know... I just...". I can't find the words, so instead I just scowl.

"That aggression puts all of us at risk, not just you," says Jayden.

Killian nods, his expression dark. "And you think that stunt will make Dylan choose you? More likely it'll drive her away, toward Kai or away from all four of us."

Their words hit me like a sack of bricks. Have I really jeopardized everything—my spot on the team, my friendships, my chance with Dylan?

I drop my head into my hands, elbows on my knees. How could I let my emotions take over like that? I'm supposed to be better than this. Smarter, more disciplined.

But seeing Dylan cheer for Kai just sent me over the edge. I want her to look at me that way, to see the hard work and passion I'm pouring into this sport, into us.

No more excuses. I need to get my act together. I can't keep letting jealousy dictate my actions.

Tomorrow I'll apologize to Kai and the whole team. And I'll find a way to make it up to Dylan, to prove I'm worthy of her faith in me. I can show her my best self again. I have to.

I take a deep breath as I enter the locker room after practice. The chatter and banter that usually fills the space is muted today. Everyone's still processing what went down on the pitch. A few people glance in my direction, but then immediately look away.

Kai's at his locker, packing his gear. Now's the time. I approach slowly, rehearsing the apology I've been preparing.

"Kai. Hey."

He glances up, his expression unreadable. I plow ahead before I lose my nerve.

"I wanted to say I'm really sorry about earlier. That high tackle was way out of line. I let my emotions get the better of me and I shouldn't have."

Kai studies me for a moment, then nods. "We all muck things up sometimes when we see red. Just keep it clean next time, yeah?"

I let out a breath I didn't know I was holding. "Yeah, definitely. It won't happen again." This seemed too easy. If I were him, I would be holding a grudge against me, possibly indefinitely. If the head coach had seen what I did, there's a chance I could have been removed from the team, no questions asked. If Kai wanted to pursue it, he probably could.

With the air somewhat cleared between us, the atmosphere in the locker room lightens up. The usual banter resumes as guys start teasing each other about highlights from practice.

But I'm only half listening. My thoughts keep drifting back to Dylan. The hurt and disappointment on her face after my tackle haunts me.

In letting my emotions get the better of me, I not only jeopardized both my and Kai's rugby careers, I also risked losing the girl I love. I may have, and if that's the case, I could never forgive myself.

I meant what I said to Kai. I'm going to be better—as a teammate, and hopefully, as someone worthy of Dylan's affection. I'll find a way to make it up to her, to show her my best self again.

I just hope it's not too late to regain her trust.

Her trust and belief in me is the one thing I can't bear to lose.

CHAPTER 49

Dylan

The living room is a disaster zone, strewn with workout gear, textbooks, and empty takeout containers—the chaotic aftermath of our busy lives. In moving here, I thought I might help them clean things up, but instead it's almost like I've acclimated to their more... relaxed way of living. I sink into the lumpy couch, absently spinning a rugby ball in my hands. The silence hangs heavy, punctuated only by the ticking clock.

My thoughts churn like whitewater rapids, replaying today's practice over and over. The whistle, Noah's dirty high tackle. He should have been dragged off the field. My chest tightens. Will I ever escape petty team politics and just play rugby?

But this time, it's almost worse than before. This isn't some bureaucratic office drama, this is personal. The men who claim to want nothing more than to be with me, fighting over me and compromising their ability to play rugby at one of the highest levels.

Suddenly, the opening chords of Justin Bieber's "Sorry" blast through the quiet, making us all jolt. Killian peers out the window, brow furrowed. Jonah joins him, peering out the window with interest at the loud sounds.

"Is that...Noah with a boombox?" His voice drips with disbelief.

I scramble over to join him and sure enough, there's Noah hoisting a boombox over his head like John Cusack in Say Anything. A grand, ridiculous gesture I can't help but chuckle at.

"What's he trying to pull?" Jayden snorts, though his lips quirk into a smile.

The song continues, muffled but unmistakable. As the lyrics wash over me, memories surface—riding with Kai as this song played...un derstanding dawns.

"Wait, this is your song with Noah!" I exclaim. Kai's eyes widen in recognition. We dissolve into laughter at Noah's well-intentioned but epically mis-targeted apology.

When Noah shuffles in, boombox under his arm, his sheepish hopefulness makes me bite back another laugh.

"That was..." I shake my head, grinning, "something else, Noah."

"Yeah, okay, okay. I know that was over the top," he says. "But I needed to make things right. Kai, I'm really sorry about that tackle today. And for causing so much drama."

"Why the boom box, though? I have to ask! Have you been on an 80s movies binge or something?"

"Well, I figured the locker room apology wasn't enough, all things considered. I needed to do something more. And when I thought about it, and about you, Kai, in general, well, I just couldn't get this song out of my head."

The tension melts away as we gather around Noah, teasing him mercilessly, but with understanding. Looks like I'm not the only one seeking redemption here. For now, we're just teammates again.

Noah rubs the back of his neck, and his cheeks are very flushed. "So we're good?" He glances around, making eye contact with each of us, his eyes eventually landing on Kai.

Kai sticks out his hand, and Noah does the same. Their hand shake is solid and seems authentic. Nobody's wrist is like a limp fish. Nobody tries to prove they're stronger than the other by crushing their hand bones. I'm shockingly proud of them in this moment.

"Agreed?" Noah quirks a brow at me.

"Agreed," I nod. "And no more boomboxes, Noah. Next time, just talk to us, okay?"

The others laugh, and even Noah snorts. "Deal," he says.

He turns to me, true remorse in his eyes.

"Dylan, I let my own insecurities make me act like a jerk, and that wasn't fair to you. You deserve to be seen for the amazing player you are, not dragged into my petty issues."

I'm touched by his sincerity. After feeling overlooked for so long, this means a lot.

"It's okay, Noah," I say. "I think we all let this rivalry go too far. How about we put it behind us and focus on working together?"

Noah's shoulders relax in relief.

"Absolutely. And no more boomboxes, I promise." He grins.

Kai claps him on the back. "We're good, man. Just leave the love songs for me from now on." He winks, and Noah blows him a kiss.

The exchange makes my heart full. Maybe there's hope for us after all, without anyone trying to kill the other.

We settle onto the couch, the earlier tension gone. Noah queues up a movie while Killian brings over snacks. Curled up with these guys, their easy banter washing over me, I feel lighter than I have in a long time.

Maybe I've finally found where I belong. A family of choice that sees me. Somewhere I can just be myself. For now, the serious and life-changing conversations can wait. For now, we all need space to just be.

I smile as the opening credits roll, the scent of popcorn filling the air. Kai and Killian bicker lightheartedly over what toppings to add—Killian preferring furikake and Kai preferring mountains of butter and salt—while Noah flips through our stacked DVD collection.

"Seriously though, I can't believe you pulled a *Say Anything* move," Killian laughs. "That takes some guts."

Noah groans. "Don't remind me. I'll be hearing about this for weeks. The idea seemed better in my head."

"Are you kidding? That's instant legend status," I say. "Noah's Boombox Ballad is going down in—not just team, not just apartment, but *club* history... because you know for sure the women's team will be finding out about this!" Despite my efforts to keep a straight face, a Cheshire cat-sized grin beams from ear to ear.

Noah tosses a pillow at me, his eyes glinting with humor.

"Laugh it up, Dylan. Just remember, I know where you sleep."

Kai nudges him with a grin. "Careful, she might like that." He turns to me. "And sorry I won't be able to make your game. I'll be back as soon as I can, I promise."

I feel my cheeks flush as the others hoot and holler. But it's a rush, being part of their casual flirtatious energy. Kai's needing to leave tomorrow to deal with a family emergency isn't ideal, but I'd never ask him to stay in the circumstances.

As the movie starts, I lean into Noah's shoulder. Maybe I misjudged him initially. Underneath that cocky exterior is a pretty stand-up guy. We all make mistakes, but it's someone's ability to take accountability and own their actions, and stop repeating them, is what makes someone a good person to me.

With these four, I feel like I can drop my guard. Speak my mind, be bold, even be vulnerable.

They see me as more than just the tough quirky female jock, they see me as a true athlete, an equal. But also a confidante, a friend... and someone each of them enjoys spending naked time with. I really have no complaints.

I close my eyes, letting the sounds of their laughter wash over me.

This right here—this feels like home. More serious conversations still need to be had, but I'll take this for now.

CHAPTER 50

Dylan

The roar of the crowd surrounds me as I take the field, the energy coursing through my veins. This is my moment. Stay focused, Dylan. Eyes on the prize. I go through my pre-game routine, visualizing each play, each tackle. This is my shot to show what I can do, to prove my worth.

The whistle blows and we're off. I explode into action, firing on all cylinders. I time my hits perfectly, sending opponents flying. When we form the scrum, I drive with everything I've got, churning those legs.

"Great work, Dylan!" Coach shouts. "Keep it up!"

I'm in the zone. This is rugby. This is me. I belong here.

Time whizzes by. By now, we're already nearly halfway through the first half and it's a tight match. As we set up for a scrum, I size up their hooker. She's got a reputation for playing dirty.

The ref blows the whistle and we clash together, eight bodies tangled in combat. I drive forward with all my might when suddenly I feel a sharp, twisting pain in my neck. Their hooker is boring in illegally, wrenching my head to the side.

As I realize what's happening, a lightning bolt of agony shoots through me. I cry out and collapse, clutching my neck. The whistle blows, halting play.

"Medic!" my teammate shouts. "Dylan's down!"

I try to move, but the pain paralyzes me. This can't be happening. Not now, when I was finally proving myself.

A medic rushes over, checking me urgently.

The pain is intense, shooting and throbbing at the same time. Fuck. It's my neck as well... the thing connecting my spine to my brain. This can't be good.

The medic secures my neck in a brace as I lie immobilized on the turf. His grim expression tells me all I need to know—this is bad. Really bad.

As the ambulance sirens wail in the distance, panic rises in my chest. My rugby career, everything I've worked for...could it really end here, like this?

The medic squeezes my shoulder reassuringly. "We're going to take good care of you, Dylan," he says. "Just try to stay still for me, okay?"

I nod slightly, blinking back tears, and immediately regret trying to move my neck as pain sears through my body. The ambulance arrives and they load me in.

Jayden

My heart is in my throat as I watch Dylan command the field. She's incredible, a force to be reckoned with. But I know how much she's endured to get here, and now seeing her shine fills me with so much pride and relief. She's finally getting the chance she deserves.

I'm on my feet in an instant when I see Dylan go down, my heart seizing in my chest. My world collapses as I see her collapsing to the ground.

I bolt down the stands, taking the steps two at a time. Not like this. She can't be hurt like this!

Reaching the field, I see her lying there motionless. Noah and Killian are right behind me, their faces etched with the same dread I feel.

"Dylan!" I cry out, dropping to my knees beside her. Her eyes find mine, filled with fear and agony. "Just hold on," I tell her. "We're right here with you."

I take her hand in mine, stroking her hair very carefully to avoid moving her head or neck. We'll get through this, together. Dylan's the strongest person I know. She has to pull through this. She just has to.

We insist on riding with Dylan to the hospital. Seeing her strapped to a stretcher, her neck braced, fills me with dread. I clasp her hand, stroking it gently.

"Thanks guys," she whispers hoarsely. "...stick with the team, the game..."

Killian shakes his head. "Forget the game, Dylan. You're all that matters right now."

Noah stays close, carefully watching her face for any flicker of pain. I know how hard this is for him. For all of us.

At the hospital, they swiftly wheel Dylan into the emergency room, a team of doctors and nurses swarming around her.

Noah, Killian and I sink into the waiting room chairs, shell-shocked. Noah stares blankly at the wall, jaw clenched. Killian paces restlessly, running his hands through his hair.

I lean forward, elbows on my knees, and drop my head into my hands.

"If anyone can pull through this, it's Dylan," I say, my voice hollow. "But seeing her like this...it's unbearable."

Noah's expression is grim. "She'll pull through," he says, almost like he's trying to convince himself. "She has to."

After what feels like an eternity, a doctor finally emerges. His face is grave as he explains the severity of Dylan's neck injury and what it could mean for her mobility, her career.

My heart drops into my stomach. Beside me, Noah goes pale.

"Her rugby career," I say in dismay. "Everything she's worked for ...could it really all end like this?"

The doctor holds up a hand. "It's still too early to say. The next few hours are critical. We'll know more then."

With that, he turns and heads back through the double doors, leaving the three of us suspended in agonizing uncertainty.

CHAPTER 51

Noah

Watching her lying there, she's a dichotomy.

I've never met someone so small, yet so fierce. So feisty yet so level-headed when she needs to control her team.

And it's only now that I realize how much she's changed me.

At first, the attention from fangirls was flattering. I ate it up, not ever giving a care that it wasn't my intellect and witty personality that was keeping these girls fluttering around me.

I let my ego do its thing, allowing myself to be stroked by these people both figuratively and literally.

But now, I see these interactions for what they were. Empty, hollow, vapid. Little fruit flies flitting around what they perceive to be a future pay day. Professional rugby comes with money, and they know that. It also comes with a certain level of notoriety and fame, and they're attracted to that. To *that*. Not to me. To people like them, rugby players are as interchangeable as a spare tire.

But then there's Dylan. Talented in her own right. Someone who has fought hard to be where she is. Who has shown resilience and persistence and tenacity, even in the face of challenges where most people would have thrown their hands up in the air and given up on their dreams.

She doesn't dwell on the people that wronged her, or the things that haven't gone her way. She's human enough to acknowledge they've occurred, of course, but that woman gets up every goddamn day and takes life by the balls harder than many people ever will.

The fact that she's so goddamn gorgeous is just icing on the cake.

So, while sharing a woman with multiple other men—let alone my teammates—would ordinarily feel so very wrong, with Dylan, it feels right.

Staring down at her sleeping form bubbles up so many emotions. Regret for all the things I didn't say, for my resistance to everything since the first day she got here. Resistance to letting myself to feel all that simmered just below the surface. Allowing my doubts and past hurts to cloud my judgements, even though none of those things were Dylan's fault and happened long before I even knew she existed.

That all changes today. Right fucking now. Because she's mine. Ours. And if anybody so much as looks at her in the wrong way, they're dead.

And if—when—she wakes up and decides she wants to get back on her feet and pursue her professional rugby career? We'll all be there, in the front row, cheering her along all of the way.

Proud.

Because that's how you treat a queen.

Dylan

I wake with a start, my heart pounding. The sterile white walls and beeping monitors slowly come into focus through blurry eyes. Hospital. I'm in the hospital. Alone.

My breathing quickens as I take in the empty room. No teammates crowded around my bedside with get-well-soon balloons and inappropriate jokes. No coaches checking in with grave concern in their eyes. No one.

I grab for my phone, my fingers fumbling over the screen. No service. Of course.

Panic rises in my chest. I'm stranded on this island of starch white sheets without a lifeline to the outside world. Abandoned. Again.

I squeeze my eyes shut and try to steady my breathing, but the monitors betray me, beeping faster in time with my racing heart. This sterile white room feels more like a prison than a place of healing.

I have to get out of here. Now. Before I'm trapped in this cold, lonely place forever.

Just as I'm about to rip the IV from my arm and make a run for it, the door bursts open.

"Surprise!" Noah, Killian, and Jayden chorus, sauntering into the room.

My jaw drops. They're wearing my women's rugby practice jerseys, the tiny polyester stretched obscenely tight across their massive chests and bulging biceps.

Killian flexes, the seams threatening to split. "We wanted you to feel at home."

Noah does a little twirl, his stomach spilling out from underneath the too-short hem. "We found these back at the apartment. Aren't we pretty?"

Jayden strikes a bodybuilder pose, the jersey barely containing his pumped up pecs. "We thought about getting you flowers instead, but we didn't want to make you sneeze."

Their ridiculous getups are so absurdly incongruous with their hulking rugby player physiques that I can't help it—I burst out laughing. It's a deep belly laugh that shakes my whole body and makes my healing neck ache, but I can't stop. Tears stream down my cheeks.

"When I said I believe in the law of abundance, I had no idea it would take quite this form," I giggle. "I guess you really can manifest anything. Even three hot rugby players in way-too-small rugby jerseys."

The three exchange satisfied grins. Mission accomplished.

When I finally catch my breath, wiping the tears from my eyes, Jayden sits on the edge of the bed.

"We know hospitals can be lonely, so we brought you something." He holds up a small black device—a wi-fi hotspot device. "Got one for every floor in this place. You'll have better internet here than at home."

Noah pulls a phone from his jersey pocket—a brand new phone, I realize. "And this is for you, the new top of the line model. And it has full bars. You can FaceTime us anytime. We'll take shifts keeping you company."

Killian squeezes my hand. "You're not alone anymore."

The panic fades, warmth flooding my chest. With these ridiculous, thoughtful men by my side, I know it's true. The isolation ends here.

I nod, overcome with gratitude.

Just then, an orderly wheels in a towering bouquet of tropical flowers—orchids, birds of paradise, anthuriums. The riot of color and scent fills the stark hospital room.

"Delivery for Ms. Dylan," he announces.

Killian lets out a low whistle. "Kai went all out, eh? Must've bought out the whole island's supply."

I breathe deep, inhaling the sweet fragrance. Kai's note reads:

My heart blooms for you. See you soon, my love.

Noah squeezes my shoulder. "We've got your back until he gets here."

Jayden pulls a deck of cards from his pocket. "Anyone up for poker? Loser has to wear the jersey for a week."

Laughing, I deal the cards. Loneliness vanishes in the presence of their playful warmth.

With my guys around me, the long nights ahead no longer seem so bleak.

CHAPTER 52

Dylan

The cozy living room comes into focus as Noah and Jayden gently guide me inside. I sink into the plush recliner they've positioned by the window, my leg elevated on a pile of pillows.

"There you go, Dylan. We've got you all set up," Noah says, his strong hands lingering on my shoulders.

Killian appears holding a tray of snacks and drinks. "Thought you could use a little refreshment after the journey home." He winks, setting the tray on the side table within my reach.

I glance around, taking in the personal touches they've added to make this space feel more like home than a frat house a tornado just ran through—photos of all of us, including Kai, on the walls. A soft blanket, my favorite books.

"You guys... you didn't have to do all this." I feel a swell of emotion.

"Of course we did. We're your team now. We're your home," Jayden says gently.

My phone chimes with a message from Kai. I smile as I read it aloud: "'Sending you sunny vibes to brighten your day as much as you brighten mine.'" I grin at the guys. "Even from halfway across the world, he finds a way to make me feel close to him."

"That's our Kai. The man is smitten," Noah chuckles.

"Clearly. And I don't mind one bit." I grin, already anticipating our nightly video call. Kai's constant encouragement has been a guiding light through all of this. With my guys surrounding me, and Kai's presence felt even from afar, I know I'll get back on my feet in no time.

Over the next few days, we settle into a comfortable routine. I'm never alone—one of the guys is always here, keeping me company.

Noah queues up my favorite movies, beats me soundly at video games, and runs potential rugby plays past me. He listens carefully, taking notes and adjusting several of his intended strategies for the upcoming away game.

Jayden challenges me to games like Battleship on our phones, and reads aloud from some of the new books he brought, his smooth voice lulling me into relaxation. At one point, I have to ask him to stop putting on funny voices because it makes me laugh so much my neck starts hurting again.

Killian keeps me well-fed, preparing healthy, delicious meals and making sure I never have to reach far for a snack or drink. He also provides daily updates on some of the animals we met at the shelter, several who have been adopted like we so badly wished for. He even makes an effort with Jonah, who has developed a habit of jumping up on his lap just about every time he sits down.

Their combined care and attention surrounds me like a warm blanket. Several large, muscly blankets of men, so different from each other except for their joint love of rugby and, well... me.

Kai's thoughtful gifts arrive daily in the mail—sweet dried fruits from his homeland, a book on mental techniques for healing, a soft knit blanket in my favorite color made especially for me by his aunties. Each night, his face lights up my phone screen and his deep, resonating voice fills my ears, providing a sense of closeness despite the distance.

"Just saw your latest pic, you're looking stronger every day hot stuff," he says during one call. "Can't wait to see that beautiful smile in person."

I feel myself blushing. "Thanks to you and the guys here, I'm starting to feel more like myself."

"We'll get you back out on the field in no time," he assures me. With my team here, and Kai's unwavering support, I know he's right. Each day, my strength returns a little more, and thoughts of our future adventures keep me motivated. With these amazing men surrounding me, I know I'll come back stronger than ever.

I nod along as Kai describes the latest match he watched, trying to focus on his words instead of how much I miss being out on the field.

"You'll be back in the heart of the scrum before you know it," he says gently, noticing my wistful expression.

"I know, I just feel so useless right now," I sigh.

Later, as the guys and I relax after dinner, I can't hide my sadness.

"What's wrong?" Noah asks.

"I just miss rugby so much," I admit. "It's hard feeling sidelined."

Killian jumps up. "I've got just the thing to get your mind back in the game," he says, pulling out a strategy board game. "Let's put that strategic brain of yours to work!"

I can't help but smile as the guys gather around the table. Their enthusiasm is contagious. We play late into the night, laughter and friendly taunts filling the air.

The next evening, Kai suggests a virtual watch party for an upcoming match. Surrounded by my teammates, their cheers and commentary make me feel like I'm really there.

As we finish up a hearty dinner prepared by Killian, I'm filled with gratitude for my guys.

"Thanks for everything, you guys. Being here with you, and Kai's messages...you've kept me going these past weeks."

Noah grasps my hand. "We're a team. We support each other, no matter what."

Jayden stretches and leans back in his chair. "You know, we should plan a big trip together once you're all healed up," he suggests. "Maybe we could visit Kai's hometown?"

My eyes light up at the thought. "That would be amazing! I'd love to see where Kai grew up."

"We could make it a real adventure—go hiking, check out the nightlife, try all the local foods," Noah adds enthusiastically.

Kai's nightly video call comes through right on time. As soon as his face appears, my heart lifts.

"Hey beautiful," he greets me. "How are you feeling today?"

I quickly fill him in on the trip idea. "What do you think? Could we all come visit you soon?"

Kai's smile is radiant. "I'd love nothing more than to show you all around. We'll have to hit the beach, the markets. Maybe I'll even take you to meet my family."

My own grin stretches wide across my face. After weeks of uncertainty, it feels amazing to have something fun to look forward to together.

"It's a plan then," I declare. "I'll be back on my feet before you know it. Then we'll embark on our next adventure—with the whole team this time."

Kai blows me a kiss through the screen. "Can't wait, love. We've got a bright future ahead of us."

It's wild how things can change so quickly, but for whatever reason, the darkness of the past few weeks seems to lift. The road to recovery doesn't feel quite so long and lonely anymore. And watching these men cooperate with each other and lavish their attention on me is doing things.

I can't wait to show them just how much I appreciate them all.

Our story is just beginning.

CHAPTER 53

Dylan

The phone rings, startling me from my brooding. It's been two weeks since I wrenched my neck in the scrum against the Barracudas, and the pain has only worsened.

"Miss Morgan? This is Dr. Chen, your physical therapist." His voice is brisk and businesslike as always. "I've reviewed your latest scans, and it looks like we'll need to intensify your treatment. You'll need to increase your heat therapy and follow each session with icing. Plus, you'll need to come into the clinic more than you have been. This type of injury can't just be treated at home."

"Even more heat and ice?" I groan. The lads are already hovering around me constantly, waiting on my every beck and call. Now they'll be setting timers and creating a full schedule to ensure I follow the doc's orders.

"It's the only way to reduce inflammation and ease the pain so you can get back on the pitch," Dr. Chen says sternly. "No rugby for at least a month otherwise."

I bite back another groan. A month without rugby might just kill me. "Alright, I'll do it."

"Excellent. Keep me posted on your progress, and we'll see about adjusting things again in a few weeks." He hangs up before I can reply.

Jayden, Killian and Noah are watching me with identical expressions of concern. I know they listened in on the call, probably huddled around the phone to catch every word.

"Did he say a month without rugby?" Jayden asks, appalled. The other two pale in unison. My injury is nearly as upsetting to them as it is to me. They've appointed themselves my personal nurses, waiting on me hand and foot.

"A month of rest and then physical therapy," I confirm. "But the heat and icing will help speed up the healing."

Noah's jaw firms with determination. "Then heat and icing it is. Timers are set for every two hours. You just say the word, Dylan, and we'll give you whatever you need." His smoldering gaze promises far more than pain relief. My inner thighs clench in response and I have to look away.

These men will be the death of me, in more ways than one. But I can't deny I'm grateful for their attentiveness. For the first time, I feel like my worth extends beyond my performance on the pitch. To Jayden, Killian, Noah and Kai, I'm more than just a rugby player. I'm the woman they all love and want to care for and protect. It's a heady feeling, and one I'm still getting used to. But I could get used to this.

The next day, the guys present me with a gift. A rugby referee whistle.

"You blow this whenever you need anything," Jayden says. "Food, drink, heat, ice, pain meds, a shoulder rub." He waggles his eyebrows. "Or anything else you might desire."

Killian smirks. "Anything at all. We're at your beck and call, angel."

Noah's expression is more serious. "You just focus on healing. Let us handle your every need."

Touched, I blink back the sting in my eyes. "You guys, this is too much."

"Nonsense," Jayden scoffs. "You'd do the same for us."

"And more," Killian adds softly.

Noah takes my hand, his rough palm enveloping my own. "You're not in this alone, Dylan. We're here for you, every step of the way."

I squeeze his hand, a lump forming in my throat. After years of struggling to prove my worth, it's almost too much to comprehend, having not one, but four, amazing men who love and support me so unconditionally, even when one of them is far away. But I'm learning to accept it. And with them by my side, this injury that once seemed catastrophic now feels more like a temporary setback. Together, we can overcome any obstacle. My heart swells with equal parts love and gratitude for these men who have made me part of their world. Looks like my time on the sidelines won't be so bad after all.

A few hours later, my neck is throbbing. Noah checks his watch. "Time for more ice. I'll grab a fresh bag."

"Let me help," Jayden says. Before I can protest, he scoops me into his arms.

Killian tucks a pillow under my head. "Comfortable, love?"

I nod, settling in. Jayden lowers me until I'm cradled in his lap, my head resting in the crook of his neck.

Noah returns and tears open the ice pack, slipping it under my neck. I gasp at the cold, but Jayden's warmth offsets the chill.

"Too cold?" Noah asks, concerned.

"No, it's perfect." The contrast is oddly pleasurable. I close my eyes, focusing on the sensations.

A moment later, there's a new sensation—the slide of ice along my collarbone. My eyes fly open to find Noah trailing the ice up my neck, his eyes molten. I shiver, but not from the cold.

"Shh," Jayden murmurs, running his hands up and down my arms. "Relax."

The ice continues its path, leaving a trail of goosebumps in its wake. Noah slides an ice cube into his mouth, then leans down to capture my lips in a searing kiss. I moan into his mouth as the chill of his lips mingles with the heat of his tongue.

Another set of hands, Killian's, come around to tease my nipples through my shirt. I gasp, arching into his touch, momentarily forgetting my injury. A sharp pain shoots through my neck and I cry out.

The sensations stop immediately. "Dylan, are you alright?" Noah asks, panic lacing his voice.

Jayden rubs soothing circles on my temples. "We're so sorry, baby."

I crack one eye open. All three of them look stricken. I manage a weak smile. "My own fault. Got a bit carried away."

"We shouldn't have—" Killian begins.

"Hush," I interrupt. "I'm fine. And that was...incredible, until the end. Maybe we try again in a few days?"

Noah chuckles. "You're impossible."

"And you love me for it," I tease.

"That we do," Jayden says softly, kissing my forehead. "That we do."

CHAPTER 54

Dylan

The aroma of sizzling bacon and freshly brewed coffee envelops me as I enter the cluttered kitchen. Noah dances around the stove, spatula in hand, while Jayden and Killian lounge at the table, cradling their mugs.

"Morning, sleepyhead," Noah chirps with a grin. "Saved you a seat."

I slide into the empty chair between Jayden and Killian, their shoulders brushing mine in a familiar, comforting way. On the laptop screen, Kai's pixelated face comes into focus. He looks different for some reason, but I can't quite put my finger on it. Maybe the wi-fi is just acting up.

"There she is," he says, voice crackling over the speakers. "Thought you were gonna sleep through breakfast."

"And miss Noah's famous scrambled eggs? Not a chance." I bump Jayden with my shoulder. "Scoot over and give me some room, would ya?"

Jayden chuckles but obliges, making space for me at the crowded table. As we dig into the feast Noah's prepared, the conversation flows easily, punctuated by laughter and playful jabs.

"Seriously, Dylan's the only one who can make my scrambled eggs just right," Noah says. "Y'all burn them every time."

"Hey, I make a mean omelet," Jayden protests.

Kai's pixelated head bobs in agreement. "Dude makes a killer omelet."

I spear a bite of perfectly fluffy eggs, catching Noah's gaze. "Gotta side with them on this one. Your eggs are unbeatable."

Noah winks, and warmth floods my cheeks. Even after all this time, his attention still makes me blush.

As the plates empty, Jayden clears his throat. "Okay, serious talk time." He meets my gaze. "We've been doing some thinking..."

Noah reaches across the table, clasping my hand. "We put you in a tough spot, Dylan, making you choose. That was wrong of us." His thumb brushes my knuckles.

On the screen, Kai nods. "And none of us want to go on without having you in our lives. We've realized that much."

My breath catches, pulse quickening. After weeks of agonizing over an impossible decision, could they really be suggesting...?

I take a deep breath, gathering my thoughts. This could change everything.

"I've been doing some thinking too," I say slowly. "And I realized I don't want to choose. I love you guys, all of you." I look from Noah to Jayden, to Kai's pixelated face. "And I want to try to make this work. On all our terms."

They all look at me, and everyone nods except Noah.

"Each of you gives me something different. Something that I need."

Noah frowns. "So what, you think you're so special no individual person is good enough for you? That you need three...four... of us to give you what you require as a person? That sounds a bit egotistical, doesn't it? What if we need three, four, women of our own?"

"Do you?"

"Well... no." His brows knit together.

"You have to let your ego go. You have to think about our situation and what it means for you, for us, without worrying whether it makes you look less... big and strong and alpha. The fact I am in love with multiple men doesn't take away any of my love for you. It doesn't detract from the quality of our relationship, it enhances it. Can't you see that?"

"I guess so... is this the law of abundance you've been speaking about?" He quirks a brow.

"Yes, precisely. Law of abundance. There is enough Dylan Morgan to go around without you feeling deprived, or your money back. Does that sound like a deal?"

Noah's gaze meets mine, and he nods slowly. "It does."

Jayden's eyes widen. "For real? You'd be up for that?"

I nod, a grin spreading across my face. "Yeah. I mean, it won't be easy, but if we all communicate and respect each other's boundaries..."

"We can figure it out," Noah finishes. His eyes shine, and he brings my hand to his lips, pressing a soft kiss to my knuckles.

"I'm game if you are," Kai says. Even through the glitchy connection, I can see his smile.

Killian leans back in his chair, tattooed arms crossed over his chest. His lips quirk up. "Well, looks like we've got ourselves a very modern relationship."

Laughter ripples around the table. As we begin to discuss logistics, ground rules, all the practicalities, Kai's screen abruptly goes dark.

"Kai?" I ask. No response.

Killian frowns. "Did we lose him?"

"His connection was fine a second ago," I say, glancing between their puzzled faces. Unease prickles my skin. Where did he go?

The doorbell rings, interrupting our speculation about Kai's sudden disappearance.

"I'll get it," I say, rising from my seat. I'm not sure who'd be stopping by this early.

I open the front door and freeze. Kai stands on the doorstep, a duffel bag slung over his shoulder and a huge grin on his face. He's slightly out of breath, like he just sprinted here.

He gestures at the two large suitcases beside him, which I didn't even notice, mesmerized by his sexiness. "Room for one more?"

"Kai!" I cry. "What are you—how—"

"Surprise," he says. "I'm here. In person." His eyes twinkle with amusement and something warmer, deeper. "Couldn't miss out on all the fun."

My heart swells even as my brain spins with questions. I launch forward and hug him fiercely. He chuckles, dropping his bag to return the embrace.

"You're really here," I murmur into his shoulder. I feel his lips brush my hair.

"I'm really here."

The others appear behind me, crowding the entryway.

"No way!" Jayden crows. He pulls Kai into a one-armed bro hug.

Noah grins ear to ear. "Welcome back, man."

"Good to have you," Killian adds with a genuine smile.

Kai's eyes sweep over us, his expression softening. "Thanks. It's good to be here."

Noah claps his hands together. "Well, this is new territory. But I think we're ready for it." He meets my gaze. "Together."

The atmosphere turns celebratory as we usher Kai inside, helping him stash his things in my room for now. With his arrival, it feels like the final piece has fallen into place. The five of us, together. All in.

My heart swells with hope. With Kai here in the flesh, this crazy, wonderful relationship feels more possible than ever.

We gather around the kitchen table, the morning sun streaming in through the windows. There's a new energy in the air - a sense of optimism and togetherness.

"Alright," I say. "Ground rules. This is all uncharted territory, so communication is key."

Killian nods. "We need to keep the lines wide open. Check in with each other. Be honest."

"And make sure everyone feels heard," I add. "No one should feel left out or unwanted."

Kai reaches over and gives my hand a squeeze. "We're in this together. All cards on the table."

Jayden leans forward, expression earnest. "I think we set up a schedule. Make sure everyone gets one-on-one time, too."

Noah smiles. "Good idea. Balance is important."

I take a deep breath. "Okay. We can figure the details out as we go. Today, let's just enjoy each other's company." I glance at Kai. "We've got catching up to do."

He grins. "I want to hear everything I missed."

Noah stands, clapping his hands together. "Alright, sounds like a plan. I say we head out, soak up the day."

The others chime in agreement. As we gather our things, I feel a swell of gratitude and love for these amazing men in my life. With open hearts and open communication, we can make this work.

Kai sidles up next to me, slipping his arm around my waist. "Lead the way," he says softly. "I've got a lot of lost time to make up for."

I smile up at him, heart fluttering. With his reassuring warmth at my side, I know we've made the right choice. Together, anything is possible. This is our fresh start.

Ready for more right now? Here's a complimentary spicy bonus scene featuring Dylan and all the guys.

Ready for more RH/why choose with surfing? Check out my Blood and Sand series.

ALSO BY

Blood and Sand (Dark Reverse Harem Mafia Romance)

- Sea of Snakes(Book 1)

- Sea of Sinners(Book 2)

- Sea of Rage (Book 3)

- Sea of Pain(Book 4)

- Sinners, Rage & Pain: The Brixton Trilogy(Books 2, 3 and 4)

- Sea of Demons(Book 5)

- Sea of Redemption(Book 6)

Standalones

- Rucked (sports romance – rugby why choose)

- Pretty Lovely Lies (FBI/mafia romance, single parent, international)

- Ruthless Choices(romantic horror)

Palm Falls Series (mafia romance – interconnected standalones)

- F*CKBOYS(dark revenge romance, second chance, enemies

to lovers)

- Bronson & Wren's story (title TBC) – preorder. Releases July 2024

Billionaire's Takeover Collection

- Irreversible Decision

- Compelling Proposal

- Love Merger

- The Billionaire's Takeover Collection (all 3 of the above!)

Novellas

- Love in a Seedy Motel Room

Sign up for my newsletter herefor the latest on new releases, promos, giveaways and events!

Join me on social media:

Facebook: @heidistarkauthor

Instagram: @heidistarkauthor

TikTok: @heidistark_author

Twitter: @heidistarkauthr

Websitehttps://heidistarkauthor.com

About Heidi Stark

Heidi Stark is an indie dark romance author who grew up in New Zealand and now lives in the US.

Heidi's books are inspired by her travels and the people she meets along the way. She loves writing about badass FMCs, morally grey men, and clearly, rugby.

When she's not writing, she's reading, listening to podcasts, cuddling with Fang, learning roller derby, watching her favorite shows, cooking, or dreaming about her next book.

Learn more about Heidi Stark at her website. Sign up for exclusive content and her newsletter here.

You can also find out more about Heidi and her upcoming books on social media:

Facebook Page

Facebook Group

Instagram

TikTok

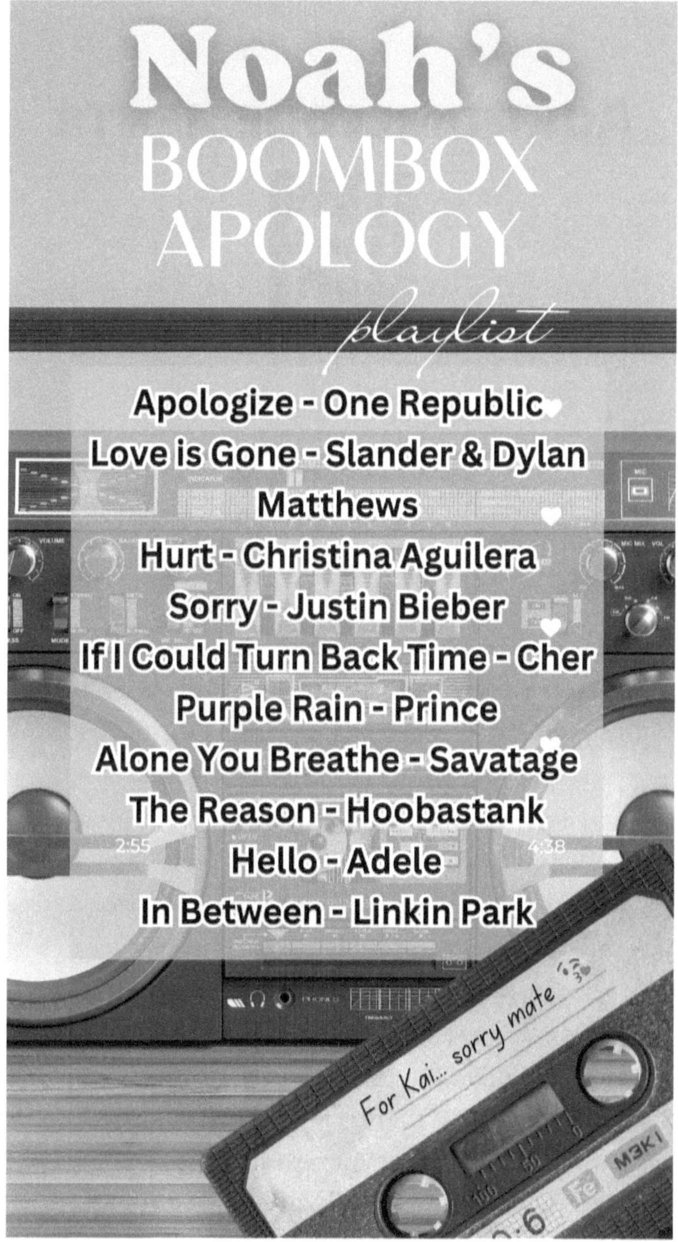

Noah's
BOOMBOX
APOLOGY
playlist

Apologize - One Republic
Love is Gone - Slander & Dylan Matthews
Hurt - Christina Aguilera
Sorry - Justin Bieber
If I Could Turn Back Time - Cher
Purple Rain - Prince
Alone You Breathe - Savatage
The Reason - Hoobastank
Hello - Adele
In Between - Linkin Park

For Kai... sorry mate

ACKNOWLEDGEMENTS

Many thanks to everyone who was part of this incredible journey, my first foray into sports romance. While the *Blood and Sand* series does feature surfing, this is the first time I've engaged in a book focused entirely on professional sports. So what better way to do it than with rugby, a sport near and dear to my heart ever since I was small.

To my father, Ross, who passed away when I was 16. I will never forget getting up with you at 2am, eating popcorn and drinking Milo, and watching South Africa devastate the All Blacks in the 1995 Rugby World Cup Final. It was so cold we had to wear beanies, or maybe that was just for fun. We may have lost the game, but it was a precious time with you that I will always cherish. You may have been gone a long time, but you have the ability to make me cry, even now, as I'm writing this. I'll always love you and I miss you heaps xoxo.

To my Uncle B, who I also miss dearly. You might not approve of some parts of this book, but I know you'd be proud of me anyway, and you'd appreciate the rugby parts. I'll never forget our time at the Bledisloe Cup match in Auckland. What a night! We will make sure E downloads this onto your Kindle right away ;)

To my friends who are incredible roller derby players, who have taught me so much about the strength of female athletes, and given me the confidence to give it a go myself. There are too many of you to name, so I'll mention T, Alexia/Nikki and all of Free State Roller Derby.

To my incredible ARC team who get as excited about my books as I do. Special mention to Bernadine, Amanda/Mrs. Swiftie, and everyone who took the time to send thoughts and ideas, stray typos, and support my way.

To my wonderful editing team.

To Rossy. Thank you for your support and for creating the chapter illustrations for each of the characters in this book.

And to the All Blacks. I may not live in New Zealand anymore, but you'll forever be my team.